The Belfast Leprecha strange stories)
By Jack Spock

Copyright © Jack Spock 2026

All rights reserved.
No part of this publication may be reproduced, distributed or transmitted in any form or by any means, including photocopying, recording, or other electronic or mechanical methods, without the prior written permission of the publisher, except in the case of brief quotations embodied in critical review and certain other non-commercial uses permitted by copyright law.

Disclaimer
This is a work of fiction. Names, characters, businesses, places, events and incidents are either the products of the author's imagination or used in a fictitious manner. Any resemblance to actual persons, living or dead, or actual events is purely coincidental.

In 'The Belfast Leprechauns (and other strange stories)' we are introduced to a wide range of fantastic characters, including a man who loves to lose in style, a woman who thrives on applause, and a married couple who pose the question: who answers the phone when it rings late at night?

Along the way we encounter a composer who cannot read or write music, an author who discovers the immense power of the blank page, and members of the aristocracy who suffer from an embarrassing wind problem.

One man has more than his fair share of jobs, another collects weird Elvis Presley memorabilia, the Beatles travel through a timeslip, and Laurel and Hardy reunite in the Twilight Zone.

We also meet a penguin in search of love a long way from his homeland, a silly serial killer and some even sillier ghosts, and a married couple who put up their Christmas decorations a bit too early in the year.

And in a quiet little leprechaun office in Belfast, Megalife loves Trumpella – but their lives are changed forever when their boss's billionaire friend declares war on the humans for clumsily trampling their fellow leprechauns underfoot…

CONTENTS

Page
005 This is Not the End of Me
017 Tomorrow Never Knows
027 A Story about Nothing
033 The Shufflebottoms of Shufflebottom Hall
038 Play Your Cards Right *(Sean and Ciara Byrne)*
043 The Decomposing Composer
048 Penny's Penguin
051 Finger on the Pulse
057 A Big Hand
062 Wallpaper *(Sean and Ciara Byrne)*
067 The Early Years of Armchair Joe and the Scrambled-Egg Kid
072 How to Sell Crap on the Internet
076 A Character in a New York Story
079 Last Orders
082 The Gallant Loser *(Sean and Ciara Byrne)*
089 The Belfast Leprechauns
145 Twice Two
158 Overheard Phone Call
161 Only Six Months until Christmas
191 Nice Weather for Hamsters *(Sean and Ciara Byrne)*
197 The Silly Ghosts
200 Line of Sight
203 Billy the Elephant
205 Say Cheese and Die
209 Early Morning Call *(Sean and Ciara Byrne)*
219 Write to the Death
224 Two Wrong Numbers
228 The Mercedes
232 Epilogue

THIS IS NOT THE END OF ME

The Fotheringays couldn't get onto dry land fast enough – the unmitigated pomposity of Lord and Lady Zeigweiller all but made their blue blood boil. Even before 'everything went arse over tit,' as he put it to his good lady wife, Lord Fotheringay had already made up his mind that he wasn't going to make the return-journey on Saturday afternoon if those two clots were on board.

'I had to use all my will-power *not* to throw the pair of them overboard late last night,' he now informed his other half, as they gazed up in awe at the Metropolitan Life Building on Madison Avenue, the tallest building in that or, indeed, any other city in the world.

'You can't just go flinging people overboard,' Lady Fotheringay protested, whilst admittedly not knowing for sure whether or not her husband was speaking in all seriousness, 'certainly not the Zeigweillers. Such outlandish behaviour would have caused an international incident. You don't want to start an unprecedented war with the Germans, do you? No, I should bally well think not.'

'Just think,' Lord Fotheringay muttered, leading his wife to wonder if he had heard a single word she had just said, 'it's less than two months since the "Big Wind" struck the Big Apple. How all these skyscrapers survived unscathed I have no idea, dearest.'

'Skyscrapers?'

'I believe that's what the natives call these huge buildings, because they quite literally scrape the sky.'

'I had no idea,' Lady Fotheringay remarked in pseudo-self-deprecation, sweeping back the blue rinse that, if anything, looked more natural than her husband's short, dark brown locks, 'I live and learn.'

'They say the new Woolworth Building is going to be even taller, once it's completed,' Lord Fotheringay stated, as if he expected his wife to swoon upon hearing this fascinating piece of information.

'*Who* says?'

'People. People who know about this sort of thing. I can't name names. I couldn't if I could.'

'Top secret government information, eh?'

'I have my sources.'

'I'm sure the president will be highly impressed, Marmaduke, even if nobody else is. He'll think you're like a *big* Lord Fauntleroy.'

'Is that yet another side-swipe at my stature?'

'Hardly,' Lady Fotheringay said, with a droll smile. Her husband was of about average height, but even after forty-five years of marriage she still thought it was funny that he always described himself as 'tall for his age'.

'Be prepared for a shock when you meet the president,' Lord Fotheringay said. 'I have it on good authority that he is one of the world's fattest political leaders, if not *the* fattest. They say he once got stuck in his own bath tub in the White House, and that he had to be prised out of the bloody thing by seven or eight men using canoe-oars.'

'I'll try not to broach the subject when we meet the man,' Lady Fotheringay said, checking her dress to feel how dry it was, in the absence of a handy change of clothing. 'Eeh, Marmaduke, I suppose that explains Teddy Roosevelt's flight a couple of years back.'

'Whatever do you mean?' he asked, also now feeling his own damp suit.

'He was the first former President of the United States ever to fly in an aeroplane,' Lady Fotheringay said. 'They would probably have invited the incumbent president to do so instead, had he not weighed three hundred and fifty-odd pounds, according to my ladies' magazine.'

'What's that in old money?'

'Old money?' Lady Fotheringay puzzled. 'Oh, about twenty-four stones, I should imagine. I wouldn't want to sit next to a man of such mighty proportions in one of those new-fangled aeroplanes... or even on an ocean-liner, for that matter.'

Lord Fotheringay let out a huge sigh, which his wife duly ignored.

'I can't believe we've travelled over three thousand miles from Oldham, Marmaduke. We're like Captain Scott travelling all the way to the North Pole.'

'The South Pole, my dear,' Lord Fotheringay corrected his good lady wife. 'He's probably there by now, maybe even on his way back home. Look up there, Minnie – can you see the clock tower?'

'Not from this distance,' she said, craning her neck and straining her eyes. 'Give me the field glasses.'

Lord Fotheringay unhooked the binoculars from his neck and handed them to his wife, knowing better than to try and advise her on how best to use them, not relishing the idea of a public ear-bashing in a foreign clime.

'We're meeting President Taft in a suite up near that clock tower, Minnie.'

'Do you think he'll like our gift, Marmaduke?' she asked, gazing up into the bright April morning sky.

'Well how could he not?' Lord Fotheringay replied. 'It's about as *personal* a gift as a body could possibly be given.'

'"Body" being the operative word,' Lady Fotheringay responded facetiously. 'I wonder what your friend Herbert would think, if he knew we were actually going to meet the President of the United States face to face?'

'Mr Asquith is a fine gentleman, as fine gentlemen go,' Lord Fotheringay commented. 'However, for me, that great country of ours will never have a better leader than his predecessor, the late Sir Henry Campbell-Bannerman.'

'Here we go again.'

'The man introduced free school meals for all children, Minnie. He was a staunch supporter of trade unions, and old-age pensions, not to mention Irish self-government.'

'Let it lie, dear. You know he's dead. Do you remember his famous last words?'

'Well of course I do. Sir Henry practically died in office, give or take three weeks. He was a true man of the people, like me. Stop sniggering. People the like of he and I are going out of fashion in the modern world. It's like the ancient Romans in North Africa all over again.'

'Whatever do you mean?' Lady Fotheringay screeched, in such a manner that it led her husband to believe she had had to mentally restrain herself from calling him a pompous little man, as, of an occasion, she was wont to do.

'The Romans killed every lion in North Africa.'

'You're not comparing yourself to a lion, are you?'

'I'm just saying,' Lord Fotheringay muttered. 'After all, when push comes to shove, you never know who among us might be here today and gone tomorrow.'

Lady Fotheringay handed the binoculars back to her husband, who manhandled them into his donkey-jacket pocket.

'I dare say the men serving under you in the Boer War didn't miss all those horrible big lions one little bit, Marmaduke, dear.'

'No, that was the *South*, Minnie. You know, you really ought to brush up on your geographical knowledge. Sharpen up your education on how and why we rule the majority of the civilized world, my little poppet.'

'I don't think concentration camps are very civilized, Marmaduke.'

'Oh, now don't start on that old chestnut again, Min.'

'Just don't mention them to President Taft, that's all I'm saying.'

'This is a new century, Minnie, with new ideas. Things have moved on. Out with the old and in with the new, and all that kerfuffle. I think the Kitcheners of this world are fast becoming old hat, if that's not too strong a term. The man is a dolt,' Lord Fotheringay carried on ranting, to fill in for his wife's surprise silence. 'Scorched earth policy my eye. People with no roots try harder to be noticed than the average man jack, and you can't get much more rootless than – why, the bombastic blackguard's family participated in the Plantation of Ireland, would you believe! He was even born there, in County Kerry, or some such backwater place. Not to mention the fact that he bats for the other team, if you know what I mean.'

'Don't go on so, dear, you'll only go raising your blood pressure again. And besides, you know only too well that the man in question is actually here in America as we speak. I hear he was booked for the return journey, at noon on Saturday.'

'Well I hope we don't bump into the blighter while we're here, Minnie.'

'I don't think that's very likely, Marmaduke. After all, I believe that America is quite a big place. I read an article in the *Daily Telegraph* saying that there are in excess of ninety million people here – that's twice the population of Great Britain.'

'Perhaps,' Lord Fotheringay replied, 'but it's only a quarter of the size of our Empire.'

'Now that's quite enough,' his wife said reproachfully. 'I don't want to hear any more of this... this *bluster*. We are abroad now, Marmaduke – let's not act like we think we rule the roost.'

'I'll say no more.'

'Jolly good show. So, do you really think the president will grace us with his presence?'

'*We* will do the gracing, Minnie. Titles like ours can pick any lock, as you know only too well. We have come this far, and no further. The Atlantic is now our line in the sand.'

They heard a sudden clattering sound, and looked up Madison Avenue to see a roofless motorcar being driven in their direction by a fellow wearing a brown leather cap, gloves and goggles. Most of the men on the streets seemed to be wearing black-and-white fedoras.

'Times are changing,' Lord Fotheringay said, as the motorized vehicle passed them by at almost running pace, and then some other vehicles came around the corner from East 23rd Street. The man at the controls of the motorcar nearest them tooted his bull-horn as if he owned the road, earning a nasty look from Lord Fotheringay. 'Oldham and New York are like two different worlds.'

Before they knew it the road was teeming with traffic, motorcars with roofs and those without, with not a horse to be seen. There was even what looked like an omnibus, with a number of glum-faced people sitting both upstairs and down, heading for Fifth Avenue, or so the sign on the front of the vehicle said.

'I've never seen a city street without horses,' Lady Fotheringay said, echoing her husband's thoughts. 'Before too long the people who make shovels will be put out of business.'

'No,' her husband begged to differ, 'they'll always need shovels, as long as people like you and I continue to live and breathe.'

'That's a charming thought, Marmaduke – thank you, once again, for speaking your mind and brightening my day.'

'I'm just being realistic, Minnie,' Lord Fotheringay said defensively. 'We are every last one of us just ashes and dust in the long run.'

'I don't think you were ever really anything else,' Lady Fotheringay said snidely.

Lord Fotheringay rolled his eyes, wishing he was able to argue the point, but he knew full well that despite being born with a silver spoon in his mouth he had totally wasted his life, and that, to make matters worse, he had dragged his childless wife down along with him. Had it been utterly foolish of him, to expect the New World to kneel down, lick his boots and welcome him with open arms?

'No horses? But look, Minnie, the street is knee-deep in… what's the correct word again?'

'Doo-doos.'

'Oy!' a man could be heard shouting, in what appeared to be an immaculate piece of timing, 'get that nag off the road!' This was immediately followed by the comforting sound of trotting hooves. Lord and Lady Fotheringay followed the line of shaking drivers' fists until their eyes arrived at the two horses tugging a high-sided wooden cart up the street. To them it was the only natural-looking vehicle on Madison Avenue, but all the motorcar drivers and pedestrians in its vicinity were glaring at it as if it was a total anachronism.

'To those people it's a ghost from the past,' Lord Fotheringay put his immediate thoughts into words, 'whereas to me, those *motorcars* are ghosts from the future.'

'Don't let everybody enjoy your ignorance,' Lady Fotheringay said, feeling embarrassed. 'I'm sure motorized vehicles in London look just the same as those ones. Don't let everybody in New York know for a fact that you are just a relative yokel.'

'Sorry, dear. On reflection, "ghosts" was the wrong word. What I should have said is, they're more like phantoms of the living.'

'It must be hard for you to accept the fact that there is actually a world outside your comfort zone,' Lady Fotheringay said as the horses and cart pulled up alongside them, incidentally making her husband feel somewhat deflated.

Two men rolled down the back shutter of the trailer, while a third man tethered the horses. Lord and Lady Fotheringay nonchalantly ambled around the rear side of the trailer in order to check that their crate, although naturally soaked, was still intact.

'How did they know who we were?'

'Because you look like Little Lord Fauntleroy,' Lady Fotheringay said with a smirk.

'What *is* your obsession with that book?' her husband asked rhetorically for the umpteenth time.

'I'm sure such eminent personages aren't ten-a-penny,' she replied to make him feel better, 'even in this great modern metropolis.'

'Fair do's,' Lord Fotheringay said, 'perhaps some of us *have* been blessed with more than our fair share of good fortune. As the Americans say, that's the way the cookie crumbles.'

'I can't believe you actually won at cards last night,' Lady Fotheringay suddenly blurted out, cutting her husband to the quick.

'I *often* win,' he bragged in response. 'Archie and Francis were simply no match for me. Although to be honest, at times I thought…'

'That they were trying to lose?' Lady Fotheringay interjected. 'You must admit, they seemed really keen to lose that painting to you in the big finale.'

'I wouldn't say "keen", Minnie. But no, they weren't exactly bawling their eyes out when they handed it over.'

'Did you know that Mr Butt was a friend of the president's before you entered the game?'

'How could I have done?' Lord Fotheringay replied properly. 'He was just another American in a smart military uniform with all the trimmings, as far as I was concerned. I don't think Archie's artist friend was too happy initially, mind you, when he put his latest painting down as the win-or-bust stake.'

'I'm sure Mr Butt knew damn well that you wouldn't want to keep the painting once you saw it. What is "Skull and Bones" anyway?'

'I think it's one of those American brotherhoods, totally hush-hush, Minnie. A fraternity, if you will.'

'Oh, do you mean like your freemasons' society?'

'Precisely, Min.'

'Do you think the president actually posed alongside… Archie… like that? In the buff, I mean? You'd think, what with Archibald wearing such a nice military uniform on the liner last night…'

'Who can ever tell these things?' Lord Fotheringay replied sagely. 'At least the huge crossbones beneath the skull hid their naughty bits. That's a blessing in disguise as far as I'm concerned.'

'I suppose so,' Lady Fotheringay said, as if there was any doubt about it. 'But do you really think Mr Taft will –'

'Oh, now please stop asking so many questions, Minnie. Mr Millet said he was going to give it to the president, so at least its final destination won't change. And in the process, it has become our foot in the door.'

'True,' Lady Fotheringay said. 'Mr Millet did seem to cheer up when you said you would make sure it reached its intended rightful owner. And, as you say, how else would you and I have got to meet the president so easily? Mind you, that Archie must be an important man in his own right, getting to associate with the president. Didn't he say last night that he was on his way back from a meeting with Pope Pius in the Vatican?'

'The elite of society do hob-nob with the rich and famous, my dear. After all, Mr Millet said that he was a close friend of the author Mark Twain.'

Lady Fotheringay beamed with delight. 'You can't get much more famous than that.'

'Twain was Millet's best man, apparently. That is some claim to fame.'

'Indeed,' Lady Fotheringay said. 'Just imagine, the man who wrote "Little Lord Fauntleroy".'

'OK, if you say so.' Lord Fotheringay noticed that his wife was rubbing her chin contemplatively. 'What are you thinking about now, dear?'

'It's...' she stumbled, 'it's almost as if they *wanted* us to deliver it for them.'

'Deliver it?'

'To the president. Maybe, subconsciously, they knew in their hearts that they wouldn't be able to make the appointment, so they sent us along instead?'

'Sent us?' Lord Fotheringay gasped. 'Nobody sends me *anywhere* to do *anything*, my dear Minnie. I am not a delivery boy.'

'Yes, but pride aside,' Lady Fotheringay said, trying to coax her highborn husband to listen to reason for once in his miserable spoon-fed life. 'It was nice of Mr Butt to get the wireless officer to send that telegraph to the White House, after you agreed to donate the picture to the president, don't you think?'

'He must have planned in advance to come to New York to collect it in person,' Lord Fotheringay reasoned. 'In which case, it must be very important to him.'

'Oh, now Marmaduke, I'm sure the president has *oodles* of portraits done.'

'Not like this one,' he replied with a wink. 'This is an election year. He probably wouldn't want the electorate to get an eyeful of him in such an undignified pose. You know how fickle the man on the Clapham omnibus is, Minnie.'

'Clapham, dear?'

'Clapham, New York, what does it matter? Why, some people are so small-minded that the very thought of a politician being a freemason would be quite enough to make them vote for his rival.' Lord Fotheringay chuckled.

'What's so funny, dear?'

'I was just thinking, if you and I weren't such incredibly nice people – such noble people, literally – we could *blackmail* Mr Taft, hanging that picture around his metaphorical neck like a millstone. I wonder how much he would be willing to pay for it?'

'Well it's all too weird for my liking,' Lady Fotheringay objected. 'If that picture is likely to be considered objectionable by one of its two subjects, why did the other one not object to it being seen, too?'

'Oh, I don't know,' Lord Fotheringay conjectured, 'perhaps he was the intended blackmailer?'

By now, the three men had transported the crate across to the Metropolitan Life Building. They were manipulating it in through the business entrance when Lord and Lady Fotheringay caught up and followed them in. The men located the service elevator and stepped into it, one of them saying 'We'll leave your crate up on the fiftieth floor, as requested.'

Lord and Lady Fotheringay entered the nearby public elevator and asked the attendant to take them up to the same floor.

'The presidential suite?' the man asked, 'Ah, you must be that English lord and lady.'

'Correct,' Lord Fotheringay said as the doors closed and the elevator commenced its long upward journey, stopping off at at least a dozen different floors to let people on and off, space permitting.

Lady Fotheringay heaved a sigh of relief when she finally stepped out onto the lavishly-decorated fiftieth floor, and saw what looked like a temporary sign reading 'presidential suite'.

'Remember, don't mention his bath tub.'

'I won't, if you don't mention aeroplanes.'

A clearly on-the-ball presidential aide approached what she called the 'esteemed visitors to our shores' and guided them into a bland meeting room with a desk and three wooden chairs, one of which was occupied by no less a man than the president himself. He put both hands on the desk and, with great difficulty, pushed himself up onto his feet. He looked as if he had just been crying.

'I'm sorry, Lord and Lady…'

'Fotheringay,' she said.

'Lord and Lady Fotheringay, it's so nice to meet you both. I can't believe you managed to make your way here all by yourselves.'

'Needs must,' Lord Fotheringay said, in what he privately considered the understatement of the century to date.

'Of course, of course,' the president said, stroking his moustache, 'I won't dwell on your troubles. Would you like to sit down?'

'Yes, Mr President.'

'Oh, just call me William, Lady Fotheringay. You don't know how thankful I am for your unbelievable act of kindness.'

'I'm sure you would have done the same for me and my good lady wife.'

'Well, I would certainly like to think so,' the president said, 'I most sincerely would. I hope I never get the chance to find out, eh?' He followed this up with a big, boisterous laugh, his jowls wobbling up and down. 'How was my dear friend, Archie? Was he… happy?'

'He was when we first met him,' Lord Fotheringay said. 'Mind you, I soon took the smile off his face.'

'I beg your pardon?' the bewildered president wheezed.

'Oh, my husband took Mr Butt to the cleaners in a game of poker, Mr President.'

'Ah, I see.'

'That was how I came to acquire his friend's painting… when he finally ran out of ready cash. But he wasn't what you might call despondent when my wife and I last saw him – far from it, as a matter of fact.'

'No, I dare say he wasn't,' President Taft said. 'He always tended to look on the bright side of life, however dire the situation.'

'He made sure everybody else did what he considered right, to the best of their abilities.'

'He was the life and soul of the party,' Lady Fotheringay said, 'although I accept that that is not a very apt idiom under the circumstances.'

'Even if they had escaped unscathed,' the president said, wiping his brow with a handkerchief, 'my expert advisor and his artistic soul-mate would never have been able to bring –' The president stopped talking when the door opened and two security men walked in, carrying the crate, one side of which had been broken off, dripping water on the maroon-carpeted floor. They suddenly looked flustered and one of them mumbled 'Sorry, Sir,' as if they hadn't expected to find the president in the room.

'Just leave it on the table,' President Taft said, and they did so, before making a hasty but silent retreat, gently closing the door behind them.

Lord Fotheringay looked almost apologetically at the huge puddle of water on the floor. 'It couldn't be helped, I'm afraid,' he said.

'Obviously not,' the president concurred wholeheartedly. 'Thank God for small mercies.'

'Mr Butt had a pistol,' Lady Fotheringay said, struggling to make herself heard above the sound of the president ferociously cracking planks of wood off the crate one at a time. 'He kept yelling out "Women and children first," and aiming his gun at any man who tried to barge his way through. I do believe he shot at least one desperate man dead.'

'He deserved it,' Lord Fotheringay insisted, as if the president doubted it for a single moment.

The president removed one final plank with a crack and what remained of the frame's body fell apart, with another gallon of salt-sea water pouring out onto the floor. With a little effort he managed to keep the eight-by-six-foot painting lying in one piece on the table, with a little help from Lord and Lady Fotheringay, who weren't at all used to manual labour.

'I was clutching my wife close to my chest,' Lord Fotheringay proudly boasted to the president, 'and by that time the half of the boat we were in was almost upright, and down close to the ice-cold water. On a whim, I shoved the crate into the water, and Minnie and I practically stepped out onto it. It rocked and rolled quite a bit, to tell you the truth, but somehow we found ourselves floating away on top of it like some sort of makeshift raft.'

Lady Fotheringay breathed a huge sigh. 'We couldn't have been more than a hundred yards away from the liner when it sank beneath the waves, thankfully drowning out the quite dreadful sound of the band playing "Alexander's Ragtime Band". The huge wave that ensued nearly dragged us down in the ship's wake, but somehow Marmaduke and I survived to tell the tale.'

'It's a pity the same can't be said for the contents of your raft,' the president said, sounding suspiciously chirpy. 'It's just a mass of blurred paint, like one of those modern abstract pieces of work. Look at it, it's impossible to make out either of the two faces, or even the large white skull above us.'
'I'm sure that's a relief,' Lady Fotheringay remarked.
'There was nothing irregular about it, I assure you,' the president insisted. 'All new members have to pose in just such an… unseemly manner for our resident artist.'
'Good luck in the election in November, President Taft.'
'Why thank you, Lady…'
'Fotheringay.'
'Lady Fotheringay, of course. So, will you be returning to England in the near future?'
'No,' Lord Fotheringay stepped in and said in a droll tone of voice, 'I'm pretty sure that the Titanic's Saturday afternoon return sailing has been cancelled.'
'We might hang around for a while,' Lady Fotheringay said, 'while our luck is in. Give my regards to Nellie.'
'I will indeed,' the president said, warmly shaking their cold hands. 'I hope your luck rubs off on me.'
'It didn't rub off on the Zeigweillers,' Lady Fotheringay said, feeling quite smug and proud of it. She stood up and walked towards the door, with her husband in close pursuit.
'For God's sake, Minnie, will you please let it lie? The ocean has them now.'
'She's welcome to them,' were the last words the president heard before Lord Fotheringay closed the door.

TOMORROW NEVER KNOWS

'With these leather-jackets, we'll rule Liverpool!' Paul foretold facetiously, stepping away from the clothes-shop counter with his old gear in a carrier-bag.

'In these leather-trousers,' John stated categorically, 'we will rule the world!' He kicked the shop door open with his new black leather boot and swaggered out onto the fog-enshrouded Bold Street right in the heart of Liverpool. 'Now all we need is a full-time drummer, and –'

John's words were drowned out by a cacophonous wall of noise from behind them, which quietened down when the shop door swung closed.

'Why…why are they playing really weird loud music inside a clothes-shop?' Paul asked.

'Good question, my dear Holmes,' John said, plucking his new blue fountain-pen down from the top of his ear and sucking it like a black clay pipe. 'I don't half agree with you. What *is* that weird fellow singing above the screeching electric-guitar sound – "Helter Skelter"?' A twinkle suddenly appeared in John's eye. 'If I didn't know better, I would say that he sounds not unlike *you* on a good day, Paul, me lad.'

'Why thank you most kindly, Sir John of Quarry Bank,' Paul replied grandiloquently. 'You know, maybe we Silver Beetles ought to do a cover-version?'

'No, Paul. Using this very fountain-pen, you and I are going to write most if not all of our own songs, once we land ourselves a manager and procure a record deal.' In so saying, John swept back his fashionable Elvis-style quiff and put the pen his beloved aunt had given him (she just didn't know it yet) back on top of his ear. 'What do we always say? "To the toppermost –"'

'"– of the poppermost!"' Paul rounded off their trusty mantra. He looked up towards the bombed-out church at the top of the street, where only last week he and his father had taken a nice stroll in the green gardens, but he could hardly make out the form of the church through the heavy fog. He returned his attention to his immediate vicinity, Bold Street's bustling hub of cafés, sweet-shops and restaurants.

'That's strange.'

'What's that, Johnny?'

'Where has the newspaper-man gone? When we went into the clothes-shop his stall was right here at the side of the road, next to the vegetable-man's usual stalls – and as you can clearly see, they have both disappeared, too.'

'I don't know about that,' Paul said, 'but what about the milk-float that had just come around the corner from Slater Street? There are no bottles of milk on any of the doorsteps.'

'I'll take your word for it,' John said, rubbing his eyes in vain.

'All the empties have gone,' Paul helped his myopic friend out.

'The milkman must have been and gone too, then,' John concluded.

'There's nothing mysterious going on here, Paolo. We Scousers take the milk in quickly of a morning, before the Liver birds come and skim off the cream.'

'Oh?' Paul said. 'Nothing mysterious? Then what the hell is *that*?'

Even without the glasses John steadfastly refused to wear (he didn't believe that even Buddy Holly or Hank Marvin made specs look cool), he didn't need to follow the direction of Paul's pointing finger to see the huge green – what was it, some sort of... *vehicle*? – with windows upstairs and down like a double-decker bus, but this was like no double-decker either he or Paul had ever clapped eyes on before. It had a door at the front that now swished open concertina-fashion, for God's sake! And the people marching nonchalantly out of it were dressed in bright red, green and yellow clothes even brighter than the ones John and Paul saw the big stars wearing in American films at the flicks every Friday night.

'It's like a flying-saucer on wheels,' John finally stopped gasping and put his thoughts into words, pulling his glasses case out of his pocket and putting his specs on so he could have a proper look at the monstrosity, which now started moving along the street. 'You can hardly even hear the engine. Where is the usual number ten bus, driven by good old Freddie Shuttleworth, with a fag hanging out of his gob?'

'Refresh my memory, John, but we *are* still in Liverpool, aren't we?' Paul asked groggily.

'I walked out of me Aunt Mimi's house not forty minutes since,' John confirmed, restoring his glasses to their case. 'Or was it forty years?'

'Eeh,' a blue-haired girl aged around eighteen or nineteen said, 'Doctor Winston O'Boogie, I presume?'

John realised that she was looking specifically at him. 'You what, love?' he said, discombobulated.

'You two look just like *them*!'

John's and Paul's eyes weren't the only things that nearly popped out of their sockets when they spotted what the young lady almost wasn't wearing – they could see everything, knees, navel and naked shoulders galore. Did her mum and dad know she was walking the streets dressed like that? She made Marilyn Monroe look like a nun.

'Who's "them"?' John finally gathered his composure and asked.

'Is your hair-colour natural, love?' Paul chipped in. 'If you don't mind me saying, you look a little bit on the young side for a blue-rinse.'

'Are you messin'?'

'Yeah, he's just messin', love. He's messin' with your blue mind, trying to blow your blue brain.'

'Divvy,' the girl said. 'You're a blue meanie. My name is Julia.'

'Just like my mum,' John said with a sigh.

'Wowee! You really do sound exactly like John Lennon.'

'Do... do I know you?'

'Does he know you?' Paul asked her too. They were a team.

'If yous two can sing,' Julia said in a thick Scouse accent, 'yous could make a fortune.'

'*I* can sing,' Paul said.

'Yeah,' John agreed, 'he does a mean "Mr Postman".'

'Don't you mean "Mean Mr Mustard"?' Julia enquired.

'"Mean mean"?'

'Sorry, John, I stand corrected, that was *your* song on "Abbey Road".'

'Where is Abbey Road? I've never set foot on it in my life.'

'No,' the bluehead laughed, seemingly as if knowingly, '*Paul* was the one with bare feet on the CD cover. Although I don't believe all that claptrap about his bare feet meaning that he was dead in real life.'

'*I'm* not dead,' Paul insisted.

'Me neither,' John concurred.

'By the way,' Julia said, 'why do you two not have mop-tops?'

'She wants to mop the floor with us, Paul.'

Julia fiddled nervously with her turquoise handbag, looking slightly confused. 'You are Beatles impersonators, aren't yous?'

'Yer ma!' Paul said to the blue-top, flashing her a cheeky smile.

'We are the *Silver* Beetles,' John kindly corrected her, 'the genuine article, formerly known as the Quarrymen, at your service. Available for school dances, church fetes and bar mitzvahs, and we even have our own amplifier.'

'Oh, I see,' Julia said, with a look on her face that said she did anything but, 'you're meant to be The Fab Four before they hit the big time? Before the days of Beatlemania? Well, I must admit, that's a novel take, lads.'

'"Fab"?' Paul puzzled. '"Four"? But there are five of us.'

'Whatever,' Julia said, as if she thought that word was a phrase that meant something all by itself. She reached deep into her handbag and pulled out what looked like a face-powder compact. 'D'you mind if I take a selfie? I'm going out on the razzle with my bestie tonight, and she won't believe it when I show her. Yous look almost like the real McCoy. I might use it as my profile picture on all my social media sites.'

'Sorry?' Paul said. 'I didn't catch a word of that.'

'I said, can I take a picture?'

'Have you got a camera in that little handbag of yours?' John asked.

'This is it, soft lad.'

She squeezed herself in between Paul and John and told them to say cheese. They reckoned they were both much more shocked than she was when a genuine flashing light appeared to emanate from the little powder-puff compact, almost as if it really was a tiny little camera. They then saw a much brighter light flashing in the corners of their eyes. It said 'police' on the side of – what looked like some sort of racing-car, going so fast down the short street that Stirling Moss himself must have been driving it. It seemed to be doing a hundred miles an hour. It wasn't sky blue, like the usual police panda cars – it was painted in multi-colours, on a mainly yellow background, and the wailing alarm coming out of it sounded more like something out of a science-fiction film than the usual 'ner-ner-

ner-ner' sound natural pandas made. Its tyres screeched as it flew around the corner of Slater Street.

'Oy! John!' a balding, morbidly-obese young man yelled out from the doorway of a café across the street. John looked across at him, and was surprised to see that he was looking at himself.

'Me?' John put his glasses on again. 'What do you want?'

'I was just thinking,' the red-faced man chortled, 'it's a pity the NYPD didn't arrive on the scene as fast as that cop car, when you were shot dead that night in 1980.'

Having said his piece, the bloated man – wearing a strange grey cardigan with a hood attached, and jeans that appeared to be falling half way down his stumpy little legs – laughed out loud and walked into the café.

'What the hell? "Beatles" with a "A"?'

Paul looked down to the corner to see what John was looking at.

'There's a real double-decker bus,' John said, 'although why it's yellow, instead of the usual lime-green, I haven't the foggiest.'

'Well, at least it has a proper doorless back entrance,' Paul said, 'just an empty space with a bus-conductor leaning on the big metal pole inside it, trying to look important.'

'Yeah,' John said, 'but have you seen the big sign on the side of the bus, between the two sets of windows?'

'"Beatles Tour Bus"?' Paul was flabbergasted. 'Who are those four guys, dressed in multi-coloured clothing?'

'They look like something clearly not of this world,' John said, in a spooky voice.

'What I want to know,' Paul pondered pragmatically, 'is have our dads formed a band behind our backs, right in front of our faces, to steal our thunder – even stealing half our band's name?'

'They look more like the "Silver-Haired Beatles", with an "A",' John said snidely. 'Those guys can't just breeze in here like John Wayne and steal our territory, like a gang of no-good claim-hoppers, as my missing dad would have said. He sailed off into the sunset just like in the cowboy films, you know, never to be seen again.'

'Did he sail away in a yellow submarine, by any chance?'

'Are you still here?' John asked, after spinning around and seeing Julia brushing her blue locks. He put his beloathed spectacles back into the case in his pocket. 'Is that a Toffees wig? I'm sure I saw a few grown men at the Stanley Park end of Goodison wearing wigs just like that, back in my younger days. I believe Paul was a blue-nose too.'

'No, this is real,' Julia said, feeling aggrieved.

Paul, meanwhile, couldn't take his eyes off the side of the bus.

'Two of those guys look just like me and you, John.'

'That's a strange coincidence,' Julia said, and then, mystifyingly, she laughed out loud like a banshee.

A song started playing through an unseen loudspeaker on the upper deck of the bus, in what sounded like absolutely pristine quality, far clearer than any record John or Paul had ever heard before. It sounded as if the acoustic guitar was coming from one side, and the singer's voice from the other, which was highly peculiar.

'He sounds just like you,' John pointed out, in case Paul hadn't noticed, as the man sang a sad ballad that was most likely called "I Believe In Yesterday". Paul stood in reverential silence and listened carefully, as if trying to take in every sad word sung and every last guitar-chord plucked.

As John had kindly refrained from uttering a word throughout, Paul returned the favour and remained totally silent when a voice suspiciously like John's, although probably slightly older, commenced singing a song about a local landmark, Strawberry Field, backed-up with some mind-bogglingly weird-sounding instrumentation.

'Where's me pen?' John asked, upon half-recognising the voice in question. He swiftly took it down from its usual resting-place above or behind his ear, then pulled a luckily-blank scrap of paper out of his pants pocket and started taking notes, not knowing that a future discovery of Paul's would make his exertions unnecessary.

Paul, meanwhile, walked up to a nearby newsagent's shop and looked in the window. Spotting one particularly interesting headline, he entered and picked up a copy of the *Liverpool Echo*. The banner headline read, "Yet more time-slips reported on Bold Street". Before buying a copy Paul checked the date and, as he almost expected, although the very idea of it made his head spin, it was sixty years hence.

'Flaming Nora,' Paul cursed, totally out of character. He wondered if he should tell John, for fear of being made fun of. He didn't yet know John well enough to know if he would even believe his own short-sighted eyes, when something totally against the laws of

physics like this occurred. Not surprisingly, he found himself wondering if maybe he was about to wake up in his own bed.
'Why are you pinching yourself, Paul?'
'Um – who is that singing?'
'As if you didn't know,' stressed the girl with the blue tresses.
'Go on,' Paul said, 'humour me.'
'Why,' Julia said, wondering why she was bothering, 'that's Ringo.'
'Ringo,' John interjected, immediately showing that he was more otherworldly-wise than Paul had suspected, 'he became our drummer?'
'What do you mean, John?' Paul asked, quite liking the idea of getting his musical accomplice to put his own far-fetched thoughts into words.
'I... I'm not sure,' John stumbled. 'But, if it's not a silly question, Paul – as you hinted at, is that *really* our fathers pasted to the side of that bus, or is it a future version of our actual selves?'
John considered Paul's virtually instant reply intriguing.
'Maybe we are from the past. Maybe we are in the future now.'
Not wanting to give John an obvious opening for the expected sarcastic reply, Paul stepped back into what used to be a clothes-shop but clearly now sold records instead, judging by the futuristic racket assaulting his eardrums from within it every time somebody opened the door, not to mention the windows strewn with posters of bands and singers he had never even heard of, such as Taylor Swift and The Weeknd ('Typo alert,' he thought to himself).
'Can I take a few more selfies with you?' Julia asked John.
'Help yourselfie,' he replied. 'You can take selfies, or whatever the Hell-fies.' He shoved the scrap of paper containing the hastily-scribbled lyrics of the double-decker bus song about a yellow submarine into his jacket pocket. 'I'll teach that to Ringo, after I ask him out of the blue to join my band with the soon-to-be-abbreviated and re-spelled name.'
John had finally stopped posing and started jotting down the lyrics to a new bus-speakers song called 'She Loves You' when Paul ran out of the shop with a smile strewn from the wisdom of years on his baby-face, and two books clutched proudly beneath his black leather-clad arm along with the local newspaper.
'You can stop writing,' Paul said, handing John a copy of 'The Beatles Song Book'. 'I've just been told that you and I are going to

become multi-millionaires over the next five or ten years, with the help of this little baby.'

'Are you messin'?'

'No, John, I'm not. Although apparently, in order to fulfil our destiny, we're going to have to change our hair-style...'

'Mop-tops.'

'Thank you, Julia. And mohair suits and Beatles boots. But don't worry, that's not really our department – Brian will take complete control of the way we look for the first few years.'

'Brian who?'

'Epstein. Apparently he runs a music shop somewhere in town. It's all in the foreword in the book,' Paul revealed, tapping his copy emphatically. 'We have to go to London to seek our fortune, with the help of a man by the name of Martin. George Martin, I think. It says he's the producer of your beloved Goons records in our day.'

'Ying tong iddle I po,' John replied, in the voice of his favourite wireless character, Neddy Seagoon. 'That sounds almost too good to be true, my erstwhile Silver Beetles bandmate. But on the other side of the sixpenny-bit, what was that about me being shot in New York again?'

'Again? You haven't been shot the first time yet,' Paul said. 'To stick with the Goons-style humour for a moment.'

'That sounds more like "Hancock's Half Hour",' John said with a sigh.

'And besides, Johnny, that's not going to happen until a couple of decades in the future – that's like a lifetime to young men like us. We'll both be little old men in our forties by then.'

'That *is* pretty old,' John agreed. 'I guess I'll just have to write all my best stuff in the early years, and then I can relax and wind down for ten or eleven years.'

'That's the spirit,' Paul said with a warm smile. He pulled the local newspaper out from under his arm and showed it to John. 'It says here,' he said, skimming through the front-page story, 'that in the summer of 1960, a few months after Bill Shankly became the manager of second-division Liverpool, a fan of the club walked out of a café here on Bold Street and found himself in the middle of a twenty-first century crowd celebrating the fact that Liverpool had just become the champions of Europe for the fifth time!'

'Yeah, right,' John said. 'As if that's ever going to happen.'

'It *did*, according to this article in the *Echo*,' Paul insisted. 'Hold on, here's another weird true story. In 1959, a struggling Liverpudlian actor stepped out of a sweet-shop on this street, and found himself surrounded by yet another huge crowd.'

'That's strange,' John said. 'I'd hate to be surrounded by huge crowds like that.'

'This one turned out to be fans of his,' Paul said, his eyes becoming wider by the second as he read the paper. 'Before going back into the sweet-shop he learned that it was thirty years later, and he was one of the stars of a Liverpool-based TV soap-opera called "Brookside".'

'Yeah,' John scoffed as Paul clumsily dropped the paper on the ground, 'that will never happen. They're all fantasists, predicting futures that will never come to fruition.'

The yellow double-decker moved on down Bold Street in the direction of the Lyceum, a long-abandoned former library and gentlemen's club known to local wits as the 'lice-ridden'. It could still barely be seen through the fog enshrouding the street.

John kissed Julia full on the lips.

'Wow!' she shrieked, not totally seriously, 'I can't believe I've just been snogged by the man they named Liverpool airport after!'

'They're going to name an airport after me?' John gulped. 'My death must have been serious.' He stepped into the record-shop, quickly followed by Paul, both of them feeling as if they were being guided by fate.

When John opened the door he heard his own voice roaring out lyrics about a revolution, and when Paul closed the door behind him they immediately found themselves surrounded by the deathly-hush of the clothes-shop in which they had not long since purchased their fashionable leather gear that was about to become old-fashioned in the eyes of youngsters around the world, thanks to them.

'We'd like to change these leather trousers and jackets for a couple of beige mohair collarless suits,' Paul told the man behind the counter. 'But we'll keep the Beatle boots.'

'Beetle boots?' the shopkeeper asked, in a confused manner. 'You'd need ten thousand for each boot.'

Ten minutes later, John and Paul stepped back out onto the street. Paul looked up towards the bombed-out shell of St Luke's Church at the top of the street, which was now a little more visible as the fog began to rise.

'It's nearly always foggy when it happens,' he told John, 'I read that in the paper.'

'You should have took it with you,' John reprimanded him.

'We don't need it,' Paul said, tapping his book, 'we have *this*. We'd better not let anyone else see it, mind you.'

As they sat reading that same book and strumming their guitars later that day, John said, 'I don't think much of "Love Me Do", Paul. It says here that our first single only squeezed into the lower reaches of the Top Twenty. Maybe we ought to just leap straight to the seventeen chart-toppers.'

'I'm not sure that would be a good idea, John,' Paul remonstrated. 'After all, if we were to cut out the number-two hits, that would put paid to the double-A sided single featuring your wonderful "Strawberry Fields Forever". I vote we do it by the book, literally,' he added, once again tapping his copy of the greatest collection of songs ever written for emphasis.

'Perhaps you're right,' John agreed. 'You sing "Penny Lane" on the flip-side.'

Paul laughed. 'We have so much work ahead of us.'

'Yeah,' John said, looking at the sacred book, 'how are we supposed to write all these hits by ourselves? Oh, Paul, if you remember, will you do me a little favour, a few years from now?'

'Name it.'

'Remind me to pay a return visit to Bold Street in the first week of December 1980, to see if I can tweak fate once more for luck. Then maybe, just maybe, they'll name the airport in Liverpool after *both* of us, instead of just me.'

'That sounds like a good deal to me,' Paul agreed wholeheartedly.

A STORY ABOUT NOTHING

Billy O'Flaherty had always known that he would one day be a writer. He had been writing since the age of fifteen. By twenty-one he could do joined-up writing. He had gone through more jotters than he had had hot dinners. Eventually he stopped eating paper and began writing on it instead.
Billy once thought of a beautiful poem, but he had no paper available so he wrote it on his left hand – no small feat, considering the fact that he wrote with his left hand. The inspiration continued on and on, all the way up his arm and down his stomach. He only ended the epic poem when he reached his toes and ran out of body-space. Then he went to his home on the outskirts of Belfast and, forgetting momentarily about his masterpiece, had a shower. C'est la vie.
Billy's first novel was rejected by four publishing companies, each of which claimed that the story was just a little too depressing. So he scrapped his autobiography and wrote a novel about trench warfare in the first world war, with instant success.
Unfortunately, while carrying his tome to the printer's with a note from the publisher requesting delivery of an initial ten thousand copies of the book, Billy was struck with a fit of inspiration. He sat down under a bridge and spent almost a full hour writing a children's version of *Lady Chatterley's Lover* on the back of his novel's pages. When he finished he decided that he didn't like the new work and – forgetting all about the masterpiece on the other side of the two hundred pages – chewed it up into little wet paper balls and threw them at people crossing the bridge above his head.
It was only when he reached the words 'the end' on the other side of the paper that he realised what he had done. He gathered all the paper balls together from the road and tried to reconstruct them, but he discovered he had clearly put them back together in the wrong order when it turned out like some horrifying sort of Jeffrey Archer novel, which he swiftly burned.
Thinking quick, Billy spent half an hour writing a novel about a Christian Scientist who worked for the Blood Transfusion Service. He ran as fast as his little legs would carry him to the printer's with

the publisher's 'print this' note. As fate would have it, the proof-reader Amadeus Johnston was a practising Christian Scientist, and when he read Billy's hastily-written novel his furore at its contents made his nose bleed profusely. His religion forbade blood transfusions, and as a result he bled to death all over the manuscript.

Coming to the conclusion that he wasn't being overly successful on the novel front, Billy returned to his first love, poetry. He came up with a lovely original poem on a bus, and began writing it down on the back of his hand. It was only when he reached the thirty-second verse on his buttocks that his fellow passengers began to scream, so he quickly scribbled it out to conceal the evidence. He then discovered one of the great facts of life: when you create a magnificent poem on your flesh the slightest drop of water will make it disappear, but when you scribble all over your body you can scrub it until your skin blisters and the stains won't go away.

Alarmed and dismayed, Billy found that his creative powers had dried up completely. Duly annoyed at his sudden lack of inventiveness his girlfriend Sally left him, at which point Billy's writing ability dried up as well. Every piece of paper he touched turned to excrement. He scrapped the toilet roll altogether and tried writing on an A4 pad, but to no avail.

Seeking inspiration, Billy turned to art. He took up an evening class and painted an almost perfect picture of a naked lady. Unfortunately he was supposed to paint the bowl of fruit in front of him and not the woman sitting next to him, so he was thrown out of the class. The naked lady was kicked out as well, for refusing to wear her artist's smock.

Where on earth could Billy find some much-needed inspiration? Maybe alcohol was the answer. For the next three weeks he totally abstained from his usual nightly bottle of vodka, but he still couldn't write a word. Gradually, however, he learned to write again. After only four months he could do joined-up writing. Then he learned to type, and six months later he had mastered joined-up typing. But he soon tired of struggling to climb inside the typewriter to type on his body, so he gave it up and used typing paper.

Still seeking inspiration Billy re-read his old autobiography, but he couldn't associate with the main character. He tried his hand at modern poetry, but no matter how he used and abused his poetic muse he couldn't prevent his stanzas from both rhyming and scanning to perfection, so he obviously had no chance of getting his poems published.

He tried writing short stories, but he couldn't get them down to less than fifty thousand words. He was getting nowhere fast. He was beginning to think he would never become a famous writer. He would probably end up a pathetic, nameless nobody, writing throwaway *Mills and Boon* books. He would rather be dead.

He tried writing a six-part TV sitcom. But as the BBC script-reader kindly explained on her rejection slip, 'Your show would only serve to make our complete sitcom output for the last fifty years appear ridiculously unfunny in comparison.'

The New Testament was getting on a bit in years – maybe he ought to up-date the Bible? Sadly, neither the Cardinal nor the Archbishop thought putting Jesus on a Harley-Davidson in modern-day New York was such a good idea.

Billy couldn't put a foot right. His horror stories made publishers laugh out loud, and his comedies made them scream. *'Why does the hero in your comedies always end up getting decapitated?'* Readett and Scrappett enquired alongside one rejection. *'And why does the beast in the closet always get the girl?'*

Billy could only write when he was depressed. But he was only depressed when he couldn't write, so he wrote more when he couldn't write than he did when he could. Paradoxically, his writing was more cheerful when he was of a depressed disposition. When he was happy he churned out totally morose work that depressed even him when he read it, and his melancholia resulted in him writing much more cheerfully.

His main problem was that he had always wanted to be a writer, and he had devoted the majority of his life thus far to the art of writing. As a result of this oversight he had never been anywhere or seen or done anything he could write about.

While others had put down in words their own first-hand experiences, such as being possessed by the devil or being kidnapped and held for five long years in a Lebanese hell-hole (the jammy gits!), nothing like that had ever happened to Billy. He had never had any earth-shattering experiences, like escaping from Alcatraz or being beaten up by Rod Hull's Emu on the *Parkinson* show. He had never been castrated by Lorena Bobbitt. Billy did everything better on paper than in real life. He even had paper sheets on his bed, in case he came up with any wonderful ideas in the middle of the night. Admittedly his cardboard pillows weren't the height of comfort – perhaps that was another reason why Sally had walked out on him?

Billy's lack of real success as an author was getting him down. He was at his lowest ebb, contemplating self-abuse, when he came to a sudden, stark realisation: to be a successful writer, you have to write about what you know. Dick Francis wrote about jockeys and Shakespeare wrote about men in tights, so Billy would follow in their footsteps and write about what he knew, and knew well.

His first book was published within the month, and it sold an incredible twenty-seven million copies worldwide. It was acclaimed as the most relaxing book ever written. People who were feeling below their best, couldn't sleep or simply wanted to relax, went out and purchased Billy's amazingly original book, *Silence*. It was a real breakthrough in the world of literature. Two hundred and forty-eight pages of nothing, sheer blankness, not even page numbers, which the buying public could read over and over again and find something different every time. They could browse through the novel, leap any number of pages and even read it backwards or sideways without in any way ruining the plot.

Seven more books filled with empty pages followed in rapid succession, making Billy a millionaire eighty times over. He knew nothing, so he wrote nothing. It was such a simple formula that he didn't know why he hadn't thought of it years ago.

He became such a prolific author that he packed in his boring office job, scrapped his typewriter and threw away all his pens. He sent two or three hundred blank A4 sheets to *Readett and Scrappett* every once in a while (Billy had the all-important final say on how many empty pages his books contained), and each one was actually better than the one before it. There was even a blank audiobook of his first novel on the shelves of all good high-street and online bookstores.

Billy won the Booker Prize for literature for his fourth novel, *Nothing*, which was later made into a blockbuster movie (with a ninety-two million pound budget), featuring not only NONE of Hollywood's top stars, but a magnificently relaxing empty screen as well.

He was still sleeping on paper bed-sheets, of course. No, not blank pages, but items of currency. Strangely enough, his returning girlfriend Sally had no complaints about the crinkling of paper beneath her as she tried to sleep at night. She especially liked the feel of the fifty-pound notes against her skin. At least Billy was now inventive enough to fully satisfy her needs, to the tune of three money-spinning void masterpieces per month.

He no longer felt depressed – quite the contrary in fact, but his cheerful disposition clearly hadn't affected his unique non-writing ability.

He was the ultimate man of many talents. He wrote countless blank columns in *The Times*. And to top that, the world's first totally minimalist newspaper, 'The -----' (which came out in thirty-two blank pages daily, with a completely empty glossy magazine on Sundays) was – needless to say – the brainchild of the great non-wordsmith himself.

Billy appeared on numerous TV chat shows around the world and, true to his image, never said a word. Like his empty books, his silence needed no translation – it was a truly universal language. The very fact that he never opened his mouth and put his foot in it made him an extremely popular choice as a future prime minister, president or ayatollah in any country of his choice. In fact his occasional political pamphlets always went down a storm, due to their lack of jargon (or any other vocabulary).

As he became revered around the world as the greatest author never to put pen to paper, Billy rewrote his previously unpublished autobiography in a more popular modern style, by simply removing all the words with a few bottles of correction fluid. He then rewrote the complete works of Shakespeare (the world's greatest writer before the extraordinary advent of Billy O'Flaherty) with the aid of an eraser and a pair of scissors.

Billy also famously dallied in the world of popular music, single-handedly deleting a complete collection of Barry Manilow's Greatest Hits and thereby creating a silent masterpiece. He then had the pop world's first-ever silent number one hit single with his faithful rendition of John Lennon's silent 1973 track, *Nutopian National Anthem*.

Billy became so enormously popular that nobody ever mentioned his name (which was precisely the way he wanted it). The only blemish on his otherwise exemplary authorship was that, since his readers were obliged to invent their own stories in their heads while enjoying a Billy O'Flaherty novel, certain nameless members of the public deciphered some less-than-complimentary remarks about themselves hidden between the non-existent lines. As a result a number of lawsuits were taken out by disgruntled readers who believed that Billy had libelled them on the blank pages of his novels.

Confounding even himself, Billy wrote a pulp romance novella for the erstwhile frowned-upon *Mills and Boon*, and the wordless gem shattered all previous sales records. Subsequently, to the delight of all true lovers of literature, it was decided that all publications on that particular label and others of its ilk would contain absolutely no words from that day on.

However, Billy himself felt that this amounted to plagiarism, and he threatened to sue any publisher who issued blank books in breach of his copyright. He even threatened to destroy the careers of fellow authors in whose books he had found the odd blank page or half-page (and in one case, the empty space between two paragraphs), for copying from his work. Not to mention the countless recording artists throughout the decades who had left too long a silent space between album tracks… some of them imitating Billy's trademark long before he was even born.

Yes indeed, Billy O'Flaherty certainly had a lot of things happening in his once-desolate life… a great deal of experiences for the author supreme to write about (or not, as the case may be).

THE SHUFFLEBOTTOMS OF SHUFFLEBOTTOM HALL

Lady Henrietta Shufflebottom would never have been able to show her face in civilised society again if she failed to turn up at the Shrimpton Castle November Ball. Non-appearance simply wasn't the done thing for a Lady of her standing.
Lord Henry Shufflebottom would have had his servants draw *Her Ladyship* to the castles, halls and mansions of England in a rickshaw, if necessary, in order to keep up the obligatory appearances. After all, Henrietta had stood by him and his slightly disconcerting toxic explosions for more years than he cared to remember, never once complaining about him showing her up in front of his peers. Their social acquaintances were his peers but, Lord Shufflebottom firmly believed, his good lady wife was most decidedly in a class above the rest.
Lord and Lady Shufflebottom were la creme de la creme of the once-proud nation's still-proud aristocracy. Indeed it had been affirmed in certain circles that an occasion couldn't quite properly be classed as anything more than a passing event if the Shufflebottoms weren't present to add a touch of *je ne sais quoi*.
Had she not been born into her esteemed position in society, it had quite correctly been whispered in high places, Lady Shufflebottom would indubitably have concluded that she had no earthly reason for existing. His Lordship, on the other hand, was less out-of-touch with the common rabble, notwithstanding the blue blood coursing imperiously through his veins.
It was rumoured in places both high and low that Lord Shufflebottom wasn't averse to consuming cold baked beans out of production-line tins with a tablespoon on arrival back at Shufflebottom Hall, after Lady Henrietta and he had passed an evening being cordially entertained by lesser members of the nobility. And Lady Henrietta herself had, it must be said, been known to drag Chef out of his chambers in the dead of night to order anything from a jar of factory-packed pickled-onions to a plateful of Brussels sprouts.

'What one chooses to devour within the confines of one's own august front portals is up to one and one alone,' Lord and Lady Shufflebottom had, on one memorable occasion, had one of the menials transcribe in a letter to *The Times*, in an effort to bring to a swift conclusion a particularly vindictive rumour that was doing the rounds in the higher echelons of society. 'The less said the better,' they added, as an adroit postscript.

Everybody who was anybody attended the November Ball at Shrimpton Castle. The soignée Lady Shufflebottom was attired in her best diamond-studded silk number. Although it was very seldom taken out of mothballs, this was an evening to savour. Lord Shufflebottom was resplendent in one of his ebony dinner jackets, with the mandatory white kerchief standing erect in his breast pocket.

Chauffeur drove slowly but surely the forty-odd miles from Shufflebottom Village to Shrimpton Hamlet. If he was lucky His Lordship might have one of the castle underlings bring Chauffeur out a carminative mug of cocoa as sunrise approached, to help him remain alert while patiently waiting for his arrant betters to satiate their palates whilst honouring Lord and Lady Shrimpton with their mighty presence.

Chauffeur was, quite correctly, drenched through to the bone as he ushered his Lord and Lady from the limousine with an umbrella in either hand.

'Do try and ensure that you don't leave a foul damp smell in the limo,' Lord Henry reprimanded Chauffeur as he shuffled subserviently away, closing the umbrellas in order to prevent them from getting any wetter than they already were.

Lady Georgina Shrimpton was a reprehensible bore. Every time she inveigled her way into Lady Shufflebottom's esteemed company she chattered about other people, and not about Lady Shufflebottom herself. It was almost as if the poor woman was of such an intensely moronic disposition that she was too embarrassed to confess that she was in utter awe of the most Ladylike Lady of them all. The sententious termagant was little short of a common fool.

At least her husband Lord Barnaby Shrimpton was, to his credit, less concerned with *people* and such piffle and more interested in admirable topics such as honourable affluence and the attendant possessions one can acquire. Lord Shufflebottom had the man treading exasperatingly on his coat tails for the major part of the evening that was in it, blatantly attempting to rise above his station in the company that he was being permitted to keep.

The nosh was so-so. The cocktails were a peculiarly blasé assortment of cheese and pickles, sausage and onion slices, and the ubiquitous cucumber and caviare. The two most venerable guests tucked in to their tummies' delight, so as not to offend their grateful host and hostess.

'Upon my soul,' Lady Shufflebottom complimented Lady Shrimpton, 'these eats are almost as good as Chef's.'

'But they *are* Chef's,' the silly woman responded grandiloquently.

Lady Shufflebottom guffawed, almost rifting in the process. 'No,' she explained, as if speaking down to a child, 'of course I meant *our* chef... we call him *Chef*.'

'But that's what we call our chef as well.'

'Well of course,' Lord Shufflebottom chipped in beneficently. 'After all, you're hardly likely to address the blackguard by his actual name, now are you?' he chortled.

'It's like the difference between, say, the Scottish Cup and *the* Cup,' Lady Shufflebottom informed her fatuous popinjay of a hostess. 'Your chef is the Shrimpton Castle chef, whereas our chef is *the* Chef.'

'Oh, is that right?'

The Shufflebottoms looked down at Lady Shrimpton's upturned nose. If she wasn't so high and mighty she could well have been mistaken for common riff-raff. *Pah.*

Halfway through the main course – duck-a-l'orange – Lady Shufflebottom started to wish she hadn't made her usual side order of sprouts. A couple of Lords were talking about the weather, and the wind-factor was extremely high. Lady Shufflebottom flashed a scornful glance at Lord Shufflebottom, and wondered what on earth was holding him back this fine night. Was he maintaining a strict silence simply in order to show her up? – The very idea was preposterous.

Lord Figley of Figley Village Green asked Lord Shrimpton whether or not the air-conditioning was switched on. Lady Shufflebottom was of the firm belief that the coarse little man was looking towards her as he spoke, and so she swiftly put him in his place with her eyes.

A quite perceptible number of the guests there present could clearly be seen removing their kerchiefs from their breast pockets and raising them up momentarily to shield their nostrils. Lady Shufflebottom attempted to circulate as speedily as possible, in the vain hope that nobody would guess it was her. But the aroma was following her around. Her name would be mud.

'Oh dear,' Lord Shufflebottom exclaimed, a tad late in the day, but better late than never. 'Deary, deary me.' He crouched down just a jot and let rip. It was loud, some would say excruciatingly so. His good Lady wife heaved a huge sigh of relief. Attention distracted yet again.

'I see potatoes are going up in price,' Lady Shrimpton uttered, blushing somewhat. She really hadn't expected Lord Shufflebottom to live up to his fast-growing reputation within the sanctity of her stately home, of all places. 'What will the personages below stairs eat?' – She nibbled on a japonica.

The drink was amusing, if nothing else. The wine couldn't have been any more than seventy years in the cellar, it was diabolically gaseous – thank heavens. Lady Shufflebottom was relying on it to make Lord Shufflebottom keep covering her tracks. She kept on slipping silent ones out, but now they would all think it was her husband once again.

'Whoops! Here I go again!' said His Shameless Lordship. He stood up on the armrest of a chaise longue and bent over and aimed directly into the gaggle of gentility. He must have squeezed good and hard because it was a modern-day classic, even by the infamous Lord Shufflebottom's standards.

'Sorry about that,' he said, getting down off the chair, 'it slipped out.'

His good Lady wife let a few more slip quietly out the back door. *Ah, that was better.* And nobody was any the wiser. They all seemed to be of the superficial assumption that sound and aroma go hand in hand. If only they knew the true secret of life, that loud ones have little or no scent.

Life was good, Lord Shufflebottom reflected without a smidgen of pomposity. The life and soul of the party at every stately home in the country was letting them out left, right and centre as was his wont, and he was making it so astoundingly obvious that ne'er a soul guessed his noble wife was doing likewise.

Henrietta Shufflebottom was just about as proud as a Lady could possibly be. What more could a man do for his woman? If Henry hadn't made himself heard so precisely, so visibly, then the Lords and Ladies there present would undoubtedly have come to realise exactly who was being so offensive to their slightly raised nostrils, and removed the Shufflebottoms from their guest lists en masse. Insulting the airwaves just wasn't the done thing, unless one went out of one's way to make it so. It was generally agreed that Lord Shufflebottom was a most hearty soul, and thus he could be forgiven virtually anything. Her Ladyship, on the other hand, was much too quiet for her own good.

Chauffeur tried his best not to look too tired as he drove the limousine home to Shufflebottom Village in the early hours of the morning. He seemed fit to pinch his nostrils at one stage, but thought better of it. One must learn never to try and rise above one's station, after all is said and done. One's betters are one's betters, and that is the end of the matter.
'I did fifteen tonight, dear,' Lord Shufflebottom chuckled as they approached Shufflebottom Hall.
'That's nothing to be proud of,' Her Ladyship chided him, secretly hoping that he would keep up the good work. 'The stench in there was absolutely abominable.'
After parking the limo in the garages, Chauffeur performed a little arithmetic in his pocketbook. Add fifteen… that brought it past the hundred mark that month, with still a week to go. Chauffeur had only guessed a hundred and twenty, so it looked like he wasn't going to win Chef's November sweepstake. Especially not if Lord and Lady Shufflebottom, as expected, opted for mushy peas and cabbage at the Buckingham Palace do on Wednesday.
Chauffeur couldn't take the pair of them anywhere without them showing him up.

PLAY YOUR CARDS RIGHT

Ciara Byrne was hovering by the curtains, trying not to be seen.
'You'll never guess who's walking up our garden path.'
'Not again?' her husband Sean groaned. 'Surely be to God it's not seven whole days since they were here last?'
'They never come on the same evening two weeks in a row,' Ciara said. 'That's how they keep managing to catch us out.' She crouched down, hoping against hope that it wasn't too late.
'I'm going to sneak out the back door,' Sean said. 'Get your coat on, sweetheart, and we'll go to the Vodka-Swiller's Handbag for a few drinks.'
'It's no use,' Ciara said, 'Mrs Kenny has just seen me. She's waving her hand at me.'
Sean faked a coughing fit. 'Tell them I'm not well,' he said, clearly clutching at straws, and he knew it. 'Say I've been dying of the flu since we got the bus home from our shopping spree in the city centre yesterday. Tell them to try again next week, and we'll be better prepared by then. We shouldn't keep letting them catch us out like this.'
There was a long, determined ring on the doorbell and Sean leapt to his feet.
'Are you venturing out there?' Ciara asked.
'No,' Sean said, 'I'm going to sneak out the back door.'
'Oh no you're not,' Ciara insisted. 'You're not leaving me here all alone with Belfast's answer to Dracula and the Bride of Frankenstein. Stay here and take your punishment like a man.'
'It's not too bad for me,' Sean whispered as the determined outsiders rang the bell again, and he found himself unable to clear his head of the picture of Quasimodo in the bell tower in an old black-and-white film. 'You're the one they expect to keep running into the kitchen like a slave, to supply them with a constant conveyor-belt loaded with cups of coffee and sandwiches, while they sit clutching their playing cards close to their pompous, overblown chests as if their lives depend on it. All at our expense, I hasten to add.'

'We're caught in a trap,' Ciara said with a despondent frown as she went out into the front hall to open the door. 'Oh, hello, you two. We were just talking about yous.'

'Nothing too bad, I hope?' Mike Kenny said, as his plastic-faced wife held her pack of cards out in front of her and went, 'Ta-da!'

'No worse than usual,' Ciara replied. 'Come in and take the huge heavy weight off your poor aching feet. We were just about to put the kettle on, boil a few eggs, slice every last onion in the house and crack open a fresh loaf of bread.'

'Good stuff,' Mrs Kenny said, unbuttoning her heavy black overcoat and whipping down the hood. 'We're absolutely famished! You get the coffee and grub, and I'll deal. I bought a brand new pack of unmarked cards this week, ha-ha. Back me up, Mike.'

'She did, she did,' he said, taking off his flat cap and stuffing it in his tweed coat pocket. He dumped his coat on top of his wife's on the armchair, so that Sean could take them and hang them up. Why they were wearing heavy overcoats on a warm summer's evening when they only lived next door was anybody's guess. They planted themselves in pride of place in the middle of Sean and Ciara's sofa.

Every week they treated every last hand with the height of reverence, like a newfound Biblical scroll. From the splitting of the deck to the dealing of the cards right through to the final denouement, they acted as if no one in the world prior to that moment in time had ever played such a vitally significant, earth-shatteringly important game of Snap. Sometimes they decided to live dangerously and play Stop the Bus and even, on one never-to-be-forgotten evening in April, Old Maid, but Snap was their game of choice on ninety-nine out of every hundred occasions.

'That was a nice cup of coffee, Ciara,' Mrs Kenny said, scratching her dull grey hair, 'although if you don't mind me saying so, I make a much nicer one myself. I suppose we all think our own coffee is the nicest. Snap! Oh no, silly me, that was a five, not a six.'

'We want our money back! We want our money back!' the intruders repeatedly sang like Northern Ireland football fans while Ciara was in the kitchen scrubbing clean the cups, saucers and plates in between games number nineteen and twenty of the usual quarter-century marathon. Sean looked at the pair of them, sitting glaring at their watches before starting the obligatory slow handclap.

After drying up, Ciara came back into the living room with a dead look in her eyes, and the tournament recommenced.

Mike was the night's big winner, going home with an extra two pounds and twenty-seven pence in his trouser pocket, one pound and fifteen pence of which he had won off his frustrated wife's back.

'We'll see you the same time next week, if you're lucky!' Mrs Kenny shouted out with her back to Sean and Ciara as she strutted down the garden path.

Ciara needed a long shower, and Sean felt almost as dirty as she did. It was as if they were trapped in the middle of a horror film, in the midst of a nightmare they couldn't wake up from. Sean thought of himself as Ray Milland in *The Premature Burial*. They didn't speak about the incident again for a few days, as it had been too harrowing an experience for the pair of them, just like every other week for what was beginning to seem like time in memoriam. The misery was never-ending.

It was five days later, and Sean was beginning to have cold sweats all over again. Ciara kept on smiling, but Sean knew that, deep down inside, she was hurting, too. Life was becoming totally intolerable.

And then Sean had his brainwave.

It began with a few passing words later that night, when he was still half asleep. Other wives would have passed off the rambling words as mere sleep-talk, but not Ciara, oh no. She picked up on it right away. By the time Sean awoke in the morning Ciara had plotted out all the intricate details in her head, like some manner of expert military strategist. And now it was time to put her master-plan into action.

As Ciara told Sean while they were drinking their morning cups of coffee, they were either going to achieve the greatest success of their interwoven lives to date, or they would fall flat on their faces and never speak about the matter again for as long as they both should live.

'Take that smug grin off your face,' Ciara said, clutching the all-important item in her left hand, with her right hand poised and ready to make a lunge to try and catch it should she accidentally drop it. 'People will think we're up to something.'

'I just can't wait to see them,' Sean said with a knowing smile.

'Neither can I,' Ciara said, 'but we *have* to wait. We have to bide our time. We don't know what their reaction is going to be, as neither man nor beast could predict that odd couple's behaviour, even at the best of times. Let's just keep our fingers crossed and hope for the best.'

'Or the worst,' Sean said, and he laughed out loud until Ciara shushed him.

The two of them felt about ten feet tall as they walked up their neighbours' front garden path, wondering if they were being watched from indoors. Sean's dream had been based around the element of surprise, although in Ciara's variation on the theme the fear factor played an equally significant role. The very thought of the terrible twosome cowering on all fours behind their curtains made Ciara feel like the greatest victor in history.

She thought she could hear despairing voices through an open window, leading her to suspect that one or two people in the house were close to tears. Her most treasured dream came true moments later, when the door was opened from within. The inhabitants had caved in to the mental anguish, after only a couple of mild presses on their doorbell.

Mrs Kenny stood back in the dark hallway holding the door open, unseen, like something out of a Hammer Horror film, but Ciara wasn't frightened. She marched into the house and Sean followed in her footsteps, pulling his collar up just a little bit to avoid having his jugular bitten, chewed or nibbled.

'We weren't expecting you,' Mike Kenny uttered theatrically as Ciara breezed intrepidly into the living room.

'Well, Mrs Kenny,' Ciara said, waving her pristine new pack of cards in the dreaded couple's faces as if it was her proudest possession in the world, 'we can't keep letting you do all the hard work, walking all the way from next door to our house carrying a big heavy pack of cards in your hand. So we decided to take the initiative and pay you a visit for a change.'

'You're so kind,' Mike Kenny said. His wife nodded her head up and down, although her face appeared to be simultaneously shaking from side to side. Ciara couldn't help noticing that Mrs Kenny's lips were turned up, whereas her mouth was turned down.

'Would you like another cheese-and-tomato sandwich?'

'Do you not have any egg-and-onion?'
'Coming up,' Mrs Kenny said, forcing a smile and rushing into the kitchen. Ciara and Sean were eating them out of house and home.
'I've changed my mind,' Ciara said a couple of minutes later, poking her head in through the kitchen door. 'I've taken quite a liking to banana sandwiches. I don't suppose you have a plateful of them handy?'
'Coming up.'
'Did I detect a sigh in Mrs Kenny's voice?' Sean puzzled. Mike trudged into the kitchen with his arms hanging limply by his sides, to try and help his poor put-upon wife. Ciara and Sean pricked up their ears. They thought they heard somebody opening the back door and sneaking out of the house.
Ten minutes later they heard voices, followed by the sound of Mrs Kenny gasping. By sheer chance, four banana sandwiches arrived on a plate three or four frantic minutes later.
'Thanks,' Ciara munched, 'I was beginning to wonder what was keeping you.'
Sean admired his wife's grit, her gumption. He loved the disgruntled look on Mrs Kenny's face, and the fact that he could have sworn he had heard Mike muttering, beneath his breath, 'Touché.'
'Game, set and match,' Ciara gloated after winning the final game of the night, rubbing the palms of her hands together in a gleeful manner. 'That even made your sandwiches worthwhile, Mrs Kenny.' She held out her cup. 'Any chance of a top-up?'
'Can I have some ice-cream?' Sean asked.

'Still no sign of them,' Sean said as he stood peeping out the window, being careful not to be seen by the gruesome twosome should they come walking up their garden path. 'How long has it been now?'
Ciara pulled Sean's hand over and looked at his watch before checking the date on that morning's *Irish News*. 'Today is the sixteenth,' she said. 'That means that, tomorrow, they won't have set foot in our house for... four years and seven months exactly.'
'Not that you're counting,' Sean chuckled.

THE DECOMPOSING COMPOSER

Needless to say, everybody has heard of Northern Ireland's most famous composer, Sammy O'Sullivan. I'm sure I don't need to delve too deeply into the extraordinary details of his bizarre death or his amazing success story here, since the tabloids have told the story back to front – and, I'm reliably informed, they intend to tell the story the right way around in the near future. However, I will touch upon just a smidgen of the great man's private life.
Strange to relate, for a man who will undoubtedly go down in history as the greatest classical composer of his generation (apart from all the ones who were much better than him), Sammy couldn't read music. He wrote all his major masterpieces down the way they sounded, much to the annoyance of his highbrow contemporaries – many of whom died long before he was born, but that didn't stop their multicoloured nostrils from literally flaring in their graves.
He wrote his music down on whatever came to hand when inspiration struck him. Unfortunately, he was always on the toilet when the aforementioned inspiration struck him, so the majority of the world's greatest museums are teeming to the rafters with sacred sheets of toilet paper – mostly unused, although there is one fascinating exception in the Louvre – containing Sammy's original scores.
Sadly, nobody has yet mastered the intricate technique of deciphering a Sammy O'Sullivan score, because he wrote in a form that was totally original and unique. It's nigh on impossible, even now, to see how the great man himself could possibly have remembered his symphonies via his hastily-scribbled notes. 'Da da da dee, dum dum dum' is the opening of his most famous ditty *Symphony Number Nine In Dee Minor*. And yet, peculiarly, the very same notes are jotted down on the lavatorial-type score for another of his countless classics, *The Dum Dum Sonata* – a completely different tempo and a completely different tune.
Thankfully, Sammy came to prominence in the era of the gramophone record, so we mere mortals can retain our old 45s and LPs to remind us of the master's tunes – which modern-day experts

have repeatedly attempted to write down in a more conventional manner, with little success. Sammy seems to have used musical notes that simply don't exist any more. 'Dum' seems to come somewhere in between 'soh' and 'lah' on the musical scale, but 'doo' has yet to be rediscovered.

'I know it's there somewhere, but I just can't find it,' one eminent musicologist was heard to yell in between screams while finally being carted off to his friendly local neighbourhood asylum.

Incredibly, Sammy was a musical virtuoso on both the spoons and the comb. The man's talents were limitless. He it was, indeed, who invented the Flarmonica – a genius (although perhaps slightly madcap) concoction of a harmonica and a bucketful of belly-button fluff.

Regrettably, Sammy was the only person able to play this most angelic-sounding of instruments. He used the Flarmonica to especially good effect on the album of the soundtrack of the motion picture about the opening and closing night of his magical opera *From Belly-Buttons To Chocolate Buttons* (the wondrous story of a confectionery manufacturer who becomes a naughty serial-killer, and does unspeakable things with his dismembered victims – I won't spoil your enjoyment by telling you what happens).

Sammy was involved in every single stage of the production of his operas. He wrote not only the tunes but also the words to both the A- and B-sides of the single of his three-minute opera about a man who has an out-of-body-experience and is subsequently arrested on a charge of indecent exposure while flying naked over his hometown (his soul is eventually sent to prison for a three-year stretch, but his body isn't allowed to visit it).

Oddly enough, considering the fact that his operatic gems had such complicated themes, his lyrics usually consisted entirely of 'Doo's and 'Dee's and 'Doo wop she bop's. I honestly don't think the great man could spell anything else.

Sammy was only too well aware that he had inherited his creative streak from his father's side of the family, because, like his whole family line before him, his father – once a top-selling author, until he was sued for stealing the words to all his novels from a dictionary – was 'a raving lunatic', or so it says on his gravestone.

They say there's a fine line between genius and madness, well Sammy was the proof of the pudding. He wasn't, to be fair, what you might commonly call a sane man. To say the very least, he was a tad eccentric. He was totally convinced that he was a reincarnation of his great hero Vincent Van Gogh – so much so that whenever anybody crossed him he threatened (if they didn't apologize instantly) to cut both his ears off, even though he clearly needed them to hold his glasses on.

'Sammy went to his grave with both his ears intact, as far as I am aware,' his doctor told the *Irish Times* a month after he died. 'Then again,' she added, 'I must confess I didn't actually count them at the time. It never crossed my mind, I was too upset. After all, how many people can honestly claim on their CVs that their best composer friend committed suicide with a dish of pilchards wrapped in cling film?'

Thankfully, Sammy didn't kill himself until late on in his life; extremely late on… in fact it was probably the last thing he ever did. Sammy was an avid collector. He had ten boxes full of avids in his favourite Eskimo girlfriend's igloo alone. He kept three cardboard boxes filled with his phlegm in his doctor's attic. She flushed it down the toilet after he died – she couldn't wait to get rid of the stuff! – but then the late, great man's fan-club belatedly informed her that she could have sold the collector's item for well over a million pounds.

He also collected anything remotely connected with lavatories. Indeed, there was a toilet in every room in his house, and in most cupboards as well. His friends used to be ever so slightly embarrassed when he invited a group of Belfast dignitaries to dinner and then proceeded to proudly demonstrate the art (for want of a better word) of excreting bodily effluent into an emerald-green portaloo on top of the dinner table halfway through the first course – which usually turned out to be the last course, incidentally. He was a rather silly man.

Certain musical experts even believe there may have been a cryptic lavatorial reference in the title of Sammy's depressingly-comic opera about the life and times of a fork-lift truck-driver, *I'm Just Going To Dump My Load*. But his doctor was quite certain that her old friend would never have stooped that low, as he was a gentleman (at least when his trousers weren't down around his ankles).

Sammy had friends both high and low – from six foot four to two foot three, you name it. Nobody disliked him. True, a great many people wanted to kill him, but they didn't actually dislike him, as such. Why, even his most fanatical supporters would just as soon have seen him slip on a banana-skin and tumble under a bus as push him under it themselves. But when he eventually snuffed it, the value of their O'Sullivan record-collections would soar astronomically.

Sammy's mother was one of his biggest fans (six foot two if she was an ounce). She had a copy of every record her son had ever released. Her collection was priceless, and when Sammy kicked the bucket its pricelessness would double. Old Mrs. O'Sullivan's rarest record, a single entitled *Wop Bop Plop*, was worth at least as much as the vinyl it was printed on – maybe even more if the hole in the middle was thrown in for free.

Then there was the picture-disc of the maestro's magnum opus, *Piano Concerto for Euphoniums*, which showed Sammy having his knees shaved by two purple-eyed midgets prior to receiving his knighthood from the Queen. This was one of only two copies issued, the other having been used by Sammy himself as a makeshift cornflakes bowl.

After gratefully accepting his long-underdue knighthood, Sir Sammy O'Sullivan developed delusions of grandeur. He started to think there was nothing under the sun that he couldn't do. Oppenheimer had split the atom? Well he would put it back together again. And Einstein's greatest achievement was $E = MC$ squared? Well, Sammy was formulating a theory called $C = ME$ cubed (if only he knew what it meant).

And he was going to rediscover the Ark (apparently Noah had lost it – how clumsy can you get), and maybe he would invent a bran-based breakfast cereal you didn't have to sit on the toilet to eat. And that was just for starters. Yes indeed, Sammy was determined to solve all of the world's major problems – just as soon as he had wrapped this dish of pilchards in cling film and applied it to his person, in a lavish attempt to reach a brand new musical note provisionally entitled 'Eek'.

Sammy was buried in a coffin made of cream-crackers and cheese. Nobody really believed that the maestro had actually intended to take his own life, although perhaps the evidence was a little on the overwhelming side. He had just completed his autobiography with a paragraph describing in great detail the actual manner of his forthcoming demise, and how he would be buried in a coffin composed of his own favourite snack. He reckoned (and not without foundation) that he had never seen a worm eat cream-crackers, certainly not with cheese.

Before cashing in her priceless Sammy O'Sullivan record-collection at Lloyd's of London, the decomposing composer's heart-broken mother insisted that he be buried in the precise manner he had predicted, otherwise his money-spinning autobiography would have been ruined.

PENNY'S PENGUIN

Penny Potterton had a pet penguin. It was the blackest and whitest penguin in the whole of Belfast. Penny loved her penguin dearly. She named him Philomena to put the other girls off him. Penny's penguin fancied every bird on the street. But the best bits of talent on Jolly Avenue wouldn't look twice at Penny's penguin, because he waddled when he walked.
The big blonde penguin-magnet across the road was a bit of all right, but what would a beautiful woman from a big city see in a shy penguin from the back end of nowhere? Women would have felt daft, walking arm-in-flipper down Jolly Avenue with a waddling penguin. Philomena wished he could up and fly away... but as every nun knows, penguins can't fly. What a cruel trick fate had played on Penny's penguin.
    Penny's penguin was pushing a shopping-trolley filled with salmon home from the supermarket. He loved to wrap his gums around a nice salmon sandwich smothered in tartar sauce. Penny's penguin clapped his flippers with glee when he had a full tummy. He liked to clap.
He had a sore belly. He had eaten too much fish. Penny's penguin would be on the toilet all night. There was no toilet-paper left, so he had to use the cardboard roll in the middle. It was very hard.
At times he wished he was back home in the Antarctic, but he had to leave because the other penguins thought he was a halfwit. He had been a very clumsy penguin. He used to keep slipping and sliding on the ice. He had hitched a ride on the first available submarine to Ireland, where Penny Potterton took the stray penguin into her home. Penny loved her penguin. Philomena was a good penguin. Apart from when he told Penny how films on the telly were going to end up. That wasn't a very nice thing for a penguin to do. It made Penny very sad. At times Penny wanted to kick her penguin's head in, for being so naughty.
Penny took her penguin to Mass every Sunday morning. Penny's penguin didn't want to go to Mass. He was a Protestant penguin, and proud of it. He didn't like nuns. He considered nuns pretenders to the

king penguin's throne, trying to steal the limelight from him with their black and white habits. But Penny's penguin was the naturally blackest and whitest penguin this side of the Irish border.

Maybe Penny was only interested in the Penguin Support Allowance she claimed from the social security office for looking after him? But he could do a decent job of work as a fisher-penguin, or maybe a police penguin. He wasn't afraid to get his flippers dirty.

Penny's penguin was watching a nature programme on the telly. It said that penguins were kept in zoos, where human beings laughed at the way they walked. Why didn't they lock Penny's penguin in a zoo, instead of peeping out through their curtains and pointing and laughing at him?

You don't bump into penguins at the frozen food section in eight out of ten supermarkets. You don't usually go for a pint and find yourself sitting next to a drunken penguin at the bar. And women generally don't dump their boyfriends in favour of a penguin. It was blatant discrimination. He had never seen a penguin play football for a top Premier League club, or even Northern Ireland. Nobody wanted to employ a penguin with flat feet and a silly flat cap.

Penny's penguin left home one cold winter's night. The following morning he awoke to find Belfast flipper-deep in snow and ice. He waddled safely across the ice while the people all around him fell flat on their faces. Now who looked like a square penguin in a round hole!

Penny's penguin noticed the curtains rustling in every house, but this time nobody was laughing. Everybody wanted to be a king penguin like Philomena. But that was only his slave name – from now on he wanted to be known as *His Royal Highness Philomena, the Penguin King of Ireland*. From this day forward, His Royal Highness proclaimed, it would snow all the time, and people would only be allowed to live in penguin-approved igloos. Fish would become the new kingdom's staple diet, apart from Fridays, when King Philomena liked a Chinese after his seven pints of lager down the pub.

Penny was overjoyed when her straying penguin returned home, suffering from hypothermia. 'Would you do me the immense honour of becoming my queen?' the king asked Penny before collapsing in a heap in the snow. It was never this cold in the Antarctic.

Penny accepted Philomena's marriage proposal. To blazes with what her neighbours thought – the king of all penguins, both north and south of the Irish border, was more human than most of the people she knew. OK, so he totally lacked facial expression, but you can't have it both ways.

Penny knew when she was on to a good thing, as she told her parents when she introduced them to the king. When would she ever again get the chance to become the queen of Ireland's blossoming penguin population?

'It would never have worked,' Penny consoled the king, as they got up off the road onto which her parents had booted them. 'I should have realised that the parents of a Catholic girl like myself would never let me marry a Protestant penguin – especially not one who wears a flat cap and waddles when he walks.'

In an effort to win the affections of Penny's parents, King Philomena changed his religion. He even became the first penguin nun in the whole of Belfast. However, as he stood in the communal shower after his first game of nuns-only rugby, he suddenly forgot that Penny had ever existed.

King Philomena was the most contented penguin nun in the whole of Belfast, bar none. He was a happy penguin.

FINGER ON THE PULSE

John Finger was always afraid that if he didn't do his little bit to help his hometown the place would simply cease to function as a whole. He liked to think that, in his own small way, he helped to keep the wheels turning in Fingertown (named, it was believed, after his great-grandfather, William Fingertown).

If there was ever a fire to be doused in the small Northern Irish town, Fireman Finger was at the ready with his one-man fire brigade. If there was a criminal to be caught, Constable Finger was waiting just around the corner with his trusty truncheon. And, come Sunday morning, Reverend Finger was always there to preach to his loyal flock.

As you may by now have gathered, John Finger was a veritable jack-of-all-trades. Petrol-pump attendant, plumber, carpet-fitter and hairdresser, you name it, he did it. He was also the local sheep-dipper, but he only worked part-time in that particular role since Farmer Finger's farm was the only one for miles around. (His uncle Jake kept a couple of sheep, but that's another story.)

The middle-aged entrepreneur's townsfolk often wondered how he managed to be so many things to so many men. Whereas most people could only manage to squeeze twenty-four hours into a single day, John Finger's days seemed to stretch on and on without end. From milking the cows at the crack of dawn to lighting the street gaslights at sunset he was always on the go. And then he seemed to spend the best part of the night prowling around the streets singing out 'Three o'clock and all's well' at the top of his voice (which was extremely irritating to the residents, because for most of the night it wasn't actually three o'clock at all), after guiding drunkards home from his public house, which he opened every evening immediately after gas-lighting time, to tend the bar without any assistance.

John Finger spent the major part of his weekdays teaching the one hundred and fifty-seven children at Fingertown's compact little school-cum-garage-cum-grocery-store (one of those typical small-town shops where a person could buy everything and anything, with or without knobs). Alas, like everyone else in the town, not one of the many hundreds of children who had passed through his one-teacher school over the years had ever managed to gain respectable employment. There simply wasn't the work. Everybody was unemployed in Fingertown (barring the obvious).

As a matter of fact, incredible as it might sound, a great many people there actually resented John Finger for occupying so many positions to the exclusion of everyone else. The man hardly ever opened the doors of his self-run job-market to the desperate public, and when he eventually did there were invariably no jobs left. Indeed, Some cynics even dared to suggest that Finger himself snapped up every half-decent post that arose.

John Finger's overwhelming confidence in his own abilities wasn't, however, totally without foundation. For example, whenever he took a day off sick the whole town seemed to grind to a clattering halt. Schoolchildren roamed the streets harassing their poor unemployed parents, the fuel-deprived traffic stood motionless, and if (God forbid) the multi-talented Finger fell ill on a Sunday, the eager morning worshippers tended to trudge around the streets like lost souls. On top of which it was best to avoid accidents and illness if Doctor Finger himself was off sick.

And yet, despite the immense amount of good work that he clearly did for the town, everybody despised him, not just the unemployed... but then again, everybody bar him *was* unemployed.

Due to the sheer intensity of his constant struggle through life, John Finger had never once managed to find time for romance. Not that it mattered, of course, because he was too jealously loathed for any woman to dare being seen dead in his company, and thus risk becoming a black-sheep like him. Neither had he ever managed to fit a holiday into his all-too-rigorous schedule. The people would have starved. Illness would have been rampant. Darkness would have reigned supreme. The Devil would have taken over the town.

All in all, John Finger *was* Fingertown. All right, so his townsfolk didn't love him... but at least they knew he was alive. *Boy*, did they know he was alive. So much so, in fact, that they wanted him dead.

John Finger was completely inconsiderate towards the petty thoughts and feelings of his petty neighbours – or as he occasionally liked to think of them, his subjects. As long as he lived and breathed, all was right with the world.

Who gave a monkey's what the scrounging masses fantasized about? Why couldn't they get up off their fat, lupine backsides and do some work once in a while? He was sick and tired of them all coming to sign on for their unemployment benefit at his social security office once a fortnight, and then going to cash their ill-gained giros at his post office. Half of them frittered their money away in his bar or his betting-office or countless other of his wasteful enterprises, and hardly any of them kept money in his bank. Meanwhile he slaved his guts out all the hours that God sent, and he rarely ever had two pennies to rub together. Maybe it was about time he started getting paid for his labours.

While Judge Finger was attending court one warm summer's evening, an unofficial select committee of Fingertown residents held a covert meeting at the town crossroads (which was in the middle of being re-tarred by John Finger construction, sole trader) to discuss ways of ridding their town of the omnipresent pariah. If he were gone, there would be more than enough work to go around the three hundred and forty-three doleful adult inhabitants.

The local comedian Dominic McKittrick, an unemployed undertaker, foolhardily suggested killing John Finger, and the ridiculous motion was accepted unanimously.

It would be the perfect crime, committed by the town as a whole against one insignificant figure. Why, even if the outside authorities ever managed to find out about the murder, what could they do? They could hardly lock a whole town up, after all. Fingertown's single cell certainly wasn't large enough to hold more than two or three people. And besides, the key to it was in the pocket of the forthcoming murder victim, and it would be buried along with him.

Since it had been his brainwave, Dominic McKittrick was given the undoubted honour of carrying out the assassination, by whatever means took his fancy. Then perhaps he could at last gain respectable employment as the undertaker he had long dreamt of one day becoming... with the late John Finger as his first customer.

At long last, John Finger Construction (sole trader) finished building the town's clandestine new prison, easily capable of holding a good five hundred inmates. And now to try it out.

No sooner had Finger the labourer downed his shovel than Dominic McKittrick raced past in his second-hand hearse, only to be arrested by Constable Finger for impersonating an undertaker. He added further charges of attempting to strangle the arresting officer, and en route to the new prison he donned his judge's wig and sent McKittrick down for three years, with only the occasionally visiting prison officer for company (when he could find the time).

But McKittrick wasn't alone for long. Later that same night the local bartender arrested seven drunken hooligans and sentenced them to four years in jail for disorderly behaviour in his public house. Add to this a couple of dozen lazy parents who were late in bringing their children to school the following morning, and the new prison *HMP Finger* was soon in full flow. So much so, that the local schoolteacher had to send the children home early so he would have the time to dish out slop for the inexplicably irascible inmates.

Furious crowds thronged the streets that night, apparently discussing the latest startling developments in Fingertown. They were duly charged with loitering with intent – another hundred-odd hungry mouths to feed. But Prison Officer Finger wasn't complaining. In fact he slept like a log that night, happy in the knowledge that he was finally beginning to earn the full respect of his lowly subjects.

John Finger had to don his fireman's outfit just after sunrise, in order to douse a blaze in his own living room. After doing that and then re-glazing his window, he entered his policeman mode once again and arrested a number of men suspected of having firebombed his house. Nobody would stand up like a man and admit to the horrendous crime, so – in judicial mode – Finger gave them all ten years' hard labour for conspiring to pervert the course of justice. Add to that (amongst others) the curmudgeonly housewives who staged an illegal demonstration in the town centre later that morning, and pretty soon the sparkling new prison was the absolute hub of all life in Fingertown.

John Finger had even had the remarkable foresight to reserve a wing specifically for the one hundred and fifty-seven children who failed miserably in their duty to turn up for school the following morning, giving the ridiculous excuse that their parents hadn't been there to get them out of bed.

John Finger finally had his comfortable little hometown all to himself.

It was the height of summer and so, with no prying eyes to size him up, John Finger took to strolling around his beloved streets in his mankini and flip-flops, lapping up the sun, making himself thoroughly at home. He spent the next few days bricking up all the roads in and out of Fingertown, to keep out any unwanted visitors. He had contemplated leaving one secret route open for himself, but decided that it was unnecessary since his little store already contained more than enough supplies to keep himself and his five hundred prisoners going for well over a year.

Ironically, Finger discovered that running a prison was hard labour in itself. He had to personally deliver all the boulders to be smashed to a pulp by the prisoners. And it was rather expensive to boot... balls and chains don't grow on trees, you know. But, luckily, Finger had at his disposal the unemployment benefits and child allowance of his five hundred prisoners to pay for all the necessities.

It must be stated here that John Finger was very good to his captives, the majority of whom openly admitted that his prison was like a home from home, only better. They had all mod cons in their cells, unlike in most of their homes. Each cell contained a comfortable armchair, a bed, a radio and a hot-water bottle, you name it, and their kindly captor had gladly supplied it. They were so happy in their confinement, in fact, that when Dominic McKittrick completed his three-year sentence he literally begged John Finger to let him stay in jail (and the great man of course concurred).

A newfound respect had evidently developed between John Finger and his loyal subjects – or as he now preferred to think of them, his *peers* (well, almost). Out of respect for their (for want of a better word) master, the prisoners even vacated a cell especially for him, so that he wouldn't have to travel all the way from his house to the prison every morning.

He could now get out of bed in jail, there to begin his day's chores by cooking breakfast for five hundred (and one, if he was ever hungry himself). Why, if he was there all day he could do absolutely everything for his poor ignorant subordinates – he could be their butler. He could do their washing, darn their smalls, change the radio channel for them, and in effect do all sorts of little jobs around their cells. Yes indeed, he could do all the work, leaving nothing whatsoever for anyone else to do, and everybody would be happy. John Finger couldn't agree more. And thus they became quite the happiest little enclosed community on earth.

John Finger the prison chef was amazed to find his job getting easier and easier as time passed by. He finally came to the stark realisation that the number of mouths he was feeding was dwindling daily, by the time it had dropped from five hundred to forty-seven within a week. But he was among friends now, for the first time in his life, and his was not to reason why.

Nobody had complained about his cooking, so how could he complain about their eating? At least his supply of food in the prison store would last a lifetime now, he thought contentedly to himself after another couple of days, when he discovered that he was apparently the only prisoner left. If he didn't know better, he might have thought that his five hundred dear, dear friends had seen fit to escape... but no, surely they loved him too much to contemplate such a thing.

*****

Fingertown is simply the happiest little town on God's good earth, what with its non-stop working ethos and every adult having a job of work, from Dominic McKittrick the undertaker to Jake Finger the sheep-dipper and bartender (a man whose nephew mysteriously went missing ten years ago).

The model village is a hive of activity, with a different face performing a different duty on every street corner. As a matter of fact, the only place in Fingertown where life seems to cease is the old, abandoned prison, long since bricked-up, which the smiling townsfolk claim has never been occupied since it was built... with maybe just the one exception.

A BIG HAND

Madge Scunthorpe has been on the stage for twenty-five years, and she will be there for another twenty-five if her captive audience lives long enough.

******

When the curtain came down on the first night of probably the best play ever written in 1971, the exhilarated audience's applause went on and on without end. The most grateful audience in the history of Irish theatre felt so privileged to have witnessed such an exemplary work of art, that they felt unworthy of a second showing.

The ten actors concerned soon got tired of standing on the stage, bowing to their adoring public. After a mere four weeks two members of the cast walked off the stage and straight into a mental hospital, believing they were obviously the finest specimens of manhood to set foot on planet Earth in almost two thousand years.
After six weeks, a third member of the bowing cast died of natural causes (he hadn't eaten since before the performance), but the applause never once faltered as they dragged his body off the stage and replaced him with a stand-in, a stunt-man who specialized in bowing.
After that, the thousand-strong audience took it in turns to leave and go to the lavatory and/or fetch food, and some of the people even slept occasionally, although they were careful not to interrupt the flow of the applause for the exceptional work of art.

Madge Scunthorpe stopped applauding for a minute and turned to her husband.
'Come on, darling, I think it's about time we went home now.'
Seamus was aghast.
'Clap, clap!' he said. 'Everybody's looking at you!'
'We've been sitting here clapping for ten years, dear… I don't think the play was *that* good.'

'Play? What play?'
'What do you think we've been sitting here applauding for all these years?' Madge asked in disbelief.
'I... I don't know,' Seamus fumbled. 'Just clap, clap... you're showing me up!'
'Hey, bozos!' A stranger shouted at the rowdy-makers. 'Stop making so much noise – you're spoiling the applause.'
'Sorry,' Seamus said subserviently, clapping ever louder.
Madge watched her husband in amazement as his hands started to bleed once more. But she loved him, so what else could she do? She started to applaud again, hoping the rest of the audience would eventually forgive and forget her little indiscretion. Not a single member of the gathering had had the gall to stop clapping in over a decade, so how on earth could she think that she was better than everybody else and be the first to do so? What was she, some sort of Communist?

By the time the nineties arrived, the outside world was beginning to ask some awkward questions. Why had seven of Belfast's greatest actors (and one stunt man) stood on a stage milking the applause for coming on twenty years, refusing all offers of work? And why, a year after that, did the two actors who had exited from stage left twenty years and forty-eight weeks ago return to the scene and recommence bowing?
There was utter uproar among the crowd when the two straying sheep returned to their flock. It was almost like the Second Coming.
'Just think,' Seamus told his middle-aged wife, making her feel totally ashamed of herself, 'if I'd listened to you eleven years ago we would have missed this extraordinary moment.'
Madge felt suitably chastised. Certain extremist sections of the audience still hadn't fully forgiven her for nearly deserting them like a rat from a sinking ship. Around a hundred members of the gathering had passed away in the intervening years, leaving a mere nine hundred-odd faithful followers. But, astonishingly, the applause seemed to be getting even louder by the year.
Neither were the cast members completely ungrateful. Some of their heads could be seen quite visibly swelling with pride and self-satisfaction as their silver anniversary approached. By which time questions were being asked in Parliament.

Five hundred bodies had by now been released from Belfast's Slaughterhouse Theatre. What strange, dark force compelled formerly decent, law-abiding citizens to clap and clap and clap until their hands fell off and they bled to death? And what were they clapping for?

The cast had whittled down to one, the eight older members and one stunt man having shuffled off this mortal coil, one by one, to rapturous applause. There were five hundred apparently sane people standing (yes, they had leapt to their feet after some twenty-three years, when the star of the show excitingly choked on his own vomit) applauding a man who, a quarter of a century earlier, had played the back end of a clothes-horse in yet another play about the Second World War and the women left at home to do the washing.

On government orders, police marksmen shot dead the sole remaining member of the cast. His bloody demise brought the house down. It was a good two years before the thunderous applause died down to a merely ecstatic level. And it was at that point that Madge Scunthorpe again attempted to test her husband's faith.

'Perhaps we should go home now,' she said snidely, 'leave while the going's good.'

But – where was he?

'Your husband died last Christmas,' a woman in the seat behind begrudgingly informed Madge when pressed. 'Now stop interrupting me – I'm trying to clap, for God's sake.'

Seamus... was *dead*? Madge was in a state of shock.

But people were looking at her. So she clapped. She clapped out loud. She clapped like she had never clapped before. She clapped until the ears of the woman in the seat behind her started to bleed.

Another three years flew by before Madge Scunthorpe again took her troublesome loud mouth in her hands and stopped smartly in her tracks. She bravely pointed out that there was nobody on the stage. Why was everybody clapping? – Luckily for her, nobody heard her.

After thirty years of non-stop clapping, the three hundred surviving members of the audience were stone deaf. All except for the woman in the seat behind Madge: the congealed blood in her ears had saved her hearing. But it wasn't much good to her, for she was as dead as a dodo's uncle.

Madge was beginning to think (not for the first time, but she wasn't about to tell anybody else that) that this whole thing was silly. Surely there was more to life than constant applause, which, to be brutally honest, hadn't been earned to such an extent? All right, the play had been quite good... but was it really *that* good? And if so, why had it closed down after only one night? The proprietors of the Slaughterhouse Theatre claimed they had intended to evict the audience as soon as the applause ended, but things hadn't gone quite according to plan.

Madge climbed up onto the empty stage. There was a temporary lull in the adulation as she commenced to speak.
'The play is over,' she yelled. 'You can all stop clapping and go home.'
After initially looking at her as if she was some sort of lunatic, the excited audience clapped even louder.
'You've wasted thirty years of your lives,' Madge screamed. 'You're all stark raving bonkers.'
The applause echoed around the Edwardian theatre. Surprisingly, Madge found that she quite liked the sound of it. They were clapping for her.
'What's black-and-white and read all over? – A newspaper.'
The audience cheered in exultation. The worse Madge's jokes got, the louder she was applauded. When she ran out of jokes she started quoting numbers from the telephone directory, and the attendant public were delighted. They adored her. She didn't want to ever leave the stage as long as she lived.

******

Madge Scunthorpe has been on the stage for twenty-five years. Although her audience is getting smaller and smaller with every passing year (at the last count there were seventeen geriatrics furiously applauding her telephone number recitals), she is happy with her lot. She has a loyal, captive audience that has stayed with her through thick and thin.
Madge has never actually performed her one-woman show outside the Slaughterhouse Theatre, and she still hasn't yet completed her first performance. But she hopes to do so one year in the not-too-

distant future, and maybe then begin a second show with which she can hopefully end her absorbing career.

But as long as there are hands to applaud Madge Scunthorpe in the theatre she has grown to love over the last fifty-five years, as long as the punters keep clapping and rolling in the aisles, then the old woman will read out encyclopaedias and dictionaries to her heart's content.

WALLPAPER

Sean and Ciara Byrne wallpapered their living room the day the UFO hovered over their house. It was the red-and-yellow wallpaper Ciara had made Sean buy for five quid a roll in the New Year sales. Ciara said it would go well with the carpet she had bought to celebrate their hamster's birthday.

They were just finishing the last wall when the flying-saucer landed in their front garden. Sean was pasting the small patches of paper onto the wall beneath the window. He hated those awkward little bits, they always seemed to take longer than the full-length ones. Ciara was moaning because Sean kept getting paste on the carpet. But as he told her when the door opened on the side of the alien craft out on their lawn, 'You can't make an omelette.' She could hardly cook at all, for God's sake.

Ciara stared out at the UFO. 'I hope that thing doesn't wreck my privet hedge.'

'*Your* privet hedge?' Sean asked in disbelief. 'Who stole it from the cemetery? Who planted it?'

Ciara said Sean was always nitpicking, like a little girl.

'Me?' he said, raging.

She laughed. 'Look at your eyes, they're popping out of your head… just *look* at them.'

'How can I look at my own eyes?' Sean asked in exasperation.

Ciara looked out into the garden for something to compare with his eyes. He hated the way she always did that. 'Your eyes are even bigger than theirs,' she laughed, pointing at the two little green men staring in their window.

'Now don't exaggerate,' Sean said, thoroughly insulted. 'Their eyes are like dishes, for God's sake. Which reminds me, when are we going to get that satellite dish? All the neighbours have one. We'll become a laughing stock if we don't get satellite TV soon.'

'When do I ever get time to watch the telly?' Ciara asked, as if Sean didn't count. 'I don't sit watching soaps all day, apart from my seven or eight not-to-be-missed favourites.'

'But I always have to go down to the Vodka-Swiller's Handbag to watch the football,' Sean argued, sitting down in his armchair. 'It's not fair.'

'Well,' Ciara argued, 'you shouldn't drink so much.' – Sean couldn't compete with female logic. 'Who the hell is that, knocking on our door at this hour of the evening?'

'Have I got x-ray eyes?'

'If it's those little green men, tell them we don't want any.'

'Who said I was going to open the door?'

'It's your turn,' Ciara argued, like a little girl. 'I paid the milkman.'

'I wish *I'd* paid the bloody milkman!' Sean snapped back, getting up out of his armchair. It wasn't a very witty riposte, but it was the best he could come up with on the spur of the moment.

'Well,' Ciara nagged, 'what did they want?'

'Ten pence for a cup of tea.'

Ciara huffed. 'You never tell me anything.'

'I've just bloody told you.'

She started wiping blobs of paste off the running board. Then she put her paste-covered green skirt into the washing machine and put her blue one on.

Ciara wasn't talking to Sean, who begrudgingly put his leather jacket on and went out to the garden shed. He was sorting out his toolbox when there was a knock on the door. It was those two little green gits again.

'I've told you once, I don't have any change. Go and get yourself a job, like the rest of us.'

They looked like four-foot frogs, standing almost erect. One of them kept scratching his naughty bits, like he had scabies or something. They had no clothes on.

'Do you mind? My wife's a woman, you know… well, just about.' Sean rubbed his chin. 'And before you say it's nothing she hasn't seen a hundred times before…'

He couldn't understand a word they said. He asked them why they couldn't learn to speak English, but he couldn't understand their reply.

The itchy one said it again. It definitely sounded like *Ten pence for a cup of tea, Guv?*

'Sean!'

He looked up the garden path. She threw a sleeping-bag out the back door.

'You can sleep in the shed, with your new friends!'

'Then where are *their* sleeping-bags?'

The garden lit up. Ciara looked up at the UFO hovering over their house and slammed the door shut. Sean expected a light to shoot out of it and beam him up. The hatch on the side of the craft opened and a little green man threw a rope-ladder out. Sean didn't know what possessed him, but he climbed up it. Anything to get away from *her*.

He looked down. 'Oy! Hands off!'

The two little thieves put his tool-kit back into the shed and followed him up the ladder. He saw Ciara standing at the back bedroom window, looking out with a big gurny gob. It looked like she was saying *Showing me up in front of the neighbours!* She closed the curtains and Sean continued his climb.

He looked down again, and saw his neighbour Mike Kenny standing in his back garden, hands on hips. Sean shouted down and asked him, 'How did Manchester United do tonight?'

'I didn't listen to the match on the radio,' Mike told him. 'I was going to watch the highlights on the telly later.' He started mowing his lawn, and Sean climbed up into the UFO.

He was amazed at how small it was inside the flying-saucer. There were seven little green midgets packed inside it like sardines. Where was Sean going to sit? Three of them got up and let him sit down, saving him from having to clip their ears. They flew slowly up the main street, narrowly missing a couple of lampposts. The driver of a double-decker bus thought they were going to crash into him, and started angrily waving his fist at them. The driver of the salmon-pink Metro-bus planted his foot on the brake and poked his head out the window.

'Get that bloody lump of tin out of here,' Sean heard him shouting. 'I hope you've got a driving-licence for that flying-saucer, you little green fecker.'

The passengers in the upper deck shook their heads and tutted. A traffic policeman looked disapprovingly up at the UFO as it hovered over Belfast City Hall. He took his notebook out of his pocket.

'Don't go above thirty miles an hour,' Sean told the little green man frantically clutching the steering-wheel. 'You don't want to get a speeding ticket on your first day in Northern Ireland.'

The alien looked at Sean and gave him a thumbs-up sign. Message received and understood. Then Sean realised that he was a *woman* driver. She was wearing green lipstick and false eyelashes. Nothing else, mind you… there's nothing worse than an alien who wears too much make-up. She had deep, four-inch-round eyes. Sean thought it was love at first sight.

She was called Blurp. What a beautiful name. She stopped at the traffic-lights and made her six chums get out. They climbed down the rope-ladder and went into the pub. Sean snuggled up next to Blurp as she put her foot down on the accelerator. Sean had to grab hold of the steering-wheel and swerve it around to the right to prevent them from crashing into the moon.

'Women drivers!' – It slipped out.

She banged her foot down on the brakes, and they came to a shuddering halt.

'Banda zorko flook!' – She was furious.

'Your revoltingly big saucer-eyes look gorgeous when you're angry…'

Sean suddenly noticed that she had big floppy ears, like a green bulldog. She was wearing little square ear-rings. They were some strange metal Sean had never seen before. Pink, it was.

She picked him up by the scruff of his ears and threw him out just over his house. He landed on the roof.

As Sean was climbing down the drainpipe into the back garden, he saw a big blue beam of light shoot out of the alien craft and zap Mike Kenny up into it. His flat cap fell off when his molecules were electrically transformed. How come the green-skinned lady had made Sean climb up the rope-ladder? She clearly didn't love him as much as she loved his next-door neighbour. To hell with her, Sean thought. There were plenty more of her sort knocking around, don't you worry.

Ciara relented and let Sean back into the house. It was obviously his sexual magnetism. And she wanted him to paint the kitchen door. The paint was a horrible yellow colour, but she liked it. Sean thought it would just look like a dirty white door. He said he would do it later, and treated Ciara to a pint down the pub. Blurp's six alien buddies were playing pool and getting pie-eyed. They had lined the side of the pool table with two-pound coins so that nobody human could get a game.

Ciara was telling her friend Mrs Kenny that she and Sean had wallpapered their living room, and Mrs Kenny was dead jealous. The lads in the pub were watching the footie highlights on the telly, but United were playing rubbish. Mrs Kenny was bemoaning the fact that her husband had run off 'to Ursa Major or Ursa Minor or Timbuk-Bloody-Tu with a wide-eyed green-skinned slut' half her age, but nobody wanted to get involved in her marital tiff so she changed the subject.

'Did you see that bloody UFO earlier on?' Mrs Kenny said, as Sean and Ciara supped their pints of lager. 'It missed our bus by inches… it could have took the bloody roof off.'

Sean was going to tell Mrs Kenny the driver's gender, but he thought better of it. Once bitten twice shy, and all that. He didn't fancy kipping in the shed, sleeping-bag or not. Manchester United scored and all the humans jumped up and down. The aliens thought they were mad. Ciara tried to take them down a peg or two.

'Are you lot not cold, running around with no clothes on?'

All the humans laughed. That would harden them. A drunkard propping up the bar started moaning about the aliens coming down to Northern Ireland stealing everybody's jobs, so Sean and Ciara decided to go home in case things turned nasty.

When they arrived home, Ciara dropped a bombshell – her mother was coming to pay them a surprise visit the following morning. So that was why she had made Sean buy the new wallpaper. That was why she wanted the kitchen door painted.

'You can do it your bloody self.'

Sean crawled off to sleep in the shed. He was going to stay there until the old battleaxe went home. He knew when he wasn't wanted.

THE EARLY YEARS OF ARMCHAIR JOE AND THE SCRAMBLED-EGG KID

Feargal Cassidy's stepfather carried his stepladder with him everywhere he went. 'You never know when it might come in handy,' he told every stranger he passed on the street.

Little did he care when, during the 1979 television strike, England's leading soap *Coronation Street* was off the air for ten weeks. He simply boarded a ferry to Liverpool, hopped on a train to Manchester and looked at the empty *Street* set over a high wall for half an hour every Monday and Wednesday night. But he was selfish. He refused to tell anybody what was happening on *Coronation Street* while they were missing it.

'A stepladder,' Feargal's stepfather often boasted, 'is the best friend a man can have.'

Nobody could argue with this one summer's day in 1981, when a panda at Belfast Zoo overpowered its guard and confiscated his machine-gun. It went on the rampage, shooting all around it while Feargal's stepfather sat on top of his stepladder watching excitedly, scoffing a bag of popcorn.

'It's a little-known fact,' he declared (showing once again just how wise he was, even then), 'that the ailuropoda melanoleuca – commonly known as the giant panda – is not adept at conquering rungs, especially of the stepladder variety. But I am.'

Feargal's stepfather had the best view of all each time he went to England and stood on the Stretford End watching Manchester United matches. Apart from the time when he had one glass of Vimto too many, and decided to hold his stepladder up above his head to let it enjoy the game for a change. He had clean forgotten about the only blot on its otherwise exemplary character... his stepladder was a Liverpool fan. The two of them were nearly eaten alive by the crowd when they heard what the loudmouth was shouting about the sworn enemy.

Feargal's stepmother was a cruel, cruel woman. She was forever nipping and punching her husband's stepladder as he cradled it in his arms in bed at night. She threatened to pickle Feargal's five-year-old collection of stale hard-boiled eggs if he ever told him – thus decreasing their collectability value by anything up to 23.5%, according to the local evaluators Schmick, Schmack and O'Shaughnessy.

With the benefit of hindsight, it's plain to see that Feargal's stepmother was jealous of the love her husband openly showed to his stepladder. Feargal spent a weekend in Dublin for the 1983 'Stalest hard-boiled egg in Ireland' competition (in which his July 1980 Co-op egg finished a magnificent second to the Reverend 'Pongypants' Parker's beloved egg 'The Lady Shufflebottom Special') and returned home to find his stepfather's stepladder covered in bruises.

Feargal's vindictive stepmother had taken advantage of his absence while his stepfather slept (so nobody could hear the screams) to beat his stepladder black and blue with a bunch of bananas she had secretly kept since 1974 for just such an occasion.

While his beloved stepladder spent two weeks in a critical condition in Belfast City Hospital, Feargal's poor stepfather locked himself away in his favourite coalbunker, a broken man. It was undoubtedly the finest day of his life when his best buddy returned home, fit and raring to face the world once again. His wife was arrested on a charge of grievous bodily harm after the stepladder told the police who had perpetrated the sickening attack.

Feargal's stepmother was sentenced to four years in prison, and during her absence it was all sweetness and light in their little red-brick house (the bricks had been blue until one night in 1978 when Feargal's drunken stepmother went out and painted the town red). Sadly, she escaped after a mere six months and set out to kill Feargal's stepfather's stepladder.

The police informed Feargal and his stepfather that the crazy woman had vowed revenge, and they put an armed guard on the Cassidy household. However, the sergeant added, the 'poor lady' was so enraged that they had little hope of being able to prevent an eventual assassination attempt on the stepladder.

Feargal's stepfather and his buddy remained down in the coalbunker for six months. But then they decided to stop enjoying themselves, and instead they kept a low profile.

Ironically, it was at that time that Feargal became a high-profile celebrity due to a sudden upsurge in interest in stale hard-boiled eggs (it was bound to happen sooner or later). You couldn't walk down the street in Belfast without seeing Feargal's face plastered on a wall hoarding somewhere or other. At one stage he was on the local news bulletins at least four or five times a week.

Stale hard-boiled eggs were taking the whole of Ireland by storm. Even Feargal was amazed by the sheer intensity of the interest they aroused. Attendances at football, rugby and gaelic matches plummeted as people stayed at home in droves at the weekend to boil eggs and time them with a stop-watch to see how long they took to go stale. The sale of stop-watches naturally rocketed, and the makers of the most popular brand sent Feargal boxes full of them as their way of saying thanks; he ended up stuffing his bed-pillows with them.

After four months of national glory, at the beginning of 1984, Feargal was awarded his own TV chat show. He introduced guests from the world of sport, art and literature, most of whom were of course obsessed with stale hard-boiled eggs... which made Feargal's job a lot easier: no prizes for guessing which single topic the majority of his conversations with football, pop and movie stars centred on.

As a personal favour to his stepfather, Feargal devoted a quarter of each of his nightly half-hour TV specials to the fascinating subject of stepladders in all their splendour. He even let his stepfather introduce these sections after the first couple of months, by which time theirs was the number one show from Cork to the Giant's Causeway. Feargal Cassidy was Ireland's favourite son (it was only a matter of time).

By now, of course, his stepfather was sporting a solid gold stepladder, although the original was still his bestest friend. He even let the Queen of England stand on the bottom rung – a great honour indeed – to reach up and award him his OBE.

Feargal bought himself and his stepfather a large mansion in Killarney, and filled it up with stale hard-boiled eggs that his adoring fans had sent him from every corner of the globe. Schmick, Schmack and O'Shaughnessy estimated their gross value at something approaching seventeen million pounds, and possibly double that now that Feargal had been associated with them.

There was a four-foot difference in the level of each room in Feargal's new mansion, which meant that – to his stepfather's utter delight – they had to use stepladders to enter and exit. It was sheer bliss.

And then the rot set in.

Feargal and his stepfather arrived home late one night, after a particularly successful episode of *The Hard-Boiled Egg and Stepladder Show*. It was the now-famous night that Feargal attained the best of both worlds, by standing on the top rung of a stepladder and determining the vintage of numerous unmarked stale hard-boiled eggs merely by their stench. Yes indeed, Feargal was truly at the peak of his powers.

As his stepfather turned the front-door key, standing on top of his stepladder, he turned around and said that something was up. Feargal looked up but he saw nothing. His stepfather had always had a sixth sense, but until then it was only insofar as stepladders were concerned.

Feargal climbed up the stepladder and hopped into the room. What he saw next fair turned his stomach. There, standing in the centre of the living room floor, was a six-foot glass jar... filled to the brim with hard-boiled eggs, pickled in vinegar.

A high-pitched scream rang out from beneath Feargal's stepfather's feet. As Feargal struggled in vain to get up off his knees he saw, through the tears streaming down his face, his distraught stepfather thumping his fist desperately up and down on his favourite old wooden stepladder, trying to revive it – but it was too late. His buddy was dead.

Feargal's evil stepmother had finally tracked them down, a year to the day (give or take a month) after escaping from jail, and shattered their very existence. 'I wish I was dead,' Feargal and his stepfather groaned in unison.

They gave that faithful old stepladder the very best funeral that money could buy.

Not long after that, Feargal's poor stepfather woke up one morning and was shocked to discover that he had a full head of snow-white hair. His incurable grief had, as I'm sure has happened to a great many mourners throughout history, completely cured his baldness. As for Feargal, he vowed never to look at or sniff another hard-boiled egg as long as he lived.

His stepmother had rushed back across the Border and handed herself in to the police the morning after she brutally slayed her husband's beloved stepladder, apparently cock-a-hoop that she had at last gained revenge for the man's adulterous behaviour. 'I wouldn't mind if it had been another woman,' she rambled insanely, 'but he fell in love with a stepladder.' The woman had no feelings of remorse whatsoever. She was deservedly shunned by her fellow inmates, owing to the cold-blooded nature of her crime.

And yet, amazingly, after only four years behind bars, the sawdust-thirsty killer was free to roam the streets once again. But as luck would have it, the next time a panda escaped from Belfast Zoo, Feargal's cruel stepmother was one of the first people to be machine-gunned to death. My, how Feargal and his stepfather celebrated that night!

'I bet she wished she had a stepladder to save her,' Feargal's stepfather gloated. As a matter of fact the man had, by that time of great joy, secretly confessed that – far from being Feargal's actual stepfather – he was his real father. For some inexplicable reason he had liked to call himself his 'step' father.

Their whole reason for living extinguished, Feargal sold his huge jar of sadistically-pickled eggs for twenty-five million pounds – 23.5% less than their unpickled value – and he and his 'father' returned to their little council house in Belfast.

Soon after that, Feargal developed a keen interest in the uses and abuses of scrambled-eggs in modern society (a subject in which he obtained a first-class honours degree at Queen's University in 1992), and his father married an armchair (a marriage made in Heaven). Of course, I don't need to tell you what happened next! The story has been told and retold so often in recent years that there can hardly be anybody alive who hasn't heard the amazing, astonishing, truly incredible tale of Armchair Joe and the Scrambled-Egg Kid!

HOW TO SELL CRAP ON THE INTERNET

I woke up one morning in the middle of August, bursting to use the loo. I climbed out of my single bed and traipsed to the lavatory, barring the door behind me by force of habit. I've lived alone in my Belfast home for five years, but a man must learn to keep his dignity at all times.

I was pulling down my pyjama bottoms in a gentlemanly manner, when I happened to glance into the loo... and spotted a huge floater! *What the hell?* I hadn't been to the toilet during the night. So who, in the name of all that's holy, had left a steaming big stool floating in my bog?

Mystified, I flushed the thing away and did my business. But I couldn't stop thinking about it all day as I sat working away in my optician's shop. Before going to bed that night, I checked just to make sure that the lavatory was as clean as could be.

Everything was going fine the following morning. But I had an eerie feeling as I walked to the loo.... a feeling that something wasn't quite right. And I was right – I found another massive poo floating menacingly in my otherwise pristine clean toilet! I almost pulled my hair out as I stood looking at it.

Thinking quick, I went downstairs to the kitchen and fetched the plastic thingumabob I use to turn over my fried eggs, and used it to scoop the offending article out of the plopper. It definitely wasn't one of mine, because I don't eat peanuts.

I wrapped the dirty thing in a roll of cling film and put it in my fridge, to await further investigation. I spent the day struggling to sell crappy black-framed spectacles for £12.99, but I couldn't find many gullible buyers.

When I got home from the optician's that evening, I couldn't bring myself to look at the excrement in my fridge. I was so upset that I couldn't even eat the frozen dinner I had bought the previous weekend. Determined to get to the bottom of the mystery, I phoned the local CCTV company and got them to install a hidden camera in my lavatory.

I slept like a log that night, but the next morning I found a less sleepy log floating in my loo. I was sure that I hadn't started sleepwalking. And my neighbours' teenaged children can be horrible little swines at times, but surely none of them would stoop so low as to sneaking into my house at night, just to crimp off a load and make safe their escape? My doors and windows all had good locks, so nobody could possibly have entered my humble abode. So who was the guilty party?

Remembering the hidden camera, I went into the spare bedroom and rewound the eight-hour video tape. I fast-forwarded through it, but I didn't notice anything out of the ordinary occurring. Not, that is, until a chubby man in a gold lamé jumpsuit suddenly appeared out of nowhere, sat down on the toilet and evacuated his bowels with a distinct 'Uh-huh-huh!' sound.

The King of rock 'n' roll squirmed his face up for a good ten minutes, until he finally turned blue. He frantically searched for the toilet roll, said 'Uh-huh-huh!' one more time, and then died on the crapper. As the King popped his clogs, his ghostly incarnation suddenly disappeared into the ether.

The only thing that was left of Elvis Presley was the huge cack I had found in my toilet that morning.

Not wanting to in any way offend Elvis's vast army of loyal fans around the world (amongst whose ranks I proudly include myself at number ninety-seven), I decided not to tell anybody that I had chanced upon a tape of his ghost sitting on my bog creating one last humungous hit for posterity.

I instead went straight to the *Belfast Telegraph*, proudly clutching the King's plop in my hand, and said to the editor: 'I bet you can't guess who did this?'

It was only after I was thrown out on my earhole by six journalists that I came to the stark realisation: nobody in their right mind would ever believe that Elvis Presley had created the artistic masterpiece squashed between my fingers, unless I showed them the proof of the pudding.

Swallowing my pride, I now confess that yes, I was the one who posted the film of 'Elvis Sitting on the John' in to *It'll Be All Right On The Night, You've Been Framed* and (latterly) *Kings Do The Funniest Things*.

Nobody really believed that it was actually Elvis, the first nine times they showed the programmes on ITV. It was only after the tenth broadcast, two or three weeks later, that an eminent musicologist announced on *Newsnight*: 'Yes, that really was the King himself going "Uh-huh-huh!" as he reeled off a brown trout that even that famous 1960s *Blue Peter* elephant would have been proud of.'

My film of Elvis pooing was shown on *News at Ten* the very next night, as definitive proof that ghosts really do exist. Experts on the subject then asked the probing question: 'Did the King do an actual dookie on the night he died while sitting on his own throne in Memphis?' This rapidly became the most-asked question on planet Earth.

Questions were even asked in Parliament. During the next sitting of Prime Minister's Question Time, the Leader of the Opposition asked the PM: 'If the Pelvis did indeed dump his load on the last night of his life, then I would like to ask the honourable member, who – in the name of all that's sacrosanct – flushed the bog after the King's toes sadly turned up?'

The Speaker of the House of Commons prevented a near riot by proclaiming in a dignified manner: 'The great Elvis Presley's last shit would have been worth millions of dollars! It would have been worth more than the rest of his estate put together!'

Luckily for me, Elvis Presley's ghost kept on stinking out my lavatory for the next three weeks, so I carefully accrued every last motion and bottled them for posterity.

A few days later I came up with the ingenious idea of selling the King of rock 'n' roll's droppings on eBay, at a starting price of fifty thousand dollars per floater. I must have raked in close to a million pounds sterling over the following three weeks... but then my luck ran out.

It was easily the saddest day of my life, when I walked nonchalantly into my crapper one day in November and found my loo totally devoid of anything even remotely resembling a major rock star's faeces.

Elvis Presley never shat in my bog again.

When I informed my bank manager of the latest sad state of affairs, she told me that I simply couldn't stop making fifty thousand American dollars a day, or my life wouldn't be worth living. 'You have to pay for the upkeep of your new walled-in castle, to keep out all the Elvis fans who are baying for your blood,' she told me. 'And doo-doos don't grow on trees, you know!'

And so, not wanting to become a laughing stock, I started creating my own masterpieces.

Yes, I admit, I have been selling my own dung to gullible Americans for the last three weeks... but what else could I do? People the world over expect to be able to buy famous pop stars' excrement on the Internet. By now, every major museum on God's good Earth gives pride of place to at least one *Elvis Presley's Last Turd* in a shiny glass case.

The first thing I do when I wake up every morning (after a peanut butter feast for my supper the night before) is go to the toilet, crimp off a steaming big crap, wrap it up in cling film and log on to the Internet.

I was just settling down into a dull routine in my castle, when I woke up this morning and the shit hit the fan. I was pulling my strides down, preparing to leave my mark on humanity once again, when – to my surprise – I spotted something really peculiar in my toilet bowl.

There they nestled, sitting in the loo as if they owned the place: a pair of £12.99 black-rimmed spectacles, just like the ones Buddy Holly used to wear...

A CHARACTER IN A NEW YORK STORY

Sam Autry was convinced he was only a character in some insane Author's short story. His whole life could be summed up in a handful of pages, and it obviously wouldn't be the best story in the book.
Sam had no qualifications, he had never had a job and he had no hobbies. Sometimes he took his eyes off the four walls and pleaded aloud with his insane Author to reveal Himself. The Writer had written about Sam on one of His dry days, when He couldn't come up with any decent ideas. Why couldn't He have written him into a story about an Everest expedition or a shipwreck?
'Throw your pen away!' he shouted, looking up at the ceiling. 'You'll never make it as a writer!'
One day soon Sam was going to take his life into his own hands – he would go out and have some fun. That would shock his cruel Author! *He* would be left sucking His pen in frustration while His creation lived the full and active life *He* wanted to lead. Maybe *Sam* should become a writer, and write about his *Author's* boring life. His Creator would be sitting there writing a story about *His* creation writing about the Author's tedious existence.
Sam had sussed his Creator out. He knew that, as a fictional character, he was practically immortal. Even if the Man writing about him plucked the Broadway Limited – coaches and sleepers and all – off track sixteen in Penn Station and used it to flatten Sam against the Staten Island ferry, readers could always turn back to the start of the story and reincarnate him. His Creator would have no such second chance – He would only live once.
Far from being a useless nobody, Sam now realised he was utterly envied by his own Creator, of all people. The Writer had lost His omnipotence in His creation's eye.
Making a major decision for the first time in his life, Sam decided that – as a character in a story still being written – he would like to be in a science-fiction-type fantasy. He would flap his arms and fly away, to the envy of all the nameless inferior characters in the story.

He raised his arms and began to flap them – and he started to fly! He flew out through the window and soared above the streets and parks of Brooklyn.

People at the funfair and on the beach at Coney Island pointed up at Sam. Young ladies sunbathing in Prospect Park licked their lips as they ogled the suddenly handsome young superhero with the power of flight.

Sam couldn't believe his luck. At last he had broken free from the shackles of his Creator's pen.

Over the next twenty-four hours the escaped character made love to countless beautiful women. His Creator had started to write a story about a man He pitied, but now He would be wishing He could change places with that once-pathetic character.

Sam looked smugly up towards the clouds as he flew over the East River with a girl in his arms. He was well aware his Writer must have been watching him, pen in hand, so he laughed out loud at Him. As Sam hovered above Manhattan he shouted a string of obscenities at the useless Creator he had finally mastered.

As long as books existed he would be there, an incredible superhero flapping his way between the pages, while his Creator grew old and died.

Sam Autry crashed into the Art Deco Chrysler Building and died instantly. His body was so badly mangled on impact with the ground that it was never discovered who he was or how he died. He was buried in an unmarked pauper's grave, and the world quickly forgot he had ever existed.

He could have lived forever, of course, but I wanted to teach him a lesson he would never forget.

I slammed my pen down on the table, sweating like a dog.

I had killed him off, but I wished I had never created Sam Autry. The most boring creation ever to emanate from my pen had leapt from the pages of my A4 pad and shoved my own mortality down my throat. Unless I scrapped the first draft of 'A Character in a New York Story' (which I clearly didn't do, as you're reading it now), Sam Autry would live over and over again every time the story was read, while I would gradually grow old and die.

My name would live on only as the Creator of Sam Autry. He had taken me by the scruff of my neck and taught me a lesson I would never forget, as punishment for giving him a life he didn't appreciate.

From now on I'll try to ensure my characters are happy with their lot. And if they're not, I'll get to them before they get to me!

LAST ORDERS

'I'm sure that object I saw in the sky wasn't of this world,' Barney O'Shea muttered to himself as he walked to the Ballybothar Arms for his usual two pints of beer. Tommy Brady was wearing a sheepskin coat just like his, he noted yet again when he passed the wheelchair-bound gentleman halfway down the hill. Tommy still had his head bowed in sorrow three decades after his wife left this mortal coil. Although their paths crossed every day, he hadn't said a word to Barney from that day to this.

Barney kept his eyes peeled to the November night sky in case some bizarre craft flew high above his head. It was only a matter of time until *They* arrived.

'Here comes the spaceman,' barman Frankie Murphy laughed as Barney stepped in out of the cold night air, plucking off his cap. He couldn't remember the last time he had felt warm blood flowing through his veins.

Frankie planted a pint on the bar in front of Barney's usual seat, in the corner nearest the door.

Have you seen any flying saucers today, Barney?' a long-haired young man leaning on the bar asked.

'Leave him alone, Gary,' Frankie said, 'you'll be old yourself one day.'

Barney frowned. Everybody treated him like an idiot. They would be sorry when the aliens arrived.

'I saw a weird object in the sky an hour ago,' Barney announced, sipping his pint, 'but you won't believe it. Some people are born non-believers, and nothing in this world can change them.'

'Or *out of this world*,' Frankie said, and his regular punters giggled. Barney hated being the butt of everybody's jokes. He hoped to God that aliens would soon come and rescue him from his shallow existence.

'Did you walk here, or did you come here by flying saucer?'

'Very funny, Father Luther.'

Barney looked at his pint and had another sip. 'I don't know why you're all so averse to the idea of aliens visiting Earth,' he said.

'There are hundreds of millions of stars, a lot of them with planets like Earth revolving around them. Some of them are *bound* to be inhabited by animals just like us.'

'Animals?'

'We might be the highest form of life on this planet, Father, but we could be like mere insects compared to the so-called *little green men* inhabiting other planets.'

'I think Barney has had enough,' young Gary Cosgrove said, and some women sitting at a table in the middle of the floor laughed themselves silly. Frankie laughed too.

'That's the longest speech Barney has made since about 1991,' Frankie said with a chuckle while drying a glass.

'All joking aside,' Father Luther uttered, cradling a glass of sherry in his hand, 'I read somewhere that scientists have discovered a planet exactly like Earth orbiting a star thirty light-years away. If intelligent beings there have telescopes made with technology far in advance of ours, maybe they can view our planet in close-up?'

'It would take light thirty years to travel from here to there,' Barney agreed. 'They might now be watching us as we were thirty years ago. They'll see me as I was when I was in my late forties.'

Frankie laughed. 'What nonsense you talk at times, Barney.'

'What do you mean, *at times*?' said Concepta Brady, propping up the bar with a glass of vodka and Coke in her hand, and laughter echoed around the pub. Even the priest chortled.

'Do you ever get the feeling that you're being watched?'

'By a higher power?' Father Luther asked the old fool. 'Why yes indeed, all the time.'

'Do you mean aliens?' Frankie asked Barney knowingly.

'Who else,' Barney replied, and Gary Cosgrove laughed out loud.

Frankie smiled and said, 'Barney is harmless.'

Barney sighed. Was that the best thing they had to say about him? Would they write 'He was harmless' on his gravestone when he eventually left this mortal coil?

'Don't worry,' Concepta Brady said. 'Whatever shenanigans you get up to tonight, the watchers on your alien planet won't see it for another thirty years. You won't be around to worry about it.'

Concepta's gin-soaked husband Tommy strode into the bar, where he looked at Barney and mumbled 'Spaceman.'

'You'll be sorry when *They* arrive,' Barney said, refusing to be downtrodden for his beliefs,' and everybody laughed out loud.

Barney walked up the hill at ten o'clock, wondering why he bothered going to the pub just to be insulted. As he undressed beside his creaky old single bed he saw, reflected in the mirror on the wardrobe, a shadowy figure walking past the door and heading down the stairs, making an unearthly groaning sound.

'The aliens will come and chase you away one day, just you wait and see,' Barney yelled out as he climbed into bed, where he listened to the groans until they faded away into the ether.

Nothing ever seemed real when the new day arrived. Barney could never tell at what point reality kicked in, if it ever did. He walked down the hill to buy his newspaper, half a pint of milk and a small loaf to help him eke out his meagre existence. While approaching the same shell of a building that he passed every morning, he again considered it amazing that the authorities hadn't yet bulldozed it, thirty years after the tragedy occurred.

He would never forget the night he saw his first UFO, as he'd had all the people sitting around the bar in the palm of his hand for two whole hours while telling them about it. Sadly, however, Last Orders had come early that night.

As he looked at the priest's name on the blue plaque in the bottom corner of the wall, alongside that of the proprietor, Francis Murphy, young Gary Cosgrove and Concepta Brady, Barney wished – not for the first time, and certainly not the last – that he hadn't been in the Ballybothar Arms that fateful November night.

THE GALLANT LOSER

Sean Byrne was a gallant loser. He believed in the old Northern Irish tradition of losing like a man instead of winning like a hamster. 'Only losers win,' he gallantly told everybody who beat him at darts. 'I lost, so I'm the *real* winner.'

Sean loved losing. It would be a dream come true if he could *just once* get to the final of a major darts tournament – preferably live on TV – and get trounced to within an inch of his life. The only problem was that, to do so, he would have to win all the preceding rounds. He was too averse to winning to avoid defeat from the very first match of every tournament he played in. 'Never miss a chance to go down with all guns blazing,' he told himself every morning. 'I love the sweet smell of failure.'

Sean loved sitting down with his beautiful blonde wife Ciara on Saturday nights to watch the football on TV. He especially loved it when a team was getting thrashed, so that he could get right behind them and hope they got smashed to smithereens. In Sean's book, there was nothing worse than when a team came back from three-nil down to win four-three. That sort of result always did his head in. 'How can I sympathize with a team that's getting hammered, if they're only going to let me down and save their own skins?' Sean whined to Ciara virtually every Saturday night.

Ciara couldn't stand sport. She thought it was silly, grown men throwing pointed bits of metal at a silly board, or poking balls around a table with a silly stick. And as for the hurdlers in the Olympics... wouldn't they get to the finishing-line a lot quicker if they removed those silly bits of wood from the track first? And the people who sat and watched it on silly boxes in the corner of their silly living rooms were even worse.

Tonight was the biggest night of the year down at the Vodka-Swiller's Handbag. Sean's darts team *We're Gonna Get Our Fecking Heads Kicked In* were playing the tournament favourites *The Champions of the World* in the first round of the Belfast City Championship. The winners were allowed to run naked through the city centre, which was the highest honour that could be bestowed upon a Belfast resident. *The Champions of the World* had good eyesight, good balance and steady hands all round. Sean's teammates were a one-legged priest and an extremely befuddled old man. They didn't even like the game, but Sean had searched the whole city to find his perfect team. They had no chance.

To make matters worse, Sean needed permission to go out gallivanting – and Saturday night was the one night of the week when Ciara liked her little hubby to wrap her wool around his hands while she knitted jockstraps and g-strings for the starving millions in Scunthorpe. God forbid that they should freeze their whatsits off on an empty stomach, just because Sean *Self, Self, Self* Byrne wanted to be given a good sound thrashing.

'It's only a silly game, you clampet,' Ciara said, searching the bedroom cupboard for her three-foot ball of pink-and-black polka-dot wool. 'And you only lose because you don't love me any more.'

'That's not the only reason,' Sean sympathized. 'Winners just don't understand. They think life is only good if you humiliate other people, but it's far better if you let them humiliate you. It's good for the soul.'

Ciara found her wool, and started wrapping it around her downtrodden husband's hands.

'I bet you've got a silly fancy woman down at that pub.'

'Don't be silly.'

'I have half a mind to let you go, to get rid of you. That silly woman is welcome to you.'

'Thank you, love.'

Sean unwrapped the wool from his fingers and put on his Saturday night underpants. They were his unlucky underpants. 'I've never won yet, wearing these – isn't it great?'

'I'll be down every half an hour to check up on you.'

'Thank you, dear.'

Sean picked up his chintzy Moroccan darts and his darts-spectacles and walked down Pub Hill to the Vodka-Swiller's Handbag. Father Finger and old Bobby Erinsborough were propping up the bar. They had been on the weewee all day, and they weren't fit to skin a cat. It was looking good.

'Don't try too hard tonight, lads,' Sean coached his team. 'As the missus says, it's only a silly game.'

'Give us a chance, Sean,' Father Finger said, 'you don't normally give us your reverse pep-talk until we're actually in the process of getting stuffed.'

'You're a couple of good lads,' Sean beamed, downing his first pint. He saw his wife peeping in the window at him and then going back up Pub Hill.

The Champions of the World had been the champions of Belfast every year since 1985, give or take forty years. But Sean knew that, deep down, they were a bunch of losers. That was why they tried so hard to win.

'Real men don't need to win,' Sean tried to persuade his teammates. 'Real men happily settle for being the dregs of society.'

Ciara arrived back home. Pub Hill was steep, going up, and she didn't like it. And besides, it shouldn't be called Pub Hill when you're going up, away from the pub. Ciara was going to apply to Belfast City Council to have it renamed *Sean And Ciara Byrne's House Hill* from the bottom upwards. That would make much more sense.

Ciara got lonely at times, living all alone on her own at home, all by herself, with only her husband and their pet hamster for company. And Sean wasn't much good, if a cat needed skinning. If only she could become one of the starving millions, and have people knit jockstraps and g-strings for her. But life was passing her by. Now she would probably never get to wear a jockstrap.

She needed a change in her life. She didn't like Ciara Byrne any more, she wanted to be somebody completely different. She was going to change herself, one hundred percent. She wouldn't change her name, because that would only confuse everybody. But she would change her whole personality.

She would still live with Sean, because he would be lost without her. And she would treat him the same way, because he seemed to like her as she was. She wouldn't act any different outwardly, as people would only pass remarks on it if she did. But inwardly, she would be a totally different person from now on.

Or maybe not.

It was brilliant, Sean and his darts team were being walloped. *The*

Champions of the World were taking *We're Gonna Get Our Fecking Heads Kicked In* to the cleaners. They had lost their first two games by a landslide, and now it was Sean's turn to throw.

He couldn't believe his luck when his first dart accidentally flew into treble-twenty. He could believe it even less when his second dart nestled alongside it... and the third dart made his opening score a maximum one hundred and eighty.

Sean stopped trying so hard to miss the board when his next throw came up, but again he scored a maximum by sheer fluke. His opponent was only scoring in the thirties, so Sean had a hefty lead.

With his next two darts, needing a hundred and forty-one to win, Sean took his glasses off. When he put them back on to see why the crowd were gasping, he realised that he had hit treble-twenty and treble-seventeen. Thirty needed to win.

Cursing his luck, Sean stood on one leg, covered his eyes with his usual throwing hand and fired the dart carelessly into the air. Double-fifteen. Game to Sean.

As the unlucky winner, Sean had to keep on playing. However hard he tried to miss the board, he kept on getting perfect scores. He won eight games in a row, throwing the darts over his shoulder, under his legs and from every conceivable ridiculous angle. Nothing was going right. If he won the next game, he would have to face the ignominy of going through to the second round.

For his first throw, Sean turned away from the board and aimed into the crowd. The dart twisted and turned in the air and seemed to somersault backwards over Sean's mousy-brown head, down towards the board and into the treble-twenty. The audience rose up and cheered ecstatically. *Trick darts*.

Sean stood on his head and fired towards the ceiling. The laws of gravity pulled the dart back down again, into its by now customary slot. For his third dart he took his shoes and socks off and aimed at his big toe. This time he hit his target at last, and it hurt. The dart rebounded off his dirty toenail and up into the sixty. He just couldn't miss.

Ciara peeped in through the bar window and saw Sean standing in front of an adoring crowd, aiming his darts at people's heads but somehow hitting the board. Darts was a *silly* game. It suddenly struck Ciara that she could go in and watch the silly game. Sean wouldn't recognize her, now that she had decided to change herself completely.

The ecstatic crowd were standing up cheering and clapping their hands, as Ciara's totally despondent husband slowly put his socks on. She couldn't believe it – her useless spouse had finally won a match.

Ciara approached the bar and bought herself a can of beer. It said *Serve at Room Temperature*. That was silly. How did the brewers know how hot the room was? Beer was supposed to be drunk cold – why didn't they write *Chill at Room Temperature*? The brewers were silly.

She stood up at the front and began swigging from her can. Sean and his silly friends were playing *We're Not Brilliant, But We're All Right* in the second round. Sean kept opening his mouth and aiming his darts into it, somehow managing to hit the board by default, to rapturous applause. He looked suicidal.

Sean's team-mates weren't getting a look in, but they seemed happy enough. 'We're stuffing them!' Bobby Erinsborough kept shouting, as if he had thrown a straight dart all night. He didn't recognize Ciara. Then again, the old man couldn't see past his own nose.

Sean won the match single-handedly, using every trick in the book in a desperate but failed attempt to lose. His team was in the final. This was his great chance to get hammered before the eyes of – if not the whole wide world – fifteen sweaty drunkards.

Sean slowly stuffed the plastic flights from the end of his darts into his mouth and chewed them up. He stood on the darts' metal shafts and bounced up and down on them. One by one, they squirmed out from under his feet and up into the treble-twenty. He hammered their points, but they wouldn't go blunt enough to not stick in treble-twenty.

People were flocking into the Vodka-Swiller's Handbag from miles around to bear witness to the art of *Sean Byrne, Trick Darts Player Supreme*. He won game after game with one hand tied behind his back, his eyes closed, and without even taking his mangled darts out of their leather pouch. His opponents *We've Never Been So Humiliated In All Our Lives* were living up to their name, after countless years of success on the Northern Ireland darts circuit. At one stage Sean was sitting at the bar downing pint after pint of Guinness while his darts did their duty, and nobody seemed to think there was anything in the least bit strange going on.

Sean was surprised to discover that he quite liked the smell of success after all. He had never been any good at anything before, so failure was all that he had ever known. When you're good at losing you may as well enjoy it. But now he could whip everybody's hide without lifting a finger, and it felt great.

In an effort to steal the limelight from his cocky darts, Sean put new flights on them and began aiming them in the general direction of the board, to make it look as if he knew how to play. But the growing audience started slow-handclapping him. 'This is boring!' they shouted out. 'Aim at our heads again, for a bit of craic!' Not wanting to upset his new army of fans, Sean did as they had asked. His darts flew all around the pub before naturally settling into the required position on the board. Winning was even easier than losing.

Sean was in love. There was a beautiful blonde sitting at the end of the bar, admiring his throwing skills. She looked a little bit like Ciara, although much more self-assured. Sean was going to leave his wife and go to live with the mysterious stranger. She was even more mysterious up-close, when Sean went to buy her a drink and fired his darts out across the crowded bar.

She said that she was called *Ciara*. Sean had once known a woman called Ciara, but he couldn't remember where or when. This woman was different than any woman he had ever known before… and yet she was very like someone that Sean thought he should remember but couldn't.

Sean's team won the tournament, and they got to run naked through the centre of Belfast. But Sean thought he deserved an even bigger prize than that – he was going for gold. He was going to win everything that he possibly could, by hook or by crook.

Sean Byrne loved winning. He believed in the old Ulster tradition of mashing his opponents to a pulp without showing any mercy. It helped that his strange new wife Ciara loved all sports, and even let Sean throw his darts down Sean and Ciara Byrne's House Hill in the general direction of the pub's dart board while she sat with her wool wrapped around his hands as she knitted hamburgers and potato waffles for the destitute strippers in Grimsby. God forbid that their tummies should rumble embarrassingly in public as they were about to get their kits off, just because Sean *Self, Self, Self* Byrne wanted to tear an opponent's head off and stick it up on a pole for safekeeping.

But at least he had a manly bloodlust – unlike Ciara's last husband, Sean somebody-or-other, who the new Ciara couldn't remember much about... except that he was the sort who would quite happily settle for second best.

THE BELFAST LEPRECHAUNS

Megalife was brave. He liked to think he was braver than everybody else in the office. His boss, Grizelda Overpants, had once told him that she honestly believed he was the bravest leprechaun in Belfast.

Mrs Overpants liked Megalife. She liked him a lot. A very lot. He was her favourite, although she would never admit it to him. She didn't want to make his head swell up like a big red tomato. She always smiled at him, and sometimes he smiled back at her. He wasn't a bad sort.

Little did Mrs Overpants know that Megalife only had eyes for Trumpella Potteringthwaite. She had lovely dark green eyes just like his Great-Auntie Bobbington's, although to be fair his Great-Auntie Bobbington's eyes had spent at least fifty years more than Trumpella's adorable ones scouting for rainbows and the inevitable pots of gold at the tail end of them.

Mrs Overpants smiled coyly at Megalife as she climbed into the little cupboard beneath the kitchen sink, at the bottom of an enormous drainpipe at the upper end of the fearsome giants' walkway called Joy's Entry. She pulled the door closed behind her for decency's sake. Megalife pushed his green-and-white hat with a bobble on top to one side and stuck his fingers in his big pointed ears in an act of apparent desperation, but alas he could still hear all the pooping and prooting sounds and the guttural grunting noises emanating from the small enclosed space between the cooker and the fridge. It almost always gave Megalife a dicky tummy when Mrs Overpants punished his ears in such an obscene manner. He closed his eyes and hummed a little twiddly-dee tune to himself, trying to picture anything or anyone but Mrs Overpants at that precise moment in time with his over-keen mind's eye.

Mrs Overpants was still feeling very shaky, very queasy, that was quite plain to hear and smell. The two-inch woman had been frightened to within an inch of her life on Thursday evening, when a gigantic rat-arsed rat shimmied up the drainpipe, making it shake from side to side. It felt as if the giant beast was about to pull the drainpipe down off the wall – the office walls were vibrating horrifyingly, and even brave Megalife was pooing his metaphorical pants and quaking in his pointy-toed dark green leather boots.

Mrs Overpants had always been every bit as afraid of the multitude of giant creatures as the next leprechaun, but now she was doubly so. Just because the vast majority of the titans who took virtual leprechaun form didn't believe that she or her friends and colleagues really existed, that was no good reason for them to tread slipshod all over the leprechauns' world as if the so-called 'humans' didn't give tuppence for the little people's thoughts and feelings. With this sad thought still rampaging around her spinning head like a rhinoceros who had just spotted his significant other giving another rhino the eye, Mrs Overpants sprayed some air-freshener down the dirty little hole in the filthy little corner of the dark little cupboard in the not-overtly hygienic kitchen. She kneed the door open, flopping out onto the blue-and-white tiles and groaning, 'Och, my poor wee aching back.' She wondered why there was an office chair sitting in the corner of the kitchen, beside the back door. It certainly wasn't a new one, it looked totally old and worn.

Not for the first time, Mrs Overpants caught Megalife unawares sitting at his desk with his eyes squeezed tightly shut and his fingers poked firmly in his ears. When she tapped him on the shoulder he almost jumped out of his pinkie-white skin. He looked up at her with a 'guilty as charged' look on his face.

'What are you doing?' Mrs Overpants asked him, looking deeply insulted.

'Nothing,' Megalife mumbled, clearly refusing to look Mrs Overpants in the eye, as if he had done something he ought to be thoroughly ashamed of.

'Why do you plug your ears,' she asked him pointedly, 'every time I —'

— Saved by the bell. Megalife scooped up the telephone a split second after it started ringing and whacked it against his ear. 'Good morning, Miniature Enterprises?'

He sat saying yes, no, I see, possibly, and as many other inconsequential mutterings as he could muster for upwards on four minutes, feigning a profound interest in the anonymous caller's dreary sales pitch long after the call had been terminated from the other end. Megalife only hung up at his end when Mrs Overpants groaned out loud and, with her shoulders hanging down practically to her knees, flicked her fingers and disappeared with the usual popping sound.

'That was close, too damned close,' Megalife muttered to himself, taking off his bobble-hat and nervously ruffling his curly red mop of hair with his fingers. He felt around his desk with his hands to see if he had any work to do that fine morning. He felt all warm and bubbly when that Friday feeling popped into his head – but then it popped out again just as suddenly and he sighed despondently. It was National Leprechaun Day, the 13th of May, but one leprechaun in particular couldn't help feeling sorry for himself. He was so jealous of Mrs Overpants and her ability to move from one place to another with the merest flick of her fingers. He, on the other hand, had to stick his hand down his pants and tweak a certain part of his anatomy in order to attain the same worthy goal. It wasn't fair. Oh well, it was better than walking.

Trumpella Potteringthwaite burst into the office like a crazy woman with a machine-gun, coming pretty darned close to plucking the door clean off its hinges. She looked for all the world as if she had just seen a ghost, if leprechaun ghosts really do exist.
Megalife could most definitely smell the delectable Trumpella's sweat the moment she barged into the room, and if anybody had asked him the pertinent question there and then he honestly wouldn't have been able to deny the fact that he simply loved it, call him perverted. Although she was only twenty and he was twenty-five Megalife loved Trumpella full-stop, if she only knew. Sweat was visibly trickling down her forehead, dripping onto her smart blue blazer and her lovely red blouse, and – maybe Megalife only imagined this part – further down onto her pretty red-and-white-striped skirt.
Trumpella crouched down and pulled up her red-and-blue-hooped socks, the toes of her winkle-picker boots curling up as she did so. As Megalife continued to watch her in silence, trying not to openly drool, she removed her black bowler-hat from her head and shook her long black hair from side to side, throwing her hat onto Megalife's desk, almost but not quite hitting his hands and breaking his fingers with it. He would have quite liked that, he thought to himself, in an admittedly kinky (she would have said disturbing) way.

'That mangy giant cat chased me all the way from my home,' Trumpella grumbled, clearly not in the best of moods. 'I nearly crashed my car three times. I think he scratched my crank-shaft the last time he attacked me, because I had trouble cranking up the engine this morning.'

'Interesting,' Megalife said, but then he seemed to think that *anything* Trumpella ever said was interesting. 'So tell me, do you still live on the other side of Belfast?'

'Yes, I have a house beside a huge drain in the ground, all the way down at the Ann Street end of Joy's Entry,' she reminded him, practically bragging about how exotically distant her home was. She wouldn't tell him which drain in the wide expanse of rocky ground exactly, as she didn't want Megalife to know her address in case he started sending her mucky photos. 'I swear on your life, Mega, one of these days I'm going to sprinkle some leprechaun dust on that giant cat and make his balls shrivel up until they're just about as tiny as yours. Nothing personal.'

'You wouldn't know it,' Megalife said pointedly, 'but mine are bigger than his.'

'His are bigger than *you*,' Trumpella pointed out.

Megalife loved it when she talked dirty, although perhaps just a little less on the personal side might have been even nicer. He would never let anybody else in the world speak to him the way she did, and he hoped she knew it, because he was kind like that. 'Oh well,' he said, 'I suppose I'd better get some work done.'

Trumpella sat down at her desk and kicked her shoes off, almost taking one of Megalife's big blue eyes out as a winkle-picker flew across the room like a constipated vampire bat. He picked it up, resisting the urge to sniff it before handing it back to her. She put her head down and started keying a boxful of invoices, her fingers moving faster than even the average leprechaun eye can see. Megalife started having one of his daydreams as he glanced back and forward at her, but Trumpella scowled at him so he got his calculator out of the top drawer and added up page after page of numbers until his fingertips felt numb.

Trumpella sniffed. 'What's that pong?'

Megalife sniffed, trying not to look at her feet. 'Oh,' his nose memory told him, 'Grizelda went to the toilet in the kitchen again. She did a number two, not that I was listening.'

Trumpella looked aghast. 'You keep saying that, but it's not funny.'
'It's true,' he protested, tucking his emerald-green sweatshirt into his jeans. 'She goes in that little cupboard –'
'– Under the sink, yes, I know, you've told me before, but you're the only one who ever says that. It sounds like you have a vendetta against her.'
'Why would I say such a ridiculous thing?' Megalife said, and surely Trumpella could see that he had a point. 'It's just a dirty little cupboard with a hole in the corner leading to who knows where. I know it sounds daft.'
'So stop saying it.'
He felt his head instinctively shaking. She never seemed to believe a word he said unless it was something she had seen with her own two eyes. He had no way of proving it. It was beginning to look as if Mrs Overpants only ever did it when only he was present on purpose, as if in an inexplicable effort to belittle him in Trumpella's eyes. Her jealousy knew no bounds. 'I'll never mention it again, even if she starts going in your drawers.'
'I don't wear drawers.'
'Really?' Megalife said, tingling with excitement like a naughty little boy.

Before Megalife had a chance to reply to his beloved Trumpella, Mrs Overpants magically reappeared in front of his desk, wearing what looked like a brand new blue-and-red-checked dress and a dark red bonnet. Trumpella glanced momentarily across to her right before returning to her invoicing.
'I've been out shopping,' Mrs Overpants said, smiling proudly at Megalife, hoping he would share her joy if only for a minute. She twirled around, 'Do you like my new gear?'
'It's lovely,' Trumpella said, feigning a delighted look with flashing teeth and beaming eyes. Mrs Overpants frowned at her. Trumpella rolled her eyes and returned to her work, feeling annoyed that their boss gave Megalife all the attention. She must have been totally sex-starved, thinking there was anything on the remarkable side about that great useless article who was only half her age. Trumpella wondered if Grizelda would still be so fond of him if she knew the things he said about her behind her back. Maybe she would be able to use it against him in future, if the atmosphere in the office didn't

improve considerably. Not that she would ever want to hurt him on purpose, unless it was good for her career.

'I bought it in Mazzarazzabazzakazza's in the city centre,' Mrs Overpants said. 'You know the shop? It's at the foot of the gigantic old postbox mountain on the other side of High Street.'

'The mountain conquered by the great leprechaun explorer Ernest Scheissenhausen in the 1990s?' Megalife asked knowingly, to show the unrequited love of his life how clever he was. 'Of course, there are two now, since that new slightly bigger, red rectangular mountain appeared beside the old round one a few years ago.'

'Ernest Scheissenhausen is going to try and climb that one tomorrow morning,' Mrs Overpants said.

'I must take my mum to Mazzarazzabazzakazza's,' Trumpella said, without even glancing at Megalife, 'she likes dresses like that too. And bonnets. Mazzarazzabazzakazza's, I'll make a mental note of that and tell her when we have our usual chat on the phone this evening.'

'It's a small world,' Megalife said, wishing Trumpella would just once show some interest in him. 'My Great-Auntie Bobbington owns that store.'

'Bobbington Mazzarazzabazzakazza is your great-auntie?' Mrs Overpants said, in a state of extreme amazement. 'Och, Megalife, I've known you for coming on seven years, and I'm pretty sure you've never mentioned that fact before.'

'She's the only billionaire leprechaun in Belfast,' Trumpella chipped in, knowing that this fact would be of great interest to Mrs Overpants, as the woman was *not totally unobsessed* with money. As she spoke she saw Mrs Overpants's eyes light up like one of the huge moons that lit up the night sky at the top of those gigantically tall poles stretching all the way up and down High Street and, conspiracy theorists said, on to infinity. 'They say she has found a pot of gold at the end of a rainbow on virtually every street in Belfast.'

'She wrote that in the deeds when she opened the store back in the Seventies,' Megalife stated.

'I can't believe you're related to that great woman,' Mrs Overpants said, smiling elatedly like a teenager who had just met a famous leprechaun rock star like Elvis Skitterington. 'Is Mazzarazzabazzakazza your surname?'

'I dunno,' Megalife confessed. 'Everyone has always just called me Megalife.'

'I don't think Mazzarabbabazzakazza is a local name, is it?'

'Not at all, Trump,' Megalife said, turning his head to the left and pumping out his feeble chest with a distinct air of pride. 'I've heard it said that Great-Auntie Bobbington is one of the Falls Road Mazzarazzabazzakazzas.'

'Oh, that lot over there,' Trumpella commented, cracking a facetious smile and then looking at Mrs Overpants to make sure it was alright. 'That's two or three miles from here, it must have taken her years to get here.'

'You certainly couldn't drive there overnight,' Megalife laughed.

As Mrs Overpants walked towards the adjoining kitchen, in a little enclave on the left-hand side of the office on Megalife's right, she noticed her favourite employee staring at her dress.

'I'd be lynched on sight if I wore a dress like that,' Megalife said in a matter of fact manner. In response to the instantaneous brace of dazed looks and dropped jaws confronting him, he elaborated, 'the colour scheme, I mean. All that red, white and blue. Everybody around my way wears green, white and gold from dawn until dusk and then some.'

Megalife was slightly taken aback when Mrs Overpants and Trumpella Potteringthwaite suddenly split their sides as one, doubling up in a shared fit of wild laughter. When they finally stopped laughing they looked at one another, and Megalife thought he detected a knowing look in their eyes. It was as if they had just bonded for the first time ever, which was a good thing – at his expense, which wasn't, particularly.

Zzzzzz was only half an hour late for work that morning. His real name was Zatarak Zoxion Zalcho Zloop Z. Zizzyzump (nobody knew what the Z stood for), but everybody called him Zzzzzz for brevity's sake, pronouncing it like the blood-curdling buzzing sound made by the four fearsome bees in the big cage at the local zoo.

'You're early this morning, Zzzzzz,' Mrs Overpants said, habitually looking up at the red-faced clock on the crème-coloured, pockmarked wall facing Megalife's desk. Zzzzzz smiled as he took off the only item of clothing he was wearing, a bowler-hat. Most of the wise leprechauns wore protection to prevent irritable birds from swooping down and pecking their little heads without fear of retribution. The bald but incredibly hirsute Zzzzzz wasn't the most coordinated member of Mrs Overpants's staff, but his colleagues put this down to his age.

In his none-too-fleeting life, Zzzzzz had travelled far and wide, climbing up and over huge red mountains in the footsteps of Ernest Scheissenhausen and descending into unexplored valleys, on a one-leprechaun mission to see the world. After a couple of glasses of claret in the local pub after work the serial father often boasted that he had seen places that weren't on any of the maps on sale in the countless leprechaun stores on High Street and Ann Street and all the humungous alleyways in between, such as the hoity-toity Pottinger's Entry, which had so many giants walking up and down it that leprechauns kept close to the walls on either side unless they had a suicidal streak.

If Zzzzzz was to be believed, during one summer holiday he had driven his car for weeks on end, knowing not where he was going, and he had ended up on a gigantic stone pathway in front of an enormous palace that surely must have made even the giant humans themselves feel small and insignificant. There, he tried to convince anyone who might possibly believe his fantastic tale, he had seen scores of those 'pesky giants' wandering around with cameras and amazed looks on their faces, staring at monoliths containing what looked like writing but it was way too high up off the ground to be read by leprechaun eyes.

To tell the truth, the majority of the leprechauns who lent Zzzzzz their ears for the duration of his magnificent journey tales assumed they were mere fantasies, figments of his vivid imagination. They found it hard to believe that such fantastic places could possibly exist in the real world, although of course nobody begrudged him the right to tell his incredible tales. If nothing else, the loveable old rogue's alleged recollections were entertainment in its finest form, especially on a cold winter's night.

'Did you do anything interesting last night, Zzzzzz?' Megalife asked, giving his calculator a welcome break while Trumpella went to put the kettle on to make Zzzzzz a nice hot cup of tea. She loved that old man.

'Funny you should ask,' Zzzzzz replied, which was his usual introduction to a splendid story or two about his evening's shenanigans. 'Sorry I'm late, Mrs Overpants.'

'I've told you at least a thousand times before, Zzzzzz, please call me Grizelda.' A special honour indeed, reserved for one special employee only.

'Why thank you, Grizelda. Wait till I tell yous what happened to me last night, and I think you might accept that I had a perfectly valid reason for my tardiness this most special of mornings. I believe you'll all find yourselves telling your grandchildren about this, my latest extraordinary adventure, in decades to come. I can hardly believe it myself, and as you all know, I once drove my Rolls-Royce no less than four miles up a long, long, perfectly straight road called a "motorway". True, I turned around and drove home again two weeks into my journey, as I was getting low on fuel – but I firmly believe that that unbelievably-wide road could only possibly have led to the very end of the world itself, and I didn't want to fall off it, and have seemingly eked out my days in this vast world in utter vain. The point is, I tried my best. I'm not afraid to dream of a whole new world out there, a world undreamt of by mortal leprechauns.'

Mrs Overpants smiled and looked again at the clock. She didn't want to appear rude, but she couldn't help wondering if any work would be done today at all, once Zzzzzz started regaling his latest in a long line of unbelievable tall tales. She often thought that it was quite ironic how much the Little People loved hearing tall tales.

'Do go on, Zzzzzz. You have us all on tenterhooks.'

'Why thank you, Grizelda,' Zzzzzz said. He smiled at Trumpella as she handed him a lovely cup of tea on a fine china saucer. He took it and sat down in the comfortable armchair in the corner facing the door.

'Are we all here?'

'I think so,' Mrs Overpants said, looking down at her new dress, hoping Zzzzzz would notice it and tell her how nice it was. 'You, me, Megalife and Trumpella. Yes, I think that's all of us.'

'I don't think there's anybody missing,' Megalife said, speaking in a louder voice than before because Zzzzzz didn't have the best of hearing when he was over two inches away from the person speaking. His hardness-of-hearing was just another of the many quirks that endeared him to people.

'Yes,' Trumpella agreed, 'I think we're all here.'

The front door opened and in wobbled a chubby, long-haired adult male, wearing a smart pinstriped suit and a bowler-hat just like Zzzzzz's. He appeared to be soaked through to the skin. Megalife looked out the window and saw dangerously-big drops of rain pouring out of the sky. He had once been knocked down and almost drowned by just such a potentially lethal raindrop. The obese man put his briefcase down on the corner of Trumpella's desk and she looked daggers at him. 'Can I help you?'
'It's... it's me,' he said in a not exactly friendly deep voice, with what appeared to be an inexplicably frustrated look on his face. Water dripped off his suit as he turned to look at Mrs Overpants and Megalife, hoping his face would spark their memories. Zzzzzz sat looking at the man in quiet contemplation, rubbing the upper part of his lengthy whiskers.
'Aren't you...' Zzzzzz said after a minute's silence. 'I think I know you, give me a moment.'
'Your pockmarked face rings a distant bell,' Megalife told the man, who now appeared to be sweating through the rain on his face. 'Haven't I seen you somewhere before?'
The wet wide man suddenly looked confused, almost as if he couldn't remember his own name. Then he excitedly stuck a finger up in the air and his eyes lit up. 'Ponkitonius Schneiderpump,' he finally revealed.
'Nice to meet you.' Mrs Overpants approached him and shook his hand, then wiped her hand on her dress.
'I work here.'
'I beg your pardon?' Mrs Overpants said. 'If it's work you're looking for I'm sorry to disappoint you, Mr Schneiderpump, but we have no openings coming up in the immediate future. If you leave your name and address with Trumpella here...'
'I've worked here for twenty-eight years.'
Mrs Overpants thought for a moment. 'Oh, I do beg your pardon,' she said, feeling quite a fool. 'I totally forgot that you existed.'
'Me too.'
'Me three.'
'Me four,' Zzzzzz said.

'I'm the head accountant,' Ponkitonius Schneiderpump said, as Trumpella, Megalife and Zzzzzz rushed to shake his hand.

'Long time no see,' Megalife said to him, trying to look friendly but finding it peculiarly hard to pull it off with aplomb.

'You had me confused there for a minute,' Ponkitonius said, wiping his perspiring brow. 'I thought I had wandered into someone else's dream.' He looked askance at the empty space in the far-right corner where his desk – on wheels, for some never-explained reason – had been situated when he left the office yesterday evening. And now that he came to think of it, some prankster had also wheeled it out yesterday afternoon when he went out to lunch.

Trumpella looked at Ponkitonius and waited for him to smile back at her. When he finally managed to do so she said, 'How could we ever forget you? We must have had a collective touch of the brain-staggers.'

Megalife went out into the back yard and wheeled in the rain-soaked desk he had erroneously wheeled out yesterday. Twice, to tell the truth. He couldn't think what had come over him. He thought he detected a 'silly boy' look on Mrs Overpants's face, but she was the one who had asked him to put the desk out with the rubbish after work, as nobody had ever sat there. That explained why there was a chair in the corner of the kitchen. 'Just as well the desk has wheels,' Megalife said, as the other two desks quite clearly didn't. 'I wouldn't fancy carrying that on my back once, never mind twice in a single day.'

'These things happen,' Ponkitonius said resignedly.

'No hard feelings?'

'Certainly not, Mrs Overpants.'

Ponkitonius sat down on his chair and loosened his tie, shuffling around in a probably hopeless attempt to get both his buttocks on the seat at the same time.

'Now, back to what happened to me last night,' Zzzzzz said, and Trumpella and Megalife dragged their chairs around their desks and across the yellow-carpeted floor towards the armchair in the corner. Realising what was about to happen, Ponkitonius stood up and wheeled his chair the length of the room. He offered it to Mrs Overpants, to save her having to go into her office to bring her own chair out. She accepted his kind offer, leaving him with nowhere to sit, but he quickly found the corner of Trumpella's desk, removing

his briefcase and replacing it with his flabby backside. Trumpella looked over her shoulder at him with a naturally disgusted look on her face, hoping against hope that he wouldn't break or soil her desk.
'Oh,' Ponkitonius said, 'before you start, Zzzzzz – anyone for tea?'
'Sorry, er…' Trumpella said, as if she had forgotten his name again, 'we're all out of sugar. By the look of you, I imagine you like to have lots of sugar in your tea?'
'Oh,' he replied in a dignified manner. 'Well, now. OK. I'll pop to the local shop to get a bag of sugar. I won't even ask if I can get it out of petty cash.'
'It's OK,' Zzzzzz said, 'I won't start until you get back.'
Ponkitonius straightened his tie and made himself scarce. Zzzzzz sat in silence for a few seconds, and Mrs Overpants looked at the clock on the wall.
'Go on,' Megalife told Zzzzzz, 'we're all ears.'
'OK,' Zzzzzz said. 'I can't think what was keeping me. I can't wait to tell yous all about my latest amazing adventure.'
They pulled their chairs even closer to him in rapt anticipation.
'Go for it,' Trumpella yelled out. She had the utmost confidence in everybody's elder's incomparable ability to spin a yarn – whether his yarns were true or false, only he could tell for sure – that would have them all glued to their seats.
'Our day's work can wait,' Mrs Overpants said, looking at the red clock and quickly waving her hand at it, as if telling it to go away and leave her alone. 'Blow our minds, Mr Zizzyzump.'

Trumpella tried to conceal a yawn behind her hand, but it was such a rare occurrence to hear someone yawning while listening to one of the exuberant Zzzzzz's stirring tales that all eyes turned to look at her.
'Now I'll get to the good stuff,' Zzzzzz said in all confidence, brushing the thick beard covering his legs. And away he went.
'After leaving work yesterday I was out hunting flies with my blunderbuss, when a robin –'
'I do so hate those ferocious beasts!'
'– swooped down out of the sky and started pecking my head,' Zzzzzz said, smiling at Trumpella. 'Now luckily I was, of course, wearing one of my exceedingly large stash of bowler-hats, so I lived to tell the tale.'

'You can't beat a bit of good hard-hat technology,' Trumpella chipped in, and Mrs Overpants wished she would stop interrupting the flow of the great orator's story.

'Well naturally, being an animal lover myself, I poked that robin right in the eye with the blunt end of my blunderbuss, and it flew away like a good bird should.'

'Phew!' Mrs Overpants said. 'As my great-grandfather always said, the bowler-hat is every good leprechaun's saviour.'

'Well,' Zzzzzz said, 'in Belfast, certainly.'

'In Belfast?' Mrs Overpants said. 'Well of course. Where else is there?'

'Ah, now you see that's the thing,' Zzzzzz said, sitting up straight and rubbing his adam's apple as if just a tiny bit nervous about his boss's possible reaction to what he was about to say. 'I firmly believe – that is, I suspect, or should I say hope and dream – that there are others of us, in other places.'

'Other places?' Mrs Overpants said. 'That's plain silly talk. How can there be other places? This is the only place. This is the world we live in.'

'Yes, the world *we* live in, but who is to say there aren't other leprechauns in other places, other worlds far, far away from here?'

Trumpella covered her mouth with her hand. She was utterly speechless. So was Megalife.

'You're a genius saying stupid nonsensical stuff, Zzzzzz,' Mrs Overpants said.

'Am I?' he asked. 'As a little refresher, how many metres away from here was Megalife's Great-Auntie Bobbington Mazzarazzabazzakazza born?'

'How would I know?'

'I'm not sure about metres,' Megalife responded to Mrs Overpants's gaze. 'They say the place she came from was about four thousand yards from here, if such a distant place could possibly exist. I think they may have fiddled the figures to make her look more mystical than all the rest.'

'See?' Zzzzzz said pointedly, as Mrs Overpants looked into his eyes once again. 'If mysterious distant places like the Falls Road and the Shankill Road really exist, then maybe – just maybe – there are also other places, twice as far away as them. Maybe even five times as far.'

The sound of disbelieving laughter rocked the office.

'I'm only saying,' Zzzzzz said, hoping he wasn't making himself sound slightly foolish. 'Maybe there are places ten, or even twenty *miles* away from here!'

Everybody looked at him as if he had just blasphemed. He decided to try it from a different angle.

'Do you believe in UFOs?'

Megalife laughed, breaking the tension that had enshrouded the office like that big bad spider's web a few months ago. 'I've never seen a UFO, Zzzzzz. Why? Have you?'

'Don't make fun of your elders,' Mrs Overpants said gently.

'Just because you've never seen one,' Zzzzzz said critically, 'that doesn't mean they don't exist. I've never seen the outer edge of Belfast, and yet I was convinced that I knew, for a verifiable fact, that if I had kept on driving that day last August I would surely have fallen off it.'

'Well of course you would,' Megalife agreed, 'but that's different.'

'Oh? How so?'

'Because it's a scientific fact, not just a theory. Everybody knows it. How could the world we live in *not* come to an end at some point? It might be five or even *six* miles away from here, if there really is such a vast distance, but nothing goes on forever. Everything has to come to an end, even time itself. But alien objects flying in the air? That's another realm of fantasy altogether, if you ask me. Only birds and flies and other flying things can fly, not great big metal things.'

'I tend to agree with Mega,' Trumpella said, slowly running her fingers through her long black hair. 'Only conspiracy theorists claim to have seen "unidentified flying objects". I mean to say, just because they saw lights moving along at a steady pace in the night sky, why does it have to be aliens? They might just have been birds.'

'Birds with lights?' Megalife asked, trying to wind Trumpella up.

'Maybe they were on fire,' she laughed, and Megalife did too. 'I'm no expert. Perhaps some birds light up at night, who knows for sure?'

'Birds don't smoke, do they?' Megalife asked, and it did his heart a world of good when Trumpella laughed out loud. 'Whatever those things are, they're too far away for leprechaun eyes to see. Why, even the best cameras that technology has to offer can't make them out.'

'Only because leprechaun lenses are too small,' Zzzzzz said sensibly, and Mrs Overpants nodded in agreement. She didn't like it when Megalife and Trumpella started the silly talk, enjoying themselves too much, on her time.

'Maybe somebody should invent a camera with a huge lens, three or even four inches wide?' Mrs Overpants suggested, as if nobody had ever thought of it before. Zzzzzz knew from personal experience that Bobbington Mazzarazzabazzakazza's experts had already worked on just such a project.

'If we had a camera that huge,' Megalife said, excited at the prospect, 'maybe we'd see a whole new world up there. Maybe birds *do* smoke cigarettes at night, that would explain the lights. Or maybe they carry torches so they can see in the dark.'

'Now you're just being silly,' Trumpella laughed as Zzzzzz shook his head.

The door leading out to the front hall opened and in walked a chubby man wearing a pinstriped suit and a bowler-hat. He was carrying a big bag of sugar, and Trumpella suspected he was going to eat it all with a big spoon. My, he was fat, she thought, feeling utterly disgusted when the very idea of what he must look like naked popped into her head. He looked shocked by the lack of recognition on everybody's faces.

'What's wrong,' he asked in a deep, unfriendly voice, 'do you not know who I am?'

Mrs Overpants spotted the office key in his hand and snatched it off him, saying 'Give me that! How dare you walk in here unannounced, whoever you are.'

'I work here,' he protested, and everybody but Mrs Overpants laughed. 'I do,' he said. 'My name is Schneiderpump, Ponkitonius Schneiderpump. I'm the head accountant in this firm. That's my desk in the far corner.'

Mrs Overpants looked to see what he was pointing at. Where had that come from? It must have been new. Maybe she would buy a chair to go with it, unless they had a spare one in the cellar.

'I've sat sweating like nobody's business, working my guts out at that desk for the best part of twenty-eight years, without a word of thanks,' the man protested, taking his hat off. His dirty brown hair reached down almost to his shoulders, and Trumpella thought it made him look absolutely ridiculous. Not that she was pass-remarkable, but what a simply horrid-looking man.

'I work here five days a week all year round,' the man tried to convince anyone who would listen to him, obviously taking them all for fools. 'Apart from when you refuse to let me in, or have me thrown out.'

'Speaking of having you thrown out,' Mrs Overpants said, as a not-so-subtle hint. 'We're not interested in your farcical words, Mr Whoever.'

'Schneiderpump,' he said, exasperated, in desperate need of a good sit-down. 'Mrs Overpants – may I call you Grizelda?' She shook her head vigorously. 'My wife is your best friend, Conkyconkytillion,' he said, clutching at straws.

'My best friend?' Mrs Overpants laughed. 'Och, that's just plain daft. I wasn't born yesterday, no matter what you might think in that strange hairy head of yours. I think I would probably know you pretty well, if you were married to my best friend Conkyconkytillion.'

'But I *am*, Mrs Overpants. I'm her husband Ponkitonius.'

'Now you know,' Mrs Overpants reflected calmly, 'my friend Conkyconkytillion did tell me that her husband was called Ponkitonius, although as she's always saying, she can't for the life of her remember why the hell she married him.'

'That's me.'

'She said she can't even remember his name half the time, and that he has an instantly-forgettable face.'

'It does sound like this guy,' Zzzzzz said.

'Oh, Ponkitonius!' Mrs Overpants said, her eyes lighting up. 'I do beg your pardon – I don't know what came over me. Why don't you join us? Zzzzzz here is just about to tell us about his latest thrilling adventure.'

'They said they didn't have any sugar in the local shop,' Ponkitonius said, to explain his long absence. 'I thought I saw some behind the counter, but I was escorted out of the shop. I had to traipse half way down Joy's Entry to buy some. Well, at least three metres. Sorry for keeping you all waiting so long. I'll just put the kettle on, and then you can begin your story, Zzzzzz. I'll make the tea myself.'

'Ponkitonius,' Trumpella remembered, smiling, although she didn't think she had ever really liked him. 'Nice to meet you again. Is that really your desk, over there in the corner?'

'Ponkitonius, of course,' Megalife said as Ponkitonius nodded affirmatively. 'How silly we must look. I can't speak for the others, but at times I have a memory like a sieve.'

'Yes,' Ponkitonius said sadly, 'most leprechauns seem to, as far as I'm concerned.'

'I was just about to talk about your Conkyconkytillion, as a matter of fact,' Zzzzzz said, as all the staff bar Ponkitonius gathered around him once again.

'This is going to be good,' Trumpella beamed gleefully, rubbing her hands together in rapt anticipation.

'It is indeed,' came a voice from the kitchen, raising a momentary look of consternation on Mrs Overpants's face.

Zzzzzz suddenly realised that he had too much leg showing, so he got up out of his comfortable armchair and spent a couple of minutes wrapping the tail-end of his beard around the lower parts of his legs, leaving only his feet and ankles showing. That was much better, much warmer.

'I hope you never get nits, Zzzzzz,' Megalife joked. Mrs Overpants looked daggers at him, as if he had just hurled the greatest insult imaginable at the charming old father of fifteen and grandfather of at least ninety.

'*Those* horrible big insects?' Zzzzzz said as he sat down, quivering at the very thought of them. 'I was infested with them once, a couple of years ago, but I pulled them out of my beard with both hands and walloped them with a big spoon. It was one hell of a mighty struggle.'

Mrs Overpants looked at the clock on the suspiciously-pockmarked wall and sighed. 'I hope you haven't sat us all down in the corner of the office to tell us about your nits? I have a business to run here, you know.'

Zzzzzz uncrossed his legs and smoothed down the beard on his thighs. 'Well hardly,' he said in mock pomposity. He looked discombobulated for a couple of seconds, as if he was having one of his rare senior moments. 'You nit,' he heard Trumpella whispering to Megalife, who smiled shyly.

Zzzzzz stared up the room on his right, as something had caught his eye. 'Who's that?' he asked.

All eyes turned to look at a rather rotund man in a pinstriped suit walking out of the kitchen, with a smug look on his not-exactly-pretty mug and a mug of tea in his hand. The long-haired yob had obviously broken in through the back door and made himself a totally illegal cuppa as if he owned the place. The cheek of some people.

'Get that burglar out of my office!' Mrs Overpants screeched, and Megalife gulped. He estimated the lump of criminal blubber to weigh all of half an ounce. But then his hormones kicked in and he realised that this was his chance to be a big hero in front of the beautiful eyes of his beloved.

'Be my hero!' Mrs Overpants ordered Megalife, as if she had misread his mind and thought he was thinking about her.

'Oy!' Megalife yelled. 'Pork-belly! Out! Now!'

'I blooming work here!' the man retorted.

'If you do, you're sacked!' Mrs Overpants joined in the yelling. She looked towards Trumpella and said, much more quietly, 'Some people, huh? He has the audacity to break into my office and try to steal a cup…' She looked at the horrible burglar again and said, 'If you damaged that back door in any way, shape or form when you were breaking in, you're going to pay for it, you, you flibbertigibbet!'

Trumpella covered her ears in a state of shock. She couldn't remember ever hearing Mrs Overpants using such crude language before. The phone started ringing, and Trumpella picked it up. 'Not now, Chops,' she quickly said before hanging up, 'I'll see you tonight. I'll take my dogs for a walk, and you can take your cat.' She was too busy eagerly waiting to see what brave Megalife was about to do to the rotund gentleman.

Zzzzzz stood up and walked calmly out of the room, keeping his eyes on the intruder before departing. Megalife wasn't overly concerned, as he had little expected his elderly friend to be much help in a fight, even though he always claimed that he had been the leprechaun world boxing champion in his younger years. No, Megalife realised with a chuckle, everybody seriously believed that *he* was the muscles of the operation, God help them. Just for a moment he thought of sticking his hand down his pants, but that would have been the coward's way out. If he were to vanish now Trumpella would probably never speak to him again. And besides, he could only travel about two metres at a time using magic – even Mrs Overpants had to flick her fingers literally hundreds of times to travel to distant places such as around the corner.

'I work here,' the bloated leprechaun tried to convince everybody.

Megalife knew he had to hit the man, and hit him hard, but he wished he wasn't so little – a wish he knew would be considered blasphemous by more extreme members of leprechaun society. But as he looked at the intruder, he couldn't help wondering why some of the Little People had to be so bloody big.

'You all love me!' the bulbous burglar bellowed in a horribly grating voice, hopping up and down so much that the legal occupants of the upper Joy's Entry drainpipe could almost feel it vibrating. 'You know my wife, Grizelda! You know me, too! Conkyconkytillion –'

Zzzzzz walked calmly in through the door and, after scouring the room with his eyes to check where everybody was, he aimed his rusty old blunderbuss at the vagabond and shot him full of lead, adding yet more pockmarks to the wall behind him. While pulling the trigger, he suddenly remembered how much he enjoyed getting to use his blunderbuss indoors – this was the twentieth time he had fired his faithful old weapon in the office in the last year or so, although he couldn't remember who he had shot with it on the previous nineteen occasions.

The stranger ran out the front door screaming blue murder, his body seemingly covered in buckshot-holes due to Zzzzzz's supreme mastery of his chosen weapon.

'He was called Conkyconkytillion,' Trumpella deduced from the bad man's last decipherable words, wiping her brow while she contemplated a job well done by Zzzzzz. She had so wanted Megalife to be the big hero of the hour, just to see if he had the balls. Now she would never know. Still, she had always really, really liked Zzzzzz, so hey-ho.

'He'll feel that in the morning,' Mrs Overpants laughed, and they all joined in.

'He got off lightly,' Megalife said, pumping out his chest and flexing his self-proclaimed muscles, not that anyone noticed. 'He'd have been a lot worse off if I'd got my hands on him, I can tell yous that for nothing.'

'So anyway,' Trumpella said, paying little or no attention to Megalife's unwarranted bragging, 'what happened next, Zzzzzz?' They all resumed their seats and awaited his reply.

'Well, as I was about to say, before I was so –' he paused. 'Was I rudely interrupted?'

'I don't remember,' Mrs Overpants said. 'I don't think so.'

Zzzzzz looked down and wondered why he was holding his blunderbuss in his hands. He put it down on the floor beside the comfy armchair.

'Who owns that hat?' Megalife asked, picking what looked suspiciously like a buckshot-riddled bowler-hat up off the floor beneath the red clock. Nobody recognised it, so he took it into the kitchen and threw it in the bin.

'As I was about to say,' Zzzzzz said, leaning back in the armchair to make himself comfortable, 'the lovely billionaire Bobbington Mazzarazzabazzakazza hand-picked Conkyconkytillion Schneiderpump to be her chief scientist, primarily because she was an absolute whizz-kid in the munitions sphere. As even the slugs on the street know, Conkyconkytillion made her own fortune in the bad old days, when she sold arms to both sides of the leprechaun divide. In trials, she once created an explosion so utterly enormous that a giant's dog started barking at the huge cloud of smoke it created, running back and forward in little sharp bursts, wondering what it was. The giant holding his lead tugged him away, telling him not to be so silly. There were reports of shaking walls and broken windows up to two feet away from the blast in the middle of Joy's Entry.'

'Conkyconkytillion Schneiderpump is such a famous scientist that you don't even need to say her surname,' Trumpella interrupted the wise old man, as if she utterly idolised Conkyconkytillion. 'When you say the name Conkyconkytillion, everybody naturally assumes that you're talking about Conkyconkytillion Schneiderpump. And she's a great singer, too.'

'My good friend Conkyconkytillion got her lungs from her mother,' Mrs Overpants chipped in.

'We all do,' Trumpella laughed cheekily, sticking out her chest.

'Under Bobbington Mazzarazzabazzakazza's tutelage,' Zzzzzz continued unabated, 'Conkyconkytillion Schneiderpump famously invented leprechaun spectacles.'

'And mirrors,' Megalife said less pertinently. 'My Great-Auntie Bobbington has covered every wall, ceiling and floor in her house with mirrors hand-crafted by Conkyconkytillion.'

'Where does your billionaire great-auntie live?' Trumpella asked Megalife in passing.

'It's that big house at the top of a doorstep in the green, amber and red light district of High Street,' he replied. 'Sometimes the flashing lights keep her awake all night. She can't figure out why the giants' enormous vehicles come to a complete standstill at all hours of the day and night, before suddenly zooming off with roaring engines. That really does her head in.'

'No leprechaun has ever safely traversed that incredible desert of a road on foot,' Mrs Overpants said sadly. 'I waited until the giant vehicles came to a complete standstill and then flicked myself across that huge expanse in seven swift flicks of my fingers. As well as my beautiful new dress I had to buy two brand new pairs of bloomers after that traumatic experience, I can tell you that for nothing.'

'Why two pairs?' Trumpella asked.

'Well, I had to come back again,' Mrs Overpants explained.

'Between them,' Zzzzzz intervened, trying to break the flow of the inane chitter-chatter, 'Bobbington Mazzarazzabazzakazza and Conkyconkytillion Schneiderpump spent the best part of a decade inventing magnifying-glasses, cameras, and all kinds of wonderful creations we take for granted nowadays. Then, four or five months ago, Conkyconkytillion revealed that she had finally succeeded in making a telescope with an incredible four-inch radius.'

'Four inches?' Trumpella gasped. 'That's not possible.'

'I looked through one of my great-auntie's telescopes a few weeks ago,' Megalife proudly announced, 'one given to her by Conkyconkytillion Schneiderpump. Believe it or not, I saw Great-Auntie Bobbington from a good three feet away, riding up High Street in the rear of her open-top chauffeur-driven limousine.' He turned and looked at Zzzzzz. 'Are you trying to tell me that Conkyconkytillion has now made a telescope that can see even further away than that?'

'A whole lot further,' Zzzzzz said, and Megalife's jaw hit the ground.

'Don't tell me it can see all the way to the far end of High Street,' Trumpella said excitedly, 'where for many decades awe-struck leprechauns claim to have seen a mysterious clock-face high up in the sky on moonlit nights?'

'No telescope could possibly see the far end of High Street,' Mrs Overpants insisted. 'Why, that must be tens of thousands of inches away.'

Megalife chuckled to himself – his boss's friendship with her so-called 'best friend' Conkyconkytillion was obviously a lot more one-sided than she let on.

Zzzzzz reached deep down into his beard and pulled out a pen and paper and began taking notes, as if he was writing his diary. But he was such a popular, good-hearted leprechaun that nobody passed any remark on his peculiar behaviour.

'I looked through the new telescope with my own eye,' Zzzzzz said after sticking his pen and paper back into his beard, and his words clearly created quite a stir in the room. 'I looked up into the sky. Unfortunately I found my attention being drawn towards an intensely bright light. The moment I actually focused the telescope on it I fell over backwards, holding my head in my hands. I felt all dizzy, and I don't even remember landing on the ground, although I bruised both my buttocks.'

'Too much information,' Trumpella giggled, finding it hard to imagine that Zzzzzz had buttocks.

'For some weird reason, I couldn't see anything at all for the next four or five minutes.'

'What was it that you looked at?' Trumpella asked. 'Was it the Hot Shiny Bright Light in the Sky?'

'The Hot Shiny Bright Light in the Sky, exactly,' Zzzzzz confirmed, smoothing down the beard enveloping his torso. 'Luckily for me it was partially covered by those Big Fluffy White Things, which indubitably prevented me from being blinded on the spot, according to Conkyconkytillion Schneiderpump. The Hot Shiny Bright Light in the Sky is hotter and shinier and brighter than any of us could ever have imagined. It must be literally *millions* of inches away.'

'What poppycock,' the ultra-skeptical Grizelda Overpants said in a forthright manner. 'The Ceiling cannot possibly be that high up.'

'Ah, now you see, there's the rub,' Zzzzzz informed her. 'I know it sounds ridiculous, but I no longer believe that there actually *is* a ceiling at the top of the sky.'

Mrs Overpants nearly fainted. Megalife laughed. Then he became all serious and said, 'It's common knowledge that the Big Fluffy White Things are an astronomical fifty feet up in the air, and the Hot Shiny Bright Light in the Sky is another fifty feet above them. No one knows which of the giants flicks the unseen switch to turn the Hot Shiny Bright Light in the Sky off and on, but there's no doubt in any sensible leprechaun's mind that it's just a big light bulb.'

'So how does the bulb move across the ceiling as the day goes on?' Trumpella asked.

'The greatest scientists in the leprechaun world have been struggling to find an answer to that puzzle since before I was in nappies,' Zzzzzz said. 'Anyhow, when I returned to the telescope I saw lots of birds flying in the sky, and – believe it or not – not one of them was smoking a cigarette, not one of them was on fire, and not one of them was carrying a torch.'

'I put it to you that you're talking through your bottom,' Grizelda pointed out.

Megalife huffed and puffed as he wheeled the superfluous desk in through the kitchen and out to the back yard.

'So,' Trumpella asked Zzzzzz with her usual cheeky grin, 'what happened to you last night?'

Zzzzzz looked somewhat nonplussed. 'Did I not get that far yet?' he asked. 'All these bloomin' interruptions. Well, now wait until you hear this. It'll make the hairs on the back of your neck –'

– The front door hadn't so much been pushed open as kicked in, judging by the ferocity with which it banged against the office wall. No, it had been pushed in by a really large wheelbarrow.

Trumpella's face came over all aglow. Mrs Overpants's frown turned upside-down in less time than it took Zatarak Zoxion Zalcho Zloop Z. Zizzyzump to say 'Conkyconkytillion Schneiderpump, as I live and breathe!' He reached out to shake the superstar scientist's hand but Trumpella beat him to it, almost knocking over the enormous tarpaulin-covered wheelbarrow that Conkyconkytillion was pushing along in front of her. How she had managed to squeeze it in through the office door, Zzzzzz had no idea.

'Hello, Conkyconkytillion,' Trumpella said in an exhilarated tone.

'I'm sorry,' Conkyconkytillion said as Megalife walked back into the office, 'I don't believe I've had the pleasure?'

'Neither have I,' Megalife muttered beneath his breath, and he spotted Trumpella frowning in his direction.
'Oh, Conkyconkytillion,' Mrs Overpants stepped in to help, 'this is my typist, Trumpella Potteringthwaite.'
'Nice to meet you, Trumpella.'
'She's your biggest fan,' Megalife told Conkyconkytillion, bringing a noticeable flush to Trumpella's cheeks. At that precise moment the black tarpaulin slipped off the top of the wheelbarrow and fell to the ground, revealing what Mrs Overpants saw as some sort of long, futuristic tubular mechanism that became really wide at one end.
'Can I have a look through that?'
'Mega,' Mrs Overpants gently reprimanded him, 'don't be cheeky to my best friend.'
'To your what now?' Conkyconkytillion asked as an aside.
'Look through what?' Mrs Overpants asked Megalife.
'It's a telescope,' he replied.
'Is everything OK, Mrs Schneiderpump?' Zzzzzz asked Conkyconkytillion, showing once again just how empathetic he was. It was common knowledge in educated leprechaun circles that he could spot trouble from twenty yards away.
'Mrs Schneiderpump?' Conkyconkytillion asked him back.
'Well,' Zzzzzz said, 'that's your name, isn't it?'
Conkyconkytillion took off her bright red top hat and rolled her long blonde hair between her fingers in a disturbed manner. 'You know,' she thought back, 'I think it is. In fact, now that you mention it, I'm sure it is. Thank you for bringing it all back to me, Zzzzzz.'
'It was nothing,' he said modestly.
Conkyconkytillion Schneiderpump sat down on the corner of Trumpella's desk. Trumpella didn't mind in the slightest – in fact she felt quite honoured to have the superstar's pert posterior in her close vicinity. Trumpella nearly drooled as she looked up close at Conkyconkytillion's beautiful gold-coloured leggings, matching mini-skirt and lovely orange duffle-coat – and her yellow-and-red-striped stilettos were to die for.
'Did you push that massive wheelbarrow all the way down Joy's Entry all by yourself?' Mrs Overpants asked, hoping that Conkyconkytillion would think she was a wonderful, caring friend for doing so. How she had managed to get it in through the office door, Mrs Overpants had absolutely no idea.

'Well, yes,' Conkyconkytillion said, 'but I kept close to the wall on this side, to avoid being trod on by those clumsy giants. But that was the least of my worries.' She turned and looked straight into Zzzzzz's eyes. 'I think I have a stalker.'

'A stalker? Oh, my good god, no,' Trumpella said.

'A strange man followed me all the way from High Street,' Conkyconkytillion said. 'I kept looking over my shoulder but he was always there, four or five paces behind me, repeatedly telling me that he loves me.'

'A groupie,' Trumpella said. 'Let's get Megalife here to beat him up.'

Megalife smiled nervously, not sure whether to be frightened or chuffed. He hoped the apple of his eye was being serious, and wasn't just making fun of him. 'No problem,' he said in a show of bravado. 'If he shows up here point him out to me, and I'll mash him to a pulp.'

'He's outside the front door,' Conkyconkytillion told Megalife, who gulped.

'What... what does he look like?'

'I... I can't remember,' Conkyconkytillion said. 'I think he's a man, of sorts.'

Zzzzzz instinctively reached down to the floor beside his comfortable old mustard-coloured armchair and picked up his beloved blunderbuss. He marched towards the exit but Megalife stepped forward and said, flexing his imaginary muscles, 'Let me deal with this, Zzzzzz.'

'My hero,' Trumpella said, smiling coyly at Megalife, who instantly went weak at the knees. To be brutally honest he wasn't at all sure why he had volunteered, apart from showing off to the girl of his dreams. Trumpella Potteringthwaite had probably appeared in more of Megalife's dreams over the last couple of years than Megalife had himself. In his fantasies it always ended in marriage, a marriage that would last for decades, with never an argument between them. Hopefully his dream would come true sooner rather than later. A kiss once every Christmas wasn't enough for Megalife any more, he wanted Trumpella all for himself.

'Be brave,' she said to him now. 'Be big and strong.'

Megalife felt, somehow, that he was trying to make amends for something he had done or failed to do quite recently, although to be honest he couldn't remember what it was. Hey-ho.

The door opened and in walked a fat, ugly man wearing a bowler-hat and an ill-fitting pinstriped suit covered in what looked like little burn-marks. He took his hat off, revealing a head of ridiculously-long hair, and he stared at Conkyconkytillion with ugly big bovine eyes. 'I love you, Conkyconkytillion,' he sobbed, and all eyes turned to her.
'Who is this fat git?' she laughed, leaping to her feet. 'I've never seen him before in my life.'
'I'm your husband,' he told her, sounding almost as ridiculous as he looked. 'I'm Ponkitonius. You've got to believe me.'
Megalife looked at Conkyconkytillion as she doubled up in laughter, wobbling on her stilettos and coming close to falling down.
'Are you not going to beat this fat slob up, Megalife?'
He looked at Trumpella. 'Beat who up?' He followed her gaze towards the obese gentleman. 'Oh, I forgot he was here,' he said, shaking his head in disbelief at his suddenly embarrassing short attention-span. 'Why, Trump? What did he do?'
'I... I don't remember,' Trumpella said, mirroring Megalife by shaking her own head.
'Who are you?' Mrs Overpants asked the stranger in an authoritative tone of voice. 'What do you mean, by barging into my office like this?'
Conkyconkytillion couldn't believe what she was seeing and hearing when the fat man pleaded with Grizelda and her employees, ridiculously trying to convince them that he worked in the office alongside them. The man was clearly as mad as a box of fleas. 'I'm the head accountant!' he insanely insisted. 'I've worked here for twenty-eight years!'
What happened next made Conkyconkytillion wonder if her long-time acquaintance Grizelda Overpants had totally lost the plot.
'Oh, I do apologise, Ponkitonius,' Mrs Overpants said to the chubby chap in a grovelling tone, 'I don't know what came over me. How could I forget my best friend's husband after all these years?' – and with a quick look to her right, 'I am so, so sorry, Conkyconkytillion.'

'Eh?' Conkyconkytillion asked, once again sitting down on the corner of Trumpella's desk. 'Sorry for what, Grizzly?' – Trumpella looked at Mrs Overpants and laughed at her 'Don't call me that in front of my staff' eyes.

'I'm sorry...' Mrs Overpants replied, giving Trumpella what she hoped the young lady recognised as a contemptuous look, 'I'm sorry for momentarily forgetting who your husband was. It must have looked extremely rude of me.'

'My husband?' Conkyconkytillion predictably asked, pressing her big red top hat down on her lap as if she thought it was her comfort blanket.

'That's me,' said the stranger, who maybe wasn't quite such a stranger after all. 'I'm your husband, Ponkitonius.'

Conkyconkytillion looked around, just to double-check that the man was indeed looking at her. 'Oh,' she said, 'right.' And then something appeared to click deep inside her head. As everybody in the office walked up to Ponkitonius and shook his hand, welcoming him back to the fold (wherever he had been, nobody knew for sure), Conkyconkytillion said, 'Oh, yes, of course. I thought you were a stalker.'

'Me? A stalker?' Ponkitonius asked, not unnaturally flabbergasted.

'Sorry,' Conkyconkytillion said. 'No hard feelings, eh?'

'Not at all,' Ponkitonius said, hugging his wife, as if he had been through this whole scenario a thousand times before and now it was second nature to him.

'Don't squash me,' Conkyconkytillion eventually said, gently nudging her big-boned husband aside and looking at him. 'What happened to your suit? It's covered in holes.'

'Oh, this?' Ponkitonius said, looking down at his jacket and trousers as if the damage done to them was of little or no consequence. 'Zatarak Zoxion Zalcho Zloop Z. Zizzyzump shot me with his blunderbuss.'

'I most certainly did not!' Zzzzzz said in an aggrieved tone, as all eyes turned to look at the blunderbuss he was holding in his hands, pointed in Ponkitonius Schneiderpump's direction. 'Oops,' Zzzzzz said, feeling ever so slightly embarrassed. 'Sorry.'

'No problem,' Ponkitonius said, as Conkyconkytillion Schneiderpump gave Zzzzzz a disapproving look.

Megalife went out and wheeled Ponkitonius's desk back into the office, blushing all the way out to the back yard and back again, muttering 'silly me' as he manoeuvred the weather-worn desk into the mustard-coloured space its exact same size in the corner of the yellow office carpet. Then he went into the kitchen to throw a loose splinter from the desk into the pedal-bin, where he found a buckshot-riddled bowler-hat. This he handed to Ponkitonius, and upon seeing him do so Zzzzzz mumbled 'Sorry about that, er… Ponkitonius.'
'Accidents will happen,' Ponkitonius replied chirpily.
'Punky what?' Conkyconkytillion asked Zzzzzz.
'Punky what?' Trumpella asked Conkyconkytillion.
'Zzzzzz said something about punky something,' Conkyconkytillion told Trumpella.
'He was talking about me,' Ponkitonius told Conkyconkytillion. 'I'm your husband, remember?'
'Oh, I give up,' Conkyconkytillion said resignedly. 'I have too many important things on my mind to be able to remember such trivialities regarding all the superfluous people in my life. Now, let's go and have a wonderful adventure!' – In so saying, Conkyconkytillion Schneiderpump wheeled her wheelbarrow back out the front door, closely pursued by Grizelda Overpants, Megalife, Trumpella Potteringthwaite, Zatarak Zoxion Zalcho Zloop Z. Zizzyzump, and the mysterious overweight stranger. By the look in Conkyconkytillion's eyes, this was going to be fun.

'Ponkitonius,' the fat man repeated every time anyone turned around and looked suspiciously at him, 'Ponkitonius, er… Schneiderpump, I think. Damn, now you've got me at it.'
'Never heard of him,' Conkyconkytillion Schneiderpump shrugged her shoulders and said. 'What does he do?'
'He's an accountant,' Ponkitonius said, feeling as if he was having an out of body experience yet again.
'He sounds like a boring git,' Conkyconkytillion said, making Ponkitonius feel about a millimetre tall. Was he *that* insignificant, that even his own wife forgot he existed every time she blinked her eyes? She hooked up with other men every time he left the house, forgetting that he existed. She even told him what she had done with them when he arrived home again. He had piled on more and more stress-related weight in recent years, every time he arrived home

from work and found his wife in bed with another man, claiming that she had no idea who Ponkitonius was. Luckily for her he wasn't the sensitive type, or he would probably have left her and found himself another woman twenty years ago.

As they rounded the corner onto High Street, Megalife spotted his best friend Chopper Longfellow the Thirteenth walking towards him. 'Hi Chopper,' he yelled over the sound of the traffic, and Chopper smiled and nodded at him.

By now Mrs Overpants had wended her way to the head of the group, as she genuinely wanted to believe that she was the leader of any pack of leprechauns she happened to be associated with, even when she quite clearly wasn't. But it kept her ego inflated, so nobody really cared. As Conkyconkytillion *Something-or-Other* knew only too well, her passing acquaintance Grizzly Overpants had absolutely no idea in which direction they were heading. Both ladies now looked around when they heard Megalife shrieking.

Trumpella had leapt into Chopper's arms the second she saw him, and now he appeared to have his tongue half way down her throat. They were standing snogging and groping one another, directly in front of Megalife, who looked practically suicidal.

Out of the corner of her eye Trumpella spotted Mrs Overpants frowning in her direction, so she quickly plucked her lips away from Chopper's and deftly removed his hands from her bottom.

'I'll see you at your house tonight,' Chopper said, looking lustily into Trumpella's eyes.

'As usual,' Trumpella laughed, walking towards Mrs Overpants like a loyal employee, leaving Megalife looking angrily at his best friend and housemate.

Three or four months ago, Trumpella had finally accepted Megalife's ongoing invitation to visit his flat after work one day, hoping that she might let her hair down and have a bit of fun with him in his own home. He had been utterly amazed when she accepted his offer. She drove Megalife to his house, where he introduced her to his best friend Chopper, who had the flat next door to his. Chopper was a single man the same age as Megalife, the only difference being that he was in a long-term relationship. Trumpella drove home shortly after that, having only spoken to Chopper in passing.

Megalife suddenly knew the truth of the matter – Trumpella had obviously sneaked back to his house at the weekends, when she knew that Megalife always went to stay with his parents in their house all the way down on Ann Street. But Chopper had a girlfriend – so why had he set out to rob his best friend Megalife of the woman he knew was the love of his life? Megalife suddenly felt dirty, he felt mentally sullied, his future dreams had just gone up in smoke. And he would probably need to find himself a new place to live.

Megalife meandered morosely behind the motley crew as Conkyconkytillion led them, ducking and diving to avoid giant feet galore, to a relatively safe spot up against the wall a few feet away from a giant who was lying, cup in hand, in an enormous sleeping-bag. Conkyconkytillion said she had personally witnessed his fellow giants, both male and female, going out of their way to avoid him, so the leprechauns were much less likely to be cruelly trod asunder at that precise position on the giants' walkway.

Under Conkyconkytillion's leadership (much to Mrs Overpants's chagrin) they all got together, utilising the very best of their muscles and adrenaline, and succeeded in setting up the telescope on a tripod on the pavement, and Conkyconkytillion then aimed it towards the far-distant upper end of High Street. After spending a minute or so focusing the lens she turned to Megalife.

'Have a look at this,' she said, expecting Megalife to be as enthusiastic as he was the time she had let him look through the telescope at some terrifying insects at the foot of his great-auntie Bobbington Mazzarazzabazzakazza's back garden. Conkyconkytillion could hardly credit the disinterested look in his eyes. In fact, being a good reader of people, she realised that he looked as if he had suddenly lost all interest in life.

'Come on, Megalife,' she tried to coax him, as Mrs Overpants looked sadly at the man in question. Grizelda didn't know the complete ins and outs of what was going on, but she had a gut feeling that Trumpella Potteringthwaite was behind this whole sad state of affairs. Maybe Megalife had a crush on her? It was quite possible, however unfortunate. Mrs Overpants herself had always had her eye on him – after all, time waits for no leprechaun, and an ageing leprechaun lady can but dream.

'We can explore the vast infinities of High Street,' Conkyconkytillion tried yet again to persuade Megalife, trying to make him get his priorities right, all the while wondering why a fat, sweaty man in a bowler-hat was standing so close to her. 'Apart from myself and your great-auntie, the only other leprechauns who have ever seen the incredible sight I'm about to show you are Ernest Scheissenhausen and Elvis Skitterington.'

'The great explorer?' Mrs Overpants asked.

'The man with the big voice! The king of rock 'n' roll!' Trumpella yelled, staring in awe at Conkyconkytillion's magnificent-looking apparatus. 'What is this thing?' she asked, totally blanking the suddenly loveless look in Megalife's eyes.

'It's a telescope,' Zzzzzz informed her, 'with – believe it or not – a four-inch lens! See, Miss Smartypants, I wasn't only imagining things when I talked about it in the office this morning. What was it you said? "Four inches? That's just stupid man's talk!" – Well this is the proof of the pudding.'

Mrs Overpants took it upon herself to step up to the mark, for the sake of the office's morale. 'I suppose I'd better lead the way,' she said, 'being office manager and all that,' and Conkyconkytillion had no objections. Neither of them heard the angrily-whispered conversation that was going on behind them.

'What I get up to behind closed doors is none of your business,' Trumpella said to her downcast workmate, 'whether it's in my own house or somebody else's.'

'Mine, for example?' Megalife asked, feeling sick to the pit of his stomach.

'Grow up,' Trumpella told him, clearly having no regrets. 'I'm not your property.'

Megalife rolled his eyes. All of a sudden he considered the love of his life to be his worst enemy, a total waste of the last two years of his life, two years he would never get back. He had held her dear to his heart for all that time, and for what? To find out that she had been stabbing him in the back for the last three or four months, using his own best friend as her weapon. He didn't know what his life was all about any more. He felt as if he had dropped down into a big hole in the ground and was falling, falling...

'It's a clock!' Mrs Overpants squealed, feeling as if she was on the verge of wetting her bloomers for the first time since she went to the Elvis Skitterington concert over twenty years ago. 'A clock, high up in the sky! A giant clock-tower – I've never seen anything like it in my life!'

'Bobbington Mazzarazzabazzakazza's spies told her that the giants call it the Albert clock,' Conkyconkytillion informed Mrs Overpants, trying to keep her voice down as low as possible in spite of the constant sound of the giants' motor-vehicles, as if she was revealing a Belfast state secret. This revelation managed to momentarily snap Megalife out of his apparent manic depression. Why, he wondered, would his Great-Auntie Bobbington have so-called 'spies' working for her? 'They say it actually has four clock-faces,' Conkyconkytillion continued, adding intrigue to mystery, 'one on each side, although to be honest I haven't got as far as checking that out for myself yet.'

'Even the giants in the distance look tiny, compared to that beautiful monstrosity of a building,' Mrs Overpants said, before kindly moving aside to let Trumpella have a look through the magical telescopic device. Mrs Overpants wondered who the fat man was, and why he was standing so close to them.

'Bloody hell!' Trumpella bellowed. Megalife had never heard her swearing before – but then, he now reckoned, she probably saved all her naughty words up until she was behind closed doors with any male leprechaun but him. Words and deeds alike.

With Conkyconkytillion's assistance, twisting and turning the telescope hither and thither, Trumpella Potteringthwaite looked left, right and centre up and down the impossibly-distant two ends of High Street and saw giant shops that looked just like their leprechaun counterparts, and giants who looked just like leprechauns, not just their giant boots, shoes and sandals. She even saw one giant wearing stilettos just like Conkyconkytillion's, except that they didn't have lovely yellow-and-red stripes like the scientific superstar's.

'From a great distance they're just like us,' Trumpella gasped, unable to believe her eyes. She even succeeded in moving the lens around slightly all by herself, in order to check out a nearer corner. 'Oh look,' she shouted, totally delighted, obviously not caring a whit about sad Megalife's feelings, 'there's my lover-boy!'

Mrs Overpants sighed. She had never realised before that Trumpella apparently had no moral compass.

Bobbington Mazzarazzabazzakazza had often mentioned to Conkyconkytillion how much her great-nephew adored his workmate Trumpella, so now the empathetic Conkyconkytillion decided to try and change the subject. 'Did you know,' she said, 'that the giants actually eat animals to make them big and strong?'
'No way!' Trumpella laughed, not removing her right eye from the telescope for an instant.
'It's true,' Conkyconkytillion revealed. 'Maybe we leprechauns ought to take a leaf out of their book?'
'I'm not eating flies, slugs and bees,' Megalife protested, making Conkyconkytillion smile – her little ploy appeared to be working.
'There are other animals,' Conkyconkytillion said. 'Spiders… ants… butterflies.'
'Robins,' Trumpella said, giggling, 'and giant cats, like the one that chased my car all the way to the office this morning.'
'Maybe we could cook a stew out of fleas?' Conkyconkytillion suggested, turning Megalife's stomach just enough to momentarily stop him pining for Trumpella.
'Or nits,' Mrs Overpants suggested whimsically.
'Not those horrid big brutes!' Zzzzzz protested.
'We could even eat our own pets,' Conkyconkytillion said, 'the moohs, and the baahs, and the cluck-clucks.'
'Blasphemy!' Zzzzzz said, wondering why a fat man was standing watching him and his colleagues. 'They are all leprechaun beasts, just like us.' He tapped Trumpella on the shoulder. 'Can I have a go now?'
'In a minute,' she replied selfishly. 'I'm looking at Chopper. Isn't he lovely? He's a real man's man – a leprechaun's leprechaun – oh no!' she screamed, quickly covering her eyes, probably just overdramatising as usual. 'No!'
Zzzzzz gently eased Trumpella away from the telescope and had his go at last. What he saw wasn't initially clear – until he saw giant fingers wiping what looked suspiciously like a brown leather-jacketed leprechaun's squashed body off his or her light, flexible rubber-soled shoe. He looked away from the telescope in disgust and saw Trumpella curled up in a ball on the floor, bawling her pretty little eyes out.
'Chopper has been trampled underfoot,' Zzzzz whispered to Megalife, who immediately held his head in his hands, rapt with

guilt. All that the great diplomat Zzzzzzz could think of saying to console Trumpella was 'It comes to us all in the end, sweetheart – I'm sorry, but that's one of the dangers of living life as a leprechaun in modern-day Belfast' – but he realised that that might not have sounded so good, so instead he erred on the side of caution and said nothing.

'Get over it,' Megalife wanted to say to Trumpella, but unlike her he had a moral compass. Besides which, his best friend had just been squashed. Life was cruel, life was strange, but strangely, perhaps cruelly, there were no tears welling up in his eyes. On reflection he realised that he ought to have consoled Trumpella on the spot, but she had told him that her relationship with Chopper the Unlucky Thirteenth was none of his business – so he did her the honour of saying nothing.

'Hey-ho,' Conkyconkytillion said with a knowing grin, 'revenge is a dish best served cold.'

'What do you mean?' Mrs Overpants asked her, with a comforting arm now wrapped around Trumpella's shoulder. 'This poor young lady has just lost the love of her life, to one of those big... brutes!'

'No she hasn't,' Megalife thought to himself, as his fleeting guilty feelings quickly abated, 'the love of her life is still very much alive and kicking – she just doesn't know it yet.' On the bright side, at least he would no longer be obliged to seek new accommodation. Sad but true, he chuckled inwardly, covering his mouth with his hand just to be on the safe side. He didn't want to antagonise the apple of his eye, the girl of his dreams, the only reason why he had ever been born. He realised that, as his best friend, it would be left to him to inform Chopper's parents about his sad demise – and his girlfriend too, for that matter, unless Trumpella wanted to tell her.

'As the old saying says,' the normally diplomatic Zzzzzz heard himself saying, just before Trumpella leapt to her feet and kneed him in the balls (with only his beard for protection – ouch!), 'worse things happen in a pond.'

Suddenly realising that moral compasses were in short supply throughout the leprechaun kingdom as a whole (their only fault), Megalife patted Trumpella three times on the head and said, 'I'm sorry for your troubles, honey. If there's anything I can do to help...'

'Yeah, right,' she replied, suddenly putting on her best angry face for some obscure reason. 'If it makes you feel any better, Chopper

Longfellow and I slept in your bed every Saturday night for the last three or four months. He only had a single bed, and so do I. Your big double bed gave us plenty of room for –'

'OK, OK,' Mrs Overpants interrupted her, 'that's quite enough, Trumpella. Will you two please stop fighting like little children? My cats and dogs don't fight half as much as you two do.'

'Oh! Wow! I don't know what came over me,' Trumpella said ironically.

'I don't want you to get too excited,' Conkyconkytillion intervened, 'but I now have an even bigger surprise for you all.'

'There you go,' Mrs Overpants told Trumpella. 'Let's not get bogged down with trivialities while we're in the presence of the greatest scientific genius on all of High Street.'

All eyes – even Trumpella's (and Zzzzzz's) tear-filled ones – focused on Conkyconkytillion.

'Yes, I have a wonderful surprise for you all,' the great woman proclaimed. 'Especially for you, Trumpella – because it's payback time!'

The gigantic cars came to a complete standstill, as they did every once in a while – and Conkyconkytillion was formulating a theory about the reason why. She swivelled the telescope around and aimed it at the two red postbox mountains all the way across the wide expanse of tarmac. 'Ah,' she said, 'here she comes now, right on cue.' She turned around and said, 'Here, Grizzly, have a look at this.'

Mrs Overpants removed her arm from Trumpella's shoulder and looked into the telescope. 'There's something…' she uttered, slightly confused, 'it seems to be flying out from between the two mountains. Is it a bird? It doesn't fly like a bird – it has no wings. And what's that spinning around on top of it?'

'It's Bobbington Mazzarazzabazzakazza's chopper,' Conkyconkytillion revealed, catching the almost instantaneous look of astonishment in Trumpella's eyes. 'Or should I say, her helicopter. I invented it – well, truth be told the giants got there first, but I had to make my smaller version from scratch. No manual for this jack-of-all-trades. Bobbington took to it like a least-sandpiper to water, she didn't even need any flying lessons – which is just as well, because that is Belfast's first and only leprechaun chopper.'

She caught the sad look in Trumpella's eyes. 'I repeat, its full name is helicopter.'
'It seems to be moving in this direction,' Mrs Overpants said in a fearful tone. 'Should we hide?'
'Not at all,' Conkyconkytillion replied with a broad smile, 'it's coming to pick us up. We are about to participate in a magnificent adventure.' Her eyes suddenly lit up like a light bulb. 'I think I've finally worked it out,' she said, gently ousting her acquaintance Grizelda from the telescope. She swivelled it around to her left and then turned it upwards until it was looking high above her head, just in time to see the red light turning amber and, a few seconds later, green. At which point – eureka! – the giant vehicles started moving. 'So that's what the lights are for,' Conkyconkytillion said, 'I should have guessed.' This discovery would end years of sleepless nights for Bobbington when Conkyconktillion explained it to her later on. 'But,' Conkyconkytillion suddenly yelled, 'the cars will hit the chopper!'
'Can you please stop using that word?' Trumpella asked the most famous person she had ever met with a sniffle. 'I'm still in mourning.'

Bobbington Mazzarazzabazzakazza was the quickest-witted leprechaun on the opposite side of High Street, and despite being well into her seventies she spotted the imminent danger just in the nick of time. She was half way across the road when she saw the traffic to her left beginning to move in her direction – panic stations! She flicked a few switches and pressed a few buttons until, by chance, the helicopter rose even higher up into the air, narrowly missing the top of a giant salmon-pink double-decker bus. She didn't want to admit it, but that had been a lucky escape by any stretch of the imagination. She made a mental note to keep her chopper away from the giants' vehicles from that moment on.

'Who the hell do you think you are? Have you no home to go to? Why do you keep following us around?'
'I'm your husband.'
Conkyconkytillion laughed her socks off.
'What's that, up in the sky?' Megalife asked, looking almost directly above his head through the telescope. 'It's like a metal tube – like

one of my mother's cigar tubes – with little wings, although the wings are not moving. And it has lights in it – and a trail of smoke coming out of its rear end!'

'Yes, I've seen them too,' Conkyconkytillion told Megalife, as Trumpella tried to shove him aside so she could have a look at the strange object. 'Believe it or not, I have a theory that there are dozens of giants inside that thing. They must fly all the way from High Street to Ann Street inside that strange contraption. I estimate it to be well over fifty feet in the air, a couple of feet above the Fluffy White Things.'

Zzzzzzz cogitated. 'Do you think those things fly at night time as well?'

'Yes indeed,' Conkyconkytillion answered, as if reading Zzzzzz's thoughts. 'You've hit the nail right on the head there, Mr Zizzyzump.'

'In that case,' Megalife deduced, formulating his own totally original theory in his own little head even while he was speaking, 'I think that maybe we can now discount the long-held theory that birds smoke cigarettes, cigars or pipes at night.'

'And they probably don't carry torches to help them see in the dark, either,' Mrs Overpants suggested, catching on quick.

'I told you years ago that they were aeroplanes,' the fat man said out of the blue, with his horrible deep, grating voice that made Trumpella's teeth grind. Conkyconkytillion couldn't help wondering why the stranger was looking at her as he spoke. 'I told you about helicopters too,' the undesirable man claimed, obviously clutching at non-existent straws. 'Why do you never remember a thing I say to you?'

'Is he talking to me?'

'I think so,' Mrs Overpants said, and Megalife, Trumpella and Zatarak Zoxion Zalcho Zloop Z. Zizzyzump nodded in agreement.

'I showed you how to make one from scratch,' the outsider said. 'I even taught Bobbington Mazzarazzabazzakazza how to fly it. Don't worry, *she*'ll remember me. *She*'ll make you realise how forgetful you are, and then you'll feel really silly. Why do you always –'

The chubby man's rambling words were, thankfully, drowned out by a huge whirring sound from the sky above their heads, almost as loud as one of the giants' electrified scooters that roared up and down the footpath at all hours of the day and night, endangering the lives of any leprechaun who hadn't kept close enough to the wall, as every leprechaun was taught to do the minute he or she was out of nappies. Trumpella's beloved purple Morris Minor had come pretty close to being squashed as flat as a pancake by giant scootering fools sneaking up in her slipstream on more than one occasion – twice, in fact – in the last week alone. She hated electric scooter-riders with a vengeance. OK, so Chopper Longfellow the Thirteenth had ridden one, but his was less than an inch in length, and that was a different kettle of *schindleria brevipinguis* altogether.

Megalife, Trumpella, Mrs Overpants and Zzzzzz reeled over backwards and cowered against the knees of the giant in the huge sleeping-bag when a UFO appeared out of the sky, with a weird thing on top of it spinning around even faster than the leprechaun eye can see. The alien craft landed on the footpath in front of them, blowing the beard wrapped around Zzzzzz's body with such a powerful gust that it almost stripped him naked. Conkyconkytillion's bright red top hat blew off her head, but she caught it mid-air and laughed.

The noise finally became less unbearable as the rapidly-circulating thingumabob on top of the UFO slowed down. A minute later a door on the side of the mainly glass and metal craft opened, and out stepped – Bobbington Mazzarazzabazzakazza!

'Phew,' Megalife said, as Zzzzzz climbed up the little ladder on the side of the craft, 'hello Great-Auntie Bobbington. I was expecting a little green leprechaun to disembark from that... what's it called?'
'It's a chopper,' Bobbington said, climbing back up the ladder.
'Stop using that word.'
'It's also known as a helicopter,' Megalife rushed to Trumpella's assistance, remembering what Conkyconkytillion had said in a quite timely manner.

Instead of looking proud of Megalife, Trumpella suddenly came over all overawed. She had never been in the presence of Belfast's only billionaire before, she had only ever seen her from a distance, riding up High Street in the back of her chauffeur-driven pink limousine.

The first thing she had noticed about the famous old lady was that she was wearing a green hat – a very tall, pointed hat, like something worn by witches in fairy tales. The long hair protruding from beneath the hat was snow-white. She was also wearing a lovely puce

dress that reached from just below her chin to just above her ankles, with a long turquoise cloak on her back, and big pink boots with elevator heels. Trumpella was not in the least bit unimpressed. She made a mental note to take her mother to Mazzarazzabazzakazza's to buy some new clothes first thing in the morning, now that Chopper was no longer around to keep her up all night playing doctors and nurses – Chopper was always the nurse, but she would let him take that secret with him to the grave. God, she missed her Chopper.
'Come on, Trump!'
'What?' She had been daydreaming again. She looked up at Megalife as he climbed in through the helicopter's glass door.
'We're all ready to go,' Megalife said, and Trumpella followed him up the little ladder.
As there was a seat to spare they had decided to bring the fat man along for a laugh – as Megalife had said when Trumpella's head was miles away, at least then it wouldn't be *all* bad, if they all got killed.
'Up, up and away!' Bobbington Mazzarazzabazzakazza said, pulling a big lever and pressing a big button, and the craft rose up into the cool Belfast afternoon air. The giant in the sleeping-bag reached out and tried to swat the helicopter like a giant fly, looking as if he thought he was only imagining it – he stared at the bottle in his hand as if he thought he might be intoxicated. Luckily for all concerned, however, the giant missed his target.
Trumpella had no fear of flying, because she had never even contemplated the possibility of flying before – maybe the fear would eventually hit her with the benefit of hindsight after they landed. She looked at Mrs Overpants, who was sitting staring at someone with what looked suspiciously like a weird look of adoration in her eyes. Trumpella naturally glanced over to her left to investigate, but instead of the expected mortal, her eyes settled upon a veritable leprechaun god.
'Oops,' Mrs Overpants said, thinking that she might have wet her fashionable bloomers for the second time in just over twenty years.
'Elvis?' Trumpella said in a state of disbelief, pinching her lovely thigh to check that she wasn't asleep. 'Elvis Skitterington?'
'In person,' the *superstar's superstar* said.
'You're my mother's hero.'

'Yeah, right,' the man in the gold lamé jump-suit said, sweeping back his big black quiff with his ring-covered hand, 'as if *you* are not going weak at the knees right now.'
'Bighead,' Megalife muttered, wondering what Trumpella could possibly see in the multi-millionaire Elvis Skitterington that she didn't see in him.
Bobbington turned around from the steering-wheel and said, 'Elvis is my best friend.'
'Mine too,' Conkyconkytillion said, and Mrs Overpants sulked.
'Apart from Grizzly Underpants here, of course,' Conkyconkytillion added with a smile, and everybody bar Mrs Overpants laughed out loud.
'You're my hero,' the fat man told the king of rock 'n' roll.
'Who is this guy?' Elvis Skitterington asked.
'Nobody knows,' Conkyconkytillion told him. 'We only brought him along in case the helicopter gets into trouble and we need to jettison some excess baggage in a hurry.'
'Ha-bloody-ha,' the fat man in the bowler-hat taking up more than his fair share of the seat said, as if he honestly believed that the woman in the red top hat was joking.
Bobbington steered the craft twenty to twenty-five feet up in the air, then took a sharp left and flew down High Street.
'Snappy Snaps,' Megalife said, finally able to see all the way up to the names of the shops on the street at long last. 'City Kitchen... Café Rosa... Bright's...'
'Cash Converters,' Trumpella said, looking to her right. 'Mace... White's Beer Hall...'
Even the giants looked relatively small, all fifty-odd of them that could be seen. Sadly, no leprechauns could be spotted from such a great height.
'Jessops... Crown Entry... Dunnes Stores,' Megalife said, feeling just about as lucky as a little leprechaun child in a sweet-shop. They flew across a huge pedestrian walkway, and then he continued, 'Starbucks... Carroll's...'
'Sports Direct,' Trumpella said, not to be outdone. 'T.K. Maxx... HMV...'
'Look,' Zzzzzz said, 'nearly all of the giants are holding little boxes up to their ears and talking to themselves. I knew there was something not quite right about those big bullies.'

'Look,' Mrs Overpants told Zzzzzz, 'some of them are staring at the little boxes as if their lives depend on it, and they're not even looking where they're going.'
'They're a menace,' Zzzzzz said.
'Costa... Guineys... McDonald's,' Megalife said, while Trumpella was saying 'Game... Barclay's... JD Sports... Spar.'
Bobbington was about to turn around the corner onto the equally huge street called Donegall Place, when a seagull swooped out of the sky and made as if to attack the helicopter, only backing away at the last moment when it realised that the rotors could have had one of its eyes out. 'Mayday, Mayday,' Bobbington yelled, as she had once seen a character do in a movie on an enormous screen, from a concealed spot underneath a giant's sofa, and Conkyconkytillion immediately rushed to her assistance, as they had planned in case of any emergency. Conkyconkytillion (the munitions expert) pressed the big red 'Do Not Press' button, and a missile shot out the front of the helicopter, seriously annoying the seagull. It looked really angry. 'Mayday,' Bobbington said once again, just to be on the safe side. Conkyconkytillion fired a second missile, which clipped the seagull's wing and made it think twice. The third missile caught the giant avian creature straight in the eye and killed it, thanks be to goodness. A couple of giants down on the ground removed their weird little silver boxes from the space beside their ears and stared at the seagull with something approaching anger on their faces, when it fell out of the sky and landed at their feet.
Undeterred, Bobbington headed on down the mysterious new street called Donegall Place.

Megalife and Trumpella Potteringthwaite hadn't even appeared to notice the dogfight with the giant seagull, so fascinated were they by the names above all the shop doors, surely never before seen by leprechaun eyes.
'Skechers... To Let... Lifestyle Sports...'
'Zara... Clarks... To Let... that company has a store on either side of the road.'
'Yangtze... Beaverbrooks...'
'Tesco... KFC...'
'Castle Lane,' Megalife said, looking at the street veering off to the left.

'Fountain Lane,' Trumpella said, looking at the turning on the right.
'Stradivarius,' Megalife said.
'That's what they call the leprechaun store where I bought my violin,' Zzzzzz said. 'I wonder if it's the same company.'
'It's bound to be,' Mrs Overpants said.
'Vodafone.'
'Primark,' Trumpella said. 'I wonder if it's pronounced Pree-mark or Pry-mark?'
'We'll probably never know,' the fat man said, and all eyes turned suspiciously towards him just for a second. Who the hell did he think he was?
'Oasis,' Trumpella continued, her eyes lighting up with wonder and delight. 'Queen's Arcade.'
'Optical Express,' Megalife said.
'That sounds like a place that *you* would like,' Bobbington said to Conkyconkytillion, who smiled back at her. It certainly was.
'River Island,' Megalife said. 'Next.'
'Boots,' Trumpella said, taking Megalife's cue. 'Oh, I got my winkle-picker boots in the leprechaun branch of that store. That's funny... that shop called Carroll's seems to have huge exaggerated leprechauns in its window, and they've all got funny hats and beards. They're making fun of us.'
'Don't take it personally, Trumpella,' Conkyconkytillion said, 'the giants will live to regret trying to humiliate us.'
'Foot Locker,' Megalife said. 'Phones4U... To Let.'
'Nationwide,' Trumpella said. 'I wonder what that word even means?'
'There really is a lot more to Belfast than is seen by leprechaun eyes,' Megalife commented.
'There certainly is,' Bobbington turned around from the steering-wheel and said, winking at Conkyconkytillion, who gave her a mysterious thumbs-up.
'It's as if the whole world picture has changed,' Mrs Overpants remarked.
'See,' Zzzzzz told her pointedly, 'I wasn't mad after all. I bet we could travel six or seven miles – yes, *miles*! – before we fell off the end of the world. Yes, even further than I drove my Rolls-Royce last summer. I *wasn't* just dreaming.'

'Nobody thought that for a minute,' Mrs Overpants said, winking at Trumpella, who wasn't even looking at her. She was too busy staring out at the big, fascinating new world. There were giants shouting and singing about life after death, they must have been preachers, although to be honest they didn't look like the most intelligent giants on the street – far from it.

They heard a loud noise, and their eyes were drawn to a really weird-looking contraption coming down the road. There were about a dozen giants – looking and sounding slightly inebriated – sitting around a rectangular vehicle of some sort, all of them cycling, as if it was bicycle-powered, and singing songs. There was a giant man at the front holding a steering-wheel, and singing along. The traffic came to a standstill, and Bobbington parked the helicopter on top of the weird yellow vehicle.

'They're playing the saddest song in the whole leprechaun lexicon,' Elvis Skitterington pointed out, 'the heartbreaking "Trampled Under Foot". I feel like crying every time I hear it.'

'I thought *you* wrote that song?' Mrs Overpants put it to Elvis.

'No,' he said, 'I believe it was composed by an unknown giant called Led Zeppelin.'

'Why is it considered such a sad song?' Trumpella asked, listening carefully to the lyrics. 'The singer is singing about love, and – from the sound of it – cars.'

'The lyric aren't important,' Elvis told her, 'it's the song title that counts. "Trampled Under Foot".'

'Tell me about it,' Trumpella sighed.

The contraption started moving again, so the quick-thinking Bobbington flew the chopper high up in the air.

'What's the matter, Zzzzzz?' Conkyconkytillion asked.

He looked her in the eye. 'Did you know that that giant bird was going to attack us?' he asked her.

'No,' she replied.

'Then why did you install missiles in your helicopter?' Zzzzzz asked her.

'Because we have always hated the giants with a vengeance,' Bobbington now interjected, as if she wasn't in the least bit ashamed of the fact. 'For far too long they have been squashing leprechauns asunder with their big feet, and other body parts. I am not in the least bit proud of the fact that my own father was flattened against a huge

circular plastic seat on top of an enormous porcelain structure by a giant's bare backside many, many years ago.'
'I agree with Bobbington,' Conkyconkytillion said. 'I, too, have lost too many friends and family members to the shoe and the boot. We simply cannot let them get away with it indefinitely. We have to fight back, in order to preserve civilization as we know it for countless future generations of leprechauns.' She then looked at the fat man. 'He is *still* staring at me,' she said, to everybody but the man in question. 'Let me know when it's time to jettison the excess baggage, Bobbington.'
Bobbington gave her the thumbs-up. Message received and understood.
'What you did to that giant bird,' Elvis Skitterington told the two women in charge, showing a sadistic streak that he had always kept hidden from his adoring fans, 'we could conceivably do to the giant men and women. I am not ashamed to admit that I have always hated those pesky giants. They constantly fail to acknowledge my talent, just because I don't have a big voice.'
'You *do* have a big voice,' Trumpella tried to convince the king of rock 'n' roll.
'Yes, for leprechaun ears,' Elvis said, speaking a great deal of sense. 'To giant ears my voice is just a little squeak. Not even that, the bastards can't even hear me at all. However, back to my main point,' Elvis said, staring out the window at the giants far below them. 'By the look of it, there are less than a hundred giants all told. We could get rid of them all with a mere four or five hundred of your missiles, Conkyconkytillion.'
'You don't think they might try and fight back?' Zzzzzz asked Elvis.
'Nah,' the king of rock 'n' roll said, 'they don't look the type. Look at the big galloots, they're spineless, with their silly electrified scooters, shopping-trolleys and beer-bellies. I reckon that if we remove the riff-raff from both High Street and Ann Street, and all the little surrounding areas, we can quite easily rule this whole world called Belfast, or my name is not Elvis Skitterington.'
'Unless there's a bigger world out there?' Zzzzzzz suggested.
'Stop that conspiracy theory nonsense,' Mrs Overpants told him, as if she was in charge of everything, even when they were flying high in the sky in a magnificent helicopter that wasn't of her making.

'Keep an eye out for the giant who trampled Chopper Longfellow the Thirteenth underfoot,' Trumpella told everybody.
'We don't know what he or she looks like,' Megalife said.
'I would recognise them anywhere,' Trumpella insisted, in an angry tone. 'He or she was wearing a white pair of light, bendy shoes with rubber soles. I've never seen anything like them before.'

Bobbington Mazzarazzabazzakazza guided the helicopter to the other side of the huge road, which was jam-packed with vehicles of all shapes and sizes, every last one of them heading from right to left. Megalife was confused by this anomaly. 'How do the giants ever get back to where they came from?' he asked all and sundry.
'Some of the wisest leprechauns in Belfast have been struggling to find an answer to that conundrum since time immemorial,' Conkyconkytillion replied, 'or at least since we first flew this far from High Street in our magical chopper two weeks ago last Thursday.'
In front of them was the most amazing sight that any leprechaun had ever seen – a building so utterly enormous that it made the giants look like insignificant little creatures, which, of course, was what the great Elvis Skitterington, for one, thought they were. They flew past a sign announcing the building as 'Belfast City Hall'. The architecture was like something none of the leprechauns present could put into words. It was like something out of their wildest dreams, with a big green dome on top – Megalife thought it looked like a huge scoop of mint-flavoured ice-cream. To its extreme left and right there were smaller green peaks, that Trumpella thought looked like a couple of giant green bell-ends.
'See,' Zzzzzz said, holding his arms wide as if to introduce the sight to disbelieving eyes, 'I didn't just dream it! Look at all those huge green fields surrounding the veritable palace – it's like something out of... well, I don't know what, with knobs on.'
'Well put,' Mrs Overpants congratulated Zzzzzz, as they all marvelled at the city hall's futuristic architecture. 'I've never seen shapes like that on a building before,' she added, stating the obvious. 'It's like a whole new world.'
'It's like something out of a fairy tale,' Trumpella cooed with delight, seemingly forgetting all her troubles.

Bobbington spun the steering-wheel around and flew up close to all the statues and monuments interspersed around the city hall, close enough for little leprechaun eyes to be at liberty – for the first time in history – to read the writing on them.

One statue, the shape of a huge grey can of beans, was dedicated to a certain 'President William Jefferson Clinton', who, it said, had visited Belfast in 1995. 'I don't remember him,' Trumpella said, but Megalife reminded her, 'He was a giant. And besides, you weren't even born then.' 'Thanks for pointing that out,' Trumpella said.

Bobbington had to fly all the way around one big circular monument in order to read the inscription etched around its side – 'First USAF landed in this city 26 Jan 1942'. 'And *we've* only just learned to fly,' Zzzzzzz said, as if he was trying to make the leprechauns in his midst feel small.

On top of one huge platform there was a statue of a man holding out an open book, posing like some sort of preacher – hopefully (assuming he was now dead) he hadn't been as dopey as the ones they had flown past on Donegall Place a few minutes ago.

Trumpella oohed and aahed at two huge, dark grey rectangular monuments with 'Litter' written on the front of them. 'They're my favourites so far,' she proclaimed in a deeply satisfied tone. 'It doesn't get much better than that.'

There was a man's head and shoulders on a rusty grey plinth, with a sign stating that it was erected by his wife. Then they came to a sign saying 'Titanic Memorial Garden' – and they all removed their hats as a mark of respect for the deceased.

They flew past a statue of what appeared to be a soldier, wearing a hat that looked like Trumpella's breakfast cereal bowl and carrying a rifle. 'Maybe he was the Titanic's security guard,' Megalife suggested. But Trumpella was much more interested in an enormous black, prison cell-type door at the top of four magnificent huge steps, with two identical green signs on it with white writing saying 'Fire exit, keep clear'. 'Those signs are so cool,' Trumpella said. 'Maybe not quite as good as the "litter" monuments, but they run them a close second.'

Zzzzzz reached deep down into his beard and pulled out a pen and paper and began taking notes, as if he was writing his diary. But he was such a popular, good-hearted leprechaun that nobody passed any remark on his peculiar behaviour.

They flew by a hard-stone gargoyle saying 'Titanic Memorial Statue'. Once again Zzzzzz took off his bowler-hat, and all the others followed his lead – not the fat man, but nobody complained because nobody even noticed that he was there any more. The statue was dedicated to the Belfast men who died on the ship. 'That's funny,' Conkyconkytillion said, 'there's a distinct absence of certain names.' This made Bobbington swerve the helicopter to one side, almost flipping it over, but she soon calmed down. She and Conkyconkytillion had to keep their cool for the matter in hand.

They flew over a long, long monument containing the names of every victim of the giant world's most infamous seafaring disaster – 'In memory of those who died on the 15th April 1912'. There must have been over fifteen hundred names, the fat accountant figured, naturally keeping his thoughts to himself to avoid being victimised. Elvis Skitterington started humming his 1990s chart-topper 'My Heart Will Go On' to himself. Mrs Overpants, Zzzzzzz, Trumpella and Megalife looked down at the monument with the utmost respect, maybe even shedding a tear. Not so Bobbington and Conkyconkytillion – they were absolutely enraged.

'Bastards,' Conkyconkytillion snarled, in what Trumpella didn't really consider a ladylike manner. That was no way for her scientific genius superstar hero to be talking, surely?

'What's the matter?' Trumpella asked her, making Mrs Overpants jealously kick herself, wishing she had thought of the question first.

'Yes, what's the matter?' Mrs Overpants asked.

'I don't know if it has escaped your attention,' Conkyconkytillion said in a furious tone of voice, looking straight into Mrs Overpants's eyes, 'but on that monument to all the victims of the disaster there is not a single mention of all the poor leprechauns who went down with the "Unsinkable Ship".'

'Most of the giants don't believe in leprechauns when we're alive,' Bobbington Mazzarazzabazzakazza said, backing Conkyconkytillion up. 'But what's worse – we have now discovered that they won't even acknowledge us in death. This is a tragedy of titanic proportions.'

'This is terrible,' Trumpella said, once again beating Mrs Overpants to the quick.

'And it's personal, Trumpella,' Conkyconkytillion told her. 'The giant who flattened your beloved Chopper will probably believe in

leprechauns all of a sudden, when he finds him stuck to the sole of his shoe.'
'Don't,' Trumpella said, wanting to cover her ears.
'By the time they realise that we *do* exist,' Bobbington said, 'we don't.'

The Big Fluffy White Things moved aside and the Hot Shiny Bright Light in the Sky shone directly into Bobbington Mazzarazzabazzakazza's eyes, almost blinding her. She covered her eyes with her arm, shrieking 'I can't see!'
Zzzzzz laughed hysterically. 'See,' he said, scratching his bare midriff, 'that was what happened to me.'
Mrs Overpants, for one, didn't get it. 'Zzzzzz,' she said, 'why does the fact that something once happened to you make it seem hysterically funny to you when it happens to someone else?'
'I'm not sure,' he said, scratching his bald bonce. 'I'm just a happy guy, I guess.'
'The same thing may have happened to you, Zatarak Zoxion Zalcho Zloop Z. Zizzyzump,' Bobbington said to him, desperately rubbing her eyelids, 'but you weren't piloting a helicopter at the time.'
'Oh bugger,' Zzzzzz said, suddenly realising the gravity of the situation, 'silly me.'
Conkyconkytillion put her hand on the steering-wheel (she and Bobbington hadn't yet decided what names to give the controls in a chopper) to make sure it didn't spin out of control.
Bobbington finally took her hand away from her eyes, able to see properly again. 'Conkyconkytillion, this is the final straw,' she said.
'You reckon now is the time to do it?' Conkyconkytillion asked.
'As good a time as any,' Bobbington replied. 'After all, we did warn them that the war would almost certainly start at some time today in our letter.'
'War?' Megalife asked. 'Who have you declared war on?' – Good question, thought Mrs Overpants, wishing she had thought of it first.
'Why, the giants, of course,' Conkyconkytillion said.
'You wrote a letter declaring war on them?' Trumpella asked, and Mrs Overpants pinched herself until it hurt.
'Yes,' Bobbington said. 'I was flying past the old postbox mountain one day, when I happened to notice a huge slot near the top of it. Utilising my modestly extra-large leprechaun brain, I deduced that

that was where the giants *post* their letters. Suddenly the name "Postbox Mountain" made perfect sense. So Conkyconkytillion and I wrote a letter declaring war on the giants, and we posted it in that self-same giant slot. Then we gave it a week, but the ignorant giants refused to even acknowledge our declaration.'

'Interesting,' Zzzzzz said, as if he was about to nit-pick with the two geniuses in their midst. 'And what size was your envelope?'

'What size?' Conkyconkytillion asked. 'Why, the normal size, of course.'

'And who did you address it to, pray tell?' Zzzzzz asked, like a detective on a case in one of his favourite library books.

'Address it to?' Bobbington asked, and Elvis Skitterington started singing his old chart-topper 'Return to Sender (Mailbox Too Big)'.

'So,' Mrs Overpants asked, perhaps a little more pertinently, 'when does the war begin?'

'It started when I saw that Titanic memorial,' Bobbington replied, and Conkyconkytillion reached forward and pressed the big red 'Do Not Press' button. A missile shot out the front of the craft, zooming straight towards a smug-looking, curly-haired giant wearing a jean jacket and track-suit bottoms. He was standing looking at the sign saying 'Titanic Memorial Garden', smoking a cigarette at least twice as long as any leprechaun. As luck would have it, the missile headed in the direction of his face. 'This'll teach him,' Conkyconkytillion said, emitting a previously-unheard evil laugh. No sooner had the jean-jacketed giant put the cigarette in his mouth than the missile scored a direct hit, knocking the lit end off and thereby extinguishing his cigarette. 'Glory to the Leprechauns!' Conkyconkytillion yelled in a victorious manner, as the giant looked sadly at his cigarette and searched in his jacket pocket for his lighter.

'Me next,' Bobbington Mazzarazzabazzakazza said gleefully, pressing the big red 'Do Not Press' button once she had her target in her sights. Alas, this time the missile wasn't such a magnanimous success. It soared towards a giant lady with way too much cleavage on show for Bobbington's liking, standing proudly shaking her long blonde hair from side to side while chatting to an admirer. The target lifted a paper cup up towards her mouth and was about to take a sip of whatever was in it, when the missile landed inside the cup with a fizzle. 'Oh I say,' the giant said, looking into her paper cup and then pouring her drink out onto the grass beneath her feet. 'I think an insect just landed in my coffee.'

'Viva les Leprechauns!' Bobbington shouted, in what sounded peculiarly like a made-up language. She and Conkyconkytillion then proceeded to take it in turns firing missiles at another half a dozen pontificating, posing and preening giants, with varying levels of success. One missile lodged undiscovered in the bun of a fifty-something giant's hair, another went down inside a younger woman's big brown boot, and the third burned an unseen but significant hole in the corner of one man's newspaper. The next two burst a chewing-gum bubble blown by a giant little boy and disappeared with a pop in an elderly man's ice-cream cone, and the final one went so far as to singe the eyebrows of a mad-looking old man wearing a big board saying 'The End is Nigh'. That particular giant of a man didn't know just how close he was to the truth, today, the thirteenth of May, of all the days of the year.

Despite this rip-roaring success, the attacks went virtually unnoticed by the rude giants. 'See,' Conkyconkytillion said, 'they refuse to acknowledge us, even when we're on the verge of bringing them to their knees.'

Can I have a go?'

'What?' Bobbington asked.

Trumpella leaned over her shoulder and pressed the big red 'Do Not Press' button – a missile shot out of the front of the helicopter, zig-zagged its way through the air, and scored a direct hit on one young woman's flabby backside. 'Bullseye!' Trumpella shouted, as the woman screamed blue murder and leapt into the air, rubbing her sore posterior.

'Why did you do that?' Bobbington Mazzarazzabazzakazza asked Trumpella. 'Not that there was anything wrong with it.'

'It's probably our most successful missile to date,' Conkyconkytillion admitted wholeheartedly.

'Isn't it obvious?' Trumpella asked with a satisfied smile. 'She is the evil giant who trampled my good friend Chopper Longfellow the Thirteenth underfoot. I would recognise those bendy, rubbed-soled shoes anywhere.'

Megalife's ears pricked up when Trumpella called Chopper her good friend. Maybe there was hope for him yet.

'Oh, by the way, Trump,' he said, 'look at that woman in the red dress.'
'Red dress?' Trumpella said. 'Why would I want to... oh. I see what you mean.'
'What about her?' Zzzzzz asked. 'Oh yes, I can see them now.'
'See what?' Mrs Overpants asked, straining her eyes to see what she was missing. 'Oh. She's wearing white, bouncy rubber shoes.'
'I believe the giants call them trainers,' Bobbington said. 'I'm going to invent the leprechaun version next week.'
'There's another one,' Mrs Overpants said, pointing at a young man wearing red 'trainers'.
'Oops,' Trumpella said, looking at the young giant she had shot with a missile, who now had her hand practically down her pants feeling her backside. 'Sorry.'
'She won't be able to hear you,' Megalife laughed, and Trumpella smiled good-naturedly. Bingo, Megalife thought, his hopes and dreams reinvigorated. He was feeling on top of the world, a good one hundred feet above ground level, when he was brought tumbling down again by a chugging sound. The engine coughed and spluttered, and then stopped altogether.
'The engine has cut out,' Bobbington Mazzarazzabazzakazza spluttered, pressing and tugging buttons and levers, to no avail.
'We're going to die,' the fat man wailed.
'Shut up,' Conkyconkytillion told him without a moment's thought.
'No, hold on a second – he's right.' No sooner had she finished speaking than the helicopter commenced to spiral out of control.
'OK, you all know the drill,' Bobbington said.
'Drill?' Mrs Overpants asked her. 'What drill?'
'We all have to use our passes to escape,' Bobbington explained.
'I'll have to make about twenty passes to reach the ground safely,' Mrs Overpants said. She flicked her fingers and disappeared.
'Is everybody ready?' Zzzzzz asked. Megalife and Trumpella nodded their heads sadly. Zzzzzz tugged his beard really hard and disappeared.
Trumpella looked at the fat man. 'I don't rate his chances,' she said cruelly.
Conkyconkytillion's eyes lit up. 'Ponkitonius?' she asked, looking at the fat man.

'She remembers me, at last!' Ponkitonius said, looking around the endangered chopper's interior at Bobbington, Megalife, Elvis Skitterington and Trumpella. 'She always comes around in times of crisis.'

Conkyconkytillion wrapped her arms around Ponkitonius and said her special pass words, 'Ibbedy babbedy boo!' – and with that they both instantly disappeared.

'Ponkitonius, of course,' Megalife remembered, not a minute too soon.

'I forgot that he existed,' Trumpella admitted, feeling slightly embarrassed.

'See,' Bobbington Mazzarazzabazzakazza said, letting go of the controls and climbing to her feet, 'Conkyconkytillion does love Ponkitonius, if only subconsciously.'

In so saying, she squeezed her left boob and disappeared, leaving only Elvis Skitterington, Trumpella Potteringthwaite and Megalife inside the rapidly-spiralling aircraft.

It all seemed to be happening so fast. The ground appeared to be moving towards them at one hell of a pace. Elvis Skitterington started singing his hit single 'Little People's Less Conversation, a Little More Action', but he looked disappointed. 'Shit,' he told Trumpella, 'I usually disappear when I sing that.' He tried 'Marie's the Name (of His Smallest Flame)', but it didn't do the trick either.

'I could listen to you singing all day long,' Trumpella told the king of rock 'n' roll, as he tried some more of his number-one hit singles, 'but perhaps now is not the right time.'

Megalife wanted to put his hand down his pants, but he was too much of a gentleleprechaun to do it in front of Trumpella. She was staring at him with big sad eyes. She suddenly sobbed, 'I've made love to all the wrong leprechauns.'

'It's your body,' Megalife told her diplomatically through clenched teeth, 'you can do whatever you want with it.'

Trumpella simply wouldn't stop crying, so Megalife kissed her full on the lips. She looked deep into his eyes, and then hugged him like she had never hugged anyone before. With tears streaming down both of their faces, Trumpella said, 'You are the one true love of my life, Mega, and you know it. You've always known it.'

'Yes, I have,' Megalife agreed. 'But I didn't know that you knew it.'

Trumpella smiled, drying Megalife's tears with the sleeve of her blue blazer. But then he took her by surprise – at such a time – by getting down on one knee and saying, 'Trumpella Potteringthwaite, will you marry me?'

The helicopter crashed into the large Titanic memorial that had so enraged Bobbington Mazzarazzabazzakazza, leaving a tiny little burn-mark in its top left corner. Once again, the rude giants wouldn't pay any attention to it whatsoever. Apparently no disaster in the leprechaun world was significant enough to make those huge galloots sit up and take notice.

The following morning's newspaper headlines were the saddest ever in the United Kingdom of High Street and Ann Street, in the great world that they called Belfast.

'Titanic Disaster – This Time It's Serious!' said the *Joy's Entry Express*, above a huge picture of Elvis Skitterington. Using the same picture, the *High Street Mirror* reported, 'Elvis Skitterington – Dead at 42.' Meanwhile the *Leprechaun Mail* ran with the headline, 'Belfast in Mourning, from High Street to Ann Street – "and Maybe Even Further Afield", Say Conspiracy Theorists.' Whereas, on a slightly different theme, 'Giant Star's Hamster Ate My Husband' was the banner headline on the front page of Belfast's best-selling leprechaun tabloid, the *Hot Shiny Bright Light in the Sky*.

That same morning, surely the saddest of all mornings in leprechaun history, the great explorer Ernest Scheissenhausen did his best to raise the spirits of the world by setting out on his greatest adventure to date – his attempt to conquer the relatively new rectangular postbox mountain on High Street, a good six or seven inches higher than his greatest previous success a good couple of feet away from it.

After spending the night drowning their sorrows with wine, produced from the vineyards of Pottinger's Entry, a more upmarket area between High Street and Ann Street, Bobbington Mazzarazzabazzakazza and her friends followed the heroic leprechaun explorer's brave ascent in Conkyconkytillion's latest invention, which she had decided to call a flying-saucer.

With Bobbington at the wheel as usual, Conkyconkytillion filmed Ernest Scheissenhausen's climb for their forthcoming invention, 'moving pictures'. No doubt their new 'cinema' would be packed out to watch the explorer's ascent, whether or not it was successful, before the week was out. The cinema was a totally original idea – neither Bobbington nor Conkyconkytillion had ever seen anything like it on their flights around Belfast.

'Where did you come up with the word "cinema"?' Zzzzzz asked.

'Great question,' Mrs Overpants said, wishing that she had thought of it first.

'Oh, as a matter of fact, that was my idea,' the fat stranger said, looking straight into Conkyconkytillion's eyes. Naturally enough, everybody in the flying-saucer burst out laughing. The vanity of men was bad enough, Conkyconkytillion thought, but *this* 'man'? The leprechaun mind boggled.

'And while we're on the subject,' the fat man added, looking out the window at the side of the gigantic postbox mountain, 'you could have hit the giants where it hurts outside the City Hall yesterday, if you had used my new nuclear weapons. My first atom-bomb, outside Poundland on Ann Street, actually set fire to a giant rat's tail.'

'What planet is this chubby fellow from?' Bobbington Mazzarazzabazzakazza asked, and everybody except the chubby fellow in question laughed their heads off.

'No, but seriously,' Zzzzzz said, taking off his bowler-hat and holding it sadly against his beard-covered heart. 'Let's think about those who didn't make it.'

'My poor great-nephew,' Bobbington said, with tears welling up in her eyes.

'Och, Trumpella was only twenty years of age,' Mrs Overpants said, trying to cry but she couldn't. 'She had her whole life ahead of her.'

They paused for a moment's silent reflection, with Bobbington's careful control of the steering-wheel the only discernible movement inside the flying-saucer.

Ernest Scheissenhausen's suction shoes nearly fell off at one stage, but he continued his brave walk up the side of the huge rectangular postbox mountain.

'Those sticky boots were a wonderful invention, Conkyconkytillion,' Bobbington told her, patting her on the back.

'Thanks,' Conkyconkytillion said. 'I don't know how I came up with the idea out of the blue like that.'

'They were my idea.'

All eyes turned towards the horrendous-looking stranger with his pockmarked face, scruffy long hair, briefcase and absolutely ridiculous-looking bowler-hat (although it did look exactly like Zzzzzz's excellent-looking one). They laughed so much that the flying-saucer nearly started wobbling in the sky, high up beside the postbox that would surely go down in history after this momentous event. 'Pull the other one,' Conkyconkytillion told the wide-bottomed man, 'it's got bells on.'

Ernest Scheissenhausen finally reached the summit of the mountain, which its discoverer Bobbington Mazzarazzabazzakazza had recently named P2, to rapturous applause from Mrs Overpants, Zzzzzz, Bobbington and the woman filming it all for posterity, Conkyconkytillion. Oh, and the totally obese gate-crasher to the party.

And then – stop the press! – Ernest Scheissenhausen clambered up and saw two people. He had been beaten to the summit by a couple of other leprechauns. Oh, the humiliation. He would never live this disgraceful moment down.

They were snogging frantically. The crew of the flying-saucer couldn't believe what they were seeing. Megalife and Trumpella pulled their lips apart momentarily, and spotted the great explorer – and the ragamuffin mob of leprechauns staring out the flying-saucer's windows, watching their every move. The flying-saucer landed on top of the postbox mountain, and out climbed Bobbington, Conkyconkytillion, Mrs Overpants and Zzzzzz (oh, and a chubby person).

'Oh, Mrs Overpants, I simply *love* your new red-and-blue boiler-suit,' Trumpella said. 'It's simply gorgeous.'

'The Mazzarazzabazzakazza's label calls it a "shell-suit",' Mrs Overpants said, 'a new fashion statement by Bobbington. But thanks anyway.' She put her hands behind her torso, as if she was in agony after spending ten or twenty minutes travelling in the flying-saucer. 'Och,' she said, 'my poor wee aching back.'

'Bobbington,' Trumpella said, 'I simply adore your puce shell-suit. It goes really well with your new puce witch's hat.'

'It's a boiler-suit,' Bobbington replied, not seeming at all chuffed. '*Witch's hat*? How very dare you.'

'And Conkyconkytillion,' Trumpella said to her scientific hero, as Megalife pined for her lips, wondering why she was wasting his precious time, 'that new dull-brown duffle-coat is to die for.'

'Ta,' Conkyconkytillion said.

'What about my four hundred and seventy-eighth bowler-hat?' the fat man asked Trumpella. She ignored his weird advances. He should have been ashamed of himself, daring to talk to her as if he thought he was her equal.

'Who is the fat man?' Megalife asked, as Zzzzzz reached deep into his beard and pulled out a pen and paper and started taking notes for his diary.

'Who cares,' Conkyconkytillion replied concisely, making the lard-bottomed gentleman visibly squirm.

Being as diplomatic as leprechaunly possible, Trumpella said to the great explorer, Ernest Scheissenhausen, 'Go away and come back tomorrow, Ernie. This is our special day and night.'

'I thought that was last night?' Megalife asked Trumpella.

'Shush,' she told him. 'As I will teach you in the months and years to come, Mega, you can't have too much of a good thing.'

And with that, the extremely wealthy Bobbington Mazzarazzabazzakazza, the supremely famous Conkyconkytillion *Something-Or-Other*, the lowly but proud office manager Grizelda Overpants, Zatarak Zoxion Zalcho Zloop Z. Zizzyzump and a mysterious load of blubber on legs gave Trumpella and Megalife the thumbs-up.

They climbed back into the craft that had taken them all the way up to the summit of the postbox mountain, P2. Bobbington and Conkyconkytillion were in such a good mood that they didn't even ignore the shameless hitchhiker, Ernest Scheissenhausen, who was standing looking at them with big sad eyes and his thumb up, and they kindly gave him a lift back to terra firma in their beloved turquoise flying-saucer.

TWICE TWO

SCENE ONE

"THE TWILIGHT ZONE" THEME PLAYS.
SCENE: A CARRIAGE IN AN OLD-FASHIONED TRAIN. THE DOOR OPENS AND OLIVER HARDY WALKS IN, BUMPING INTO "THE TWILIGHT ZONE" HOST, ROD SERLING.

OLLIE Oh, I do apologise, sir. I nearly knocked you down. I'll just… sit down here, by the window, if that's OK with you?
ROD SERLING Picture of a man, a larger-than-life man, who is unknowingly clinging on to the past. As you can see, he is wearing a bowler hat that was considered old-fashioned even in his long-gone but never-to-be-forgotten heyday.
OLLIE This little thing? Oh, I do apologize. I find it hard to keep up with the modern fashion. This stupid hat… it doesn't seem to fit on my head…
ROD SERLING This man knows he belongs in the past, but he also knows that he wasn't alone there. His until-now unsuccessful search for his long-lost friend is about to become a reality, in the Twilight Zone.
EERIE MUSIC PLAYS. STAN LAUREL STUMBLES INTO THE CARRIAGE.
STAN Oh, I've caught meself on the door. Oh, I've dropped me hat.
TRAIN GUARD *(SHOUTS, OUTSIDE THE CARRIAGE)* This train is now departing from Willoughby. Next stop, Pottsville.
THE GUARD BLOWS HIS WHISTLE AND THE TRAIN STARTS MOVING.
STAN Oh good, Pottsville. That's where I'm going.
OLLIE Why, that's where I'm going too.
STAN I recognise that voice… don't I know you?
OLLIE *(CONFUSED)* Where did that mysterious monologue-man disappear to? He seemed to vanish into thin air.
STAN He disappeared, just like a live ghost. Was that Rod Serling?
OLLIE Now *who* is Rod Serling?

STAN You know, Ollie, the fella who introduced that programme about weird little stories every week on the television?
OLLIE Don't call me Ollie. Besides which, I have no idea what programme you're referring to, Stanley. It must have been after my time. Are you wearing my hat?
STAN Is this yours? Oh, sorry.
STAN AND OLLIE CLUMSILY EXCHANGE BOWLER HATS A NUMBER OF TIMES UNTIL THEY EACH GET THE RIGHT ONE.
STAN *(LAUGHS)* Sometimes those scenes seemed to go on forever. It's so nice to meet you again at last, Babe.
OLLIE It seems like an eternity since anybody called me that, Stan.
STAN Gee, it's good to see you again, Babe. It seems like a thousand years since our last film.
OLLIE It certainly does. You look just like you did in the good old days.
STAN Neither do you too. Do you think people will still remember our films a thousand years from now?
OLLIE A thousand years? Why certainly, Stanley. People will still remember our movies a *hundred* years from now!
STAN Do you really think so, Babe?
OLLIE In-dubitably, Stan. Why, with the aid of modern technology, our wonderful fans are probably watching our movies in *colour* as we speak. Maybe even in 3D.
STAN What's 3D, Ollie?
OLLIE Oh, you know... like that Three Stooges movie you and I watched in a Nottingham movie theatre back in 1953. Do you remember? We had to wear special glasses to watch it. I think it was called "Spooks". It's like the audience are actually in the scene.
STAN I don't think I'd like that, Ollie.
OLLIE Now *why* would you possibly not like that?
STAN Well, you know... there we would be, doing our best to get a piano up an enormous flight of stairs like the one in "The Exorcist", and we'd have to keep on manoeuvring it around our lovely fans who were sitting on the stairs, eating sarsaparilla ice-cream and drinking sassafras sodas.
OLLIE You know, Stanley, you could be right.
STAN I *am* right, Ollie. The scene in "Busy Bodies" where we drive our 1918 Model T Ford through a huge band-saw might be slightly

dangerous – some of our beloved *Appreciation Society* members might well end up getting decapitated.

OLLIE That wouldn't be nice, Stan.

STAN You're darn tootin' it wouldn't be nice, Ollie. I find it hard to imagine that people in the twenty-first century consider chainsaw-based decapitations a form of entertainment.

OLLIE "Twenty-first century chainsaw-based decapitations"... you know, Stanley, that is the dumbest thing you have ever said, and you have said some pretty dumb things in the last hundred years.

STAN I certainly have, Ollie. Do you remember the time you and I were a couple of cops out on the midnight patrol, and I said –

OLLIE LOUDLY CLEARS HIS THROAT TO SILENCE STAN.

OLLIE Need I remind you, that was only a movie?

STAN Was it?

OLLIE Certainly, Stan. We died in the final scene, remember?

STAN You know, Ollie, I think you're right.

STAN'S WORDS BECOME HIGH-PITCHED, AS HE BEGINS TO LAUGH UNCONTROLLABLY.

STAN The chief of police shot us, didn't he?

OLLIE He certainly did.

STAN SUDDENLY STOPS LAUGHING.

STAN Of course we didn't die. I mean to say, how could we be here now, if we had died back then? I forget, sometimes. You know, Ollie, I don't remember as much about my own life as I do about our films. Isn't that silly?

OLLIE *(SIGHS)* I'm sure your four wives think it's hilarious.

STAN Oh, I don't like talking about the first three. Their money-demands left me virtually penniless in the latter years of my life, living in a cheap Santa Monica apartment with the love of my life, Ida.

OLLIE You made a good choice there, Stan... eventually.

SCENE TWO

STAN I'm sure I read someplace that the last two Stooges passed away in 1975, Larry and Moe.

OLLIE SIGHS.

STAN What's the matter, Ollie?

OLLIE Oh, nothing, I guess. It's just that, well, to tell you the truth, Stan, I never really liked their violent, face-slapping brand of humour.

STAN Me neither. It was too "in your face" for my tastes.

OLLIE We got it just right, thanks to your hard work. Just think of all the nights you stayed in the studio for hours on end, rewriting our gags until they were perfect, while I was out playing golf with Bing, Chico and W.C. Fields. Why, Stan, do you know that they are still showing our movies on TV to this day, coming on a hundred years later?

STAN That's nice, Babe. What about Charlie's films?

OLLIE No... no, not so much with Charlie's. I suppose, when it boils down to it, silence doesn't *really* speak volumes.

STAN Do you remember our first talkie, Ollie?

OLLIE "Unaccustomed As We Are"...

STAN "...to public speaking". I didn't really like the Marx Brothers' brand of humour, but I always liked Harpo. He was funny, and yet he never said a word in any of their movies. To this day, most people in the world have never once heard his voice. Now that's what I call loyalty to the cause.

OLLIE I suppose "Mr Bean" is almost a modern-day equivalent.

STAN Possibly, but he had other roles – speaking roles – like "Blackadder" and "Johnny English". Harpo was a silent clown, throughout his celluloid career.

OLLIE True. Do you remember the time, in "Oliver the Eighth", when I asked you if you had a pair of scissors, and you felt in all the pockets of your long coat and pulled out a pair? I reckon Harpo found that scene inspirational.

STAN I think it was my affectionate tribute to him. I'm pretty sure he did it first.

OLLIE You're too modest. In our later movie "Flying Deuces", when you started playing bed-springs like a harp...

STAN That was *definitely* a tribute to Harpo. Did you know that Harpo campaigned for JFK in 1960?

OLLIE *(SIGHS)* I'm glad to hear it.

STAN What's the matter, Ollie? Do you not like me talking about the 1960s?

OLLIE No, it's not that, Stan. I'm sure they were wonderful. It's just that, it's hard to believe that our contemporaries are all gone.

Now why does life have to be so fleeting? Even though movies can live forever, the lives of their stars are here today, gone tomorrow – and sometimes it seems as if they never existed at all. Who today remembers our lovely co-stars Charlie Hall, Mae Busch and Jimmy Finlayson?

STAN *(SADLY)* I was lost without you, Babe. It was like losing an arm, or a leg, only worse. Do you know, I never worked again after you left me. Jerry Lewis offered me a hundred thousand dollars to write sketches for him, but I turned it down. Although, in private, I did keep writing scripts for our films for the rest of my life.

OLLIE Now why on earth would you do that?

STAN I didn't know what else to do, Babe. Writing comic scripts was my life.

OLLIE Stanley, you never cease to amaze me. I can't believe you kept your name in the local area telephone directory right until the end of your days.

STAN I wanted our fans to know where to come if they wanted to say hello.

OLLIE That was a nice gesture.

STAN Thank you, Mister Hardy. Even your moustache looks exactly like it did in our peak years.

OLLIE At times I wonder if my moustache was part of the reason why we stopped being so popular in 1940, Stan.

STAN Oh, now why would you even think that?

OLLIE This was a quite common style in our heyday, until a nasty little Austrian killed the style stone dead.

STAN Charlie had the same problem.

OLLIE How come you never grew a moustache, Stan?

STAN Our fans would never have forgiven me. My character could never have looked rugged and lived to tell the tale. I don't think a slapstick/Clint Eastwood crossover would have worked.

OLLIE *(LAUGHS)* Do you remember the time when there was a rumour going around that Clint Eastwood was your son?

STAN I could never quite figure that one out, Ollie. He was making those brilliant spaghetti westerns at the time. The closest you and I ever got to a spaghetti western was singing "The Trail of the Lonesome Pine" in "Way Out West". Our old adversary James Finlayson was the bad guy in that, but he was nowhere near as bad as the character Lee Van Cleef played in "The Good, the Bad and the Ugly".

OLLIE Do you know that I once made a movie with John Wayne?

STAN And very good you were in it too. But to tell you the truth, Ollie, I feel a little bit guilty about that.

OLLIE Well, now why on earth would you feel guilty about me starring alongside *The Duke* in a movie? That doesn't make any sense. That was a great career move for me.

STAN Oh, I know that, Ollie. And you see, that's the problem. It was only because you and I eventually teamed up together in the Hal Roach Studios that you became strictly a comedy actor. If you had stuck to serious roles, you might have won an Oscar or two between the 1930s and '50s. I honestly believe that you could, would or should have been one of the greatest actors in history, given half a chance.

OLLIE Why thank you, Stanley. It's very nice of you to say so.

STAN Instead of just being my straight-man.

OLLIE Now I know you're being facetious, Stan. You know as well as I do that I was never just your straight-man.

STAN No, but in a way, Babe, you *were* the funniest straight-man ever. If you think about people – huge stars in our wake – like Bud Abbott, I don't believe he was ever funny the way you were. He didn't come close, as I'm sure he would agree. There wasn't any warmth in his on-screen relationship with Lou Costello, although Lou was a very funny man.

OLLIE He was indeed, but he wasn't at your level. I don't think many were.

STAN Groucho raised the bar.

OLLIE And then W.C. Fields drank it dry.

STAN Back home in Old Blighty, Morecambe and Wise were *both* funny. Although Eric Morecambe was obviously the comic genius in that double-act.

OLLIE Like spaghetti-westerns they were after my time, I'm afraid. I have seen them many times since, of course, with all the repeats on BBC. I wish we had met them when we did that big British tour in 1953. Do you remember?

STAN Yes, Ollie. We got to meet Norman Wisdom, he was a man after my own heart. And Arthur Askey.

OLLIE Oh, I love his movie "The Ghost Train". Did you know that it was written by *Private Godfrey* out of "Dad's Army"? Unfortunately it looks a bit dated now.
STAN *Everything* looks a bit dated now.
OLLIE Good point.
STAN I also met Peter Sellers.
OLLIE Out of those wonderful "Pink Panther" movies?
STAN That's the one, Ollie. He came to visit me in L.A. after you died.
OLLIE Please don't say that word, Stanley. It's so... final.
STAN Sorry, Babe. You know, I don't think a day went by when I didn't see one of our films on television in my last seven-and-a-half years. Every time I saw you on the screen it was like you were alive again, and half the tears I cried were tears of laughter.
OLLIE *(LAUGHS)* It's just as well you didn't bawl your eyes out like a big baby in real life, the way you did in our movies. I hope you didn't cry like that at my funeral, with that squeaky voice you used to do when you were wailing?
STAN LAUGHS.
OLLIE It's OK, Stan, I know you couldn't attend my funeral, because your own mother's funeral had been such a traumatic occasion for you. Don't worry, my wife Lucille and I both fully understood your absence.
STAN It's kind of you to say that, Babe. Thank you.

SCENE THREE

OLLIE Oh, Stan, did you know that Hanna-Barbera made over a hundred and fifty *Laurel and Hardy* cartoons?
STAN I thought they were very good. They first went to air about a year after I left that mortal coil.
OLLIE A year after *what*?
STAN After I died.
OLLIE Now Stan, I asked you not to say that word.
STAN But we were just talking about your funeral! Anyway, I was talking about me, Babe. I can talk about my own death if I want to, it's no big deal.
OLLIE That's all very well, Stanley, but it was a big deal to me. I didn't like it when you passed away.

STAN You weren't even there.

OLLIE I was always there, in spirit. Now you didn't really think I would leave you in your hour of need, did you? After all, you were there for me right to the end of my days, and you know me, I always return a favour. I like to repay my debts in full.

STAN *(CLOSE TO TEARS)* Thank you, Babe. You don't know how much that means to me.

OLLIE Oh, now don't go getting all maudlin, Stan. Always remember the joy you and I brought to the world – to generations of people we would never get to meet in person.

STAN That's a lovely thought, Babe.

OLLIE Why certainly it is. Do you know that double-acts like ours went out of fashion in later years? I think the likes of Peter Cook and Dudley Moore were just vulgar.

STAN I liked Dud in "Ten", and in "Arthur".

OLLIE That's as well may be.

STAN I've always been a big fan of Ant and Dec.

OLLIE Me too, Stanley, although with the best will in the world, they are hardly up there with the likes of Tony Hancock and Sid James in the comedy stakes. Although I believe "the lad himself" hated it when people considered him and Sid a double-act. Tony was a very unhappy man.

STAN He was probably jealous that Sid got to star in all those great British "Carry On" films, Ollie. But they were too smutty for my liking. I always preferred good clean fun. I still do. I hate slasher-movies, and everybody using the "F" word on television. Not "feck", the *bad* "F" word, to quote "Father Ted". Even pop songs have people effing and blinding in them nowadays. What was wrong with good, clean songs like "The Trail of the Lonesome Pine"?

OLLIE You're preaching to the converted there, Stan. We had a number-two hit with that song in England in 1975. We were only kept off the top of the chart by "Bohemian Rhapsody".

STAN Oh, Ollie, I loved that video!

STAN *(SINGS)* "Scaramouche, scaramouche, will you do the fandango?"

STAN I think we did quite well to be number-two behind that record.

OLLIE Yes indeed, but our song wasn't really suitable for the 1970s. It didn't quite fit in with Abba, the Bay City Rollers and Showaddywaddy.

STAN Oh, I don't know about that, Ollie. Weren't Showaddywaddy a rock 'n' roll revival band?

OLLIE Yes, Stan, but the old music they were reviving was way, way after our time.

STAN Good point.

OLLIE MAKES AN ANNOYED "HRMPH" SOUND.

STAN What's the matter, Ollie?

OLLIE How come the Beatles had you on the cover of their "Sergeant Pepper" album, but not me? The picture everybody assumes is me looks more like Fatty Arbuckle.

STAN Oh, I don't know, Ollie. Maybe it's because I was born in England?

OLLIE That's racist.

STAN I don't think racism was such a big deal in England in 1967.

OLLIE LAUGHS.

STAN What's so funny, Babe?

OLLIE The fact that you're using the past tense, when you're talking about something that happened two years after you died.

STAN Don't say that word.

OLLIE Touché. That's another nice mess you've gotten me into.

SCENE FOUR

STAN You know, Ollie, I used to love it when you did a slow-burning look straight into the camera. If an actor in any subsequent era did that, they'd have been fired on the spot. Oh, do you remember the graveyard scene in our silent film, "Do Detectives Think?"? I still think it was both funny and spooky at the same time.

OLLIE It certainly was. It was like one of the modern comedy-horror movies. We were a hundred years ahead of our time.

STAN Except we didn't go around lopping people's heads off.

OLLIE Oh, I don't know about that, Stan. If you remember, there was a throat-slasher in that movie. And at one point you were running around, looking like you'd had your head chopped off.

STAN Oh, I forgot about that. In "Habeas Corpus" we were grave-robbers.

OLLIE *(MOROSELY)* I see Charlie's body was stolen after he died.
STAN Thank God we were both cremated.
OLLIE Don't be so ghoulish, Stanley.
STAN Sorry, Ollie.
OLLIE People should have more respect for the artistes of the world. I felt really sad when John Lennon was murdered in 1980.
STAN Me too. That was the first time it really hit me that maybe I shouldn't have lived such a public life in Santa Monica in my later years, allowing our fans to telephone me, and visit me and Ida in our home.
OLLIE *(LAUGHS)* Oh, now *who* would want to shoot Stan Laurel?
STAN Who would want to shoot John Lennon?
OLLIE Good point. Even though he didn't put my picture on the cover of "Sergeant Pepper".
STAN You could probably understand, if it had been one of the Rolling Stones.
OLLIE What, if one of them had been shot instead, or if one of them had shot John Lennon?
STAN Either.
PAUSE.
OLLIE On the contrary, Stan, Fame may well have saved you from an early death.
STAN How do you figure that, Babe?
OLLIE What year were you born – 1890, wasn't it?
STAN Yes, and I went to America around about 1910.
OLLIE When you were twenty. Imagine if you hadn't been a comedy superstar in the making, and as a result, you had stayed in England.
STAN *(SADLY)* I would probably have ended up on the battlefields of Europe, along with millions of other people my age. What a senseless waste of life.
OLLIE It certainly was. It makes you wonder how many people just like us, or better than us, never got to live their dreams, their young lives cruelly snuffed out.
STAN It's a miracle that we had any audience left.

SCENE FIVE

OLLIE I always loved "The Dick Van Dyke Show" and "Some Mothers Do 'Ave 'Em". I think some of the slapstick humour in those TV show was clearly inspired by our movies.
STAN I always liked good clean, old-fashioned fun. I loved the homespun family entertainment of "The Waltons".
OLLIE Me too. Do you remember Grandma Walton, played by Ellen Corby? She actually appeared in our movie "Sons of the Desert" about forty years earlier.
STAN Yes, I remember. At the time she was married to our cinematographer, Francis Corby. To paraphrase your wife in "Sons of the Desert", "You're *not* going to the Convention, you're going to Waltons Mountain with me!" Oh – what was that song you sung?
OLLIE *(SINGS)* "Honolulu Baby, where'd you get those eyes…?"
STAN That was the B-side of our hit record in 1975. Do you remember?
OLLIE I think I preferred Queen's B-side, "I'm in Love With My Car".
STAN I bet they weren't singing about a 1918 Ford like the one we used to drive, Ollie.
OLLIE No, automobiles have changed beyond all recognition over the years. What do you call that one in "Back to the Future" again?
STAN It was a DeLorean, Ollie.
OLLIE That's the one. I wouldn't mind driving one of those jalopies.
STAN I don't think they would have let us drive it through that large band-saw in the saw mill in "Busy Bodies".
OLLIE No, probably not.
STAN Do you remember in "Sons of the Desert", when our wives thought we were on-board the Honolulu liner that had sunk? As we were hiding above them in the loft, your wife said "I feel as if they were hovering right above me". That scene touched on the supernatural.
OLLIE I was always a huge fan of the supernatural, Stanley. It was one of the regrets of my life that I never got to sit back in my comfortable old easy chair and watch "The Twilight Zone" on television, on account of my being just a little bit deceased at the

time. I have always loved stories about time-travel, aliens, and ghosts.
STAN Oh? Do you believe in ghosts, Babe?
OLLIE Well, I most positively believe that life is not the be-all and the end-all of existence. There is most definitely an afterlife, whatever form it takes. Do you remember the final scene in "The Flying Deuces", where our airplane crashed and I came back as a horse?
STAN A horse with your moustache, and wearing your hat. As I said in that film, "I'd like to come back as myself – I always got along swell with me".
OLLIE I didn't like the finale of our much later movie "The Bullfighters", where you and I were skinned alive. That was way too Wes Craven- or James Wan-like for my liking.
STAN We should have called it a day after "Saps at Sea" in 1940. Our subsequent films were so sub-standard, by our standards, that they made Abbott and Costello look like comedy geniuses in comparison.
OLLIE Do you remember their most famous radio sketch, "Who's on first?" I love those guys, but… well, even our worst critics have to admit that, apart from "Abbott and Costello Meet Frankenstein", which I loved, they were the Rolling Stones to our Beatles.
STAN I always preferred the Stones, even though they didn't put me on the cover of "Their Satanic Majesties' Request". It's funny, but Bud and Lou didn't stand the test of time. I think our best stuff was timeless.
OLLIE *(PARAPHRASING ABBOTT AND COSTELLO)* "Who's on first? Stan and Ollie's on first. Bud and Lou's on third or fourth at best – after Groucho, Chico and Harpo, and maybe Larry, Curly and Moe." To every thing there is a season – Ecclesiastes.
STAN Oh, I was thinking The Byrds.

SCENE SIX

STAN You know, Babe, I never considered us to be competing with anyone. I only ever wanted to make people laugh, and keep them laughing. If they did, I'm happy, although don't ask me to explain *how* to make someone laugh, as I have no idea.

OLLIE *(LAUGHS)* Oh, I think you have a fairly good idea, Stanley. Better than most.
STAN *(QUOTING FROM A LAUREL AND HARDY FILM)* "Thank you, Ma'am".
OLLIE *(DOING LIKEWISE)* "It's a good thing you haven't any sense".
STAN "It certainly is".
OLLIE "At last you're using *my* brains".
STAN Ollie, do you remember near the end of "Be Big", where my wife screeched "Stan-leeeee!" She sounded just like Hilda Ogden shouting to her husband in "Coronation Street".
THE TRAIN PULLS INTO A STATION.
TRAIN GUARD *(SHOUTS)* Pottsville! Next stop, Pottsville!
OLLIE *(SIGHS)* Oh, this is my stop.
STAN *Our* stop.
THEY STAND UP TO DISEMBARK.
STAN Oh look, there's that fella again. It *is* him, isn't it?
OLLIE LOOKS AROUND.
OLLIE I think so. Although as I've said before, his absolutely wonderful TV show was after my time.
ROD SERLING Picture of two men, two heroes to millions of people throughout ensuing generations.
STAN That's nice.
ROD SERLING Did I say earlier that these two men are desperately clinging on to the past? Wrong, Rod! They brought joy into countless lives in their heyday – which, in a great many people's eyes, has not ended yet, and maybe never will. Hats off to Mister Laurel and Mister Hardy... in the Twilight Zone!
'THE TWILIGHT ZONE' END-THEME PLAYS LOWLY IN THE BACKGROUND.
OLLIE What a nice man. I tip my hat to him.
STAN So do I, neither.
WOMAN'S VOICE *(SCREECHES)* Stan-leeeee!
OLLIE *(LAUGHS)* Hilda Ogden wants you, Stan.
STAN STARTS DOING HIS MOCK-BABY CRY.
STAN *(STILL CRYING BETWEEN THE WORDS)* This is another nice mess I've gotten myself into!
THE THEME TUNE ENDS.
CURTAIN.

OVERHEARD PHONE CALL

'Don't be daft, of course you're not dead. If you were dead, do you think I wouldn't have told you?

'Look, Dad, if you think you found two coins under your eyelids when you woke up, you must have been dreaming. Do you honestly think I would have wasted fifty-pence pieces like that? They would have made your eyes look like they had – how many little sides does a 50p have? No, I've never counted them, either.

'What? You found a *what*, stuck up your *what*? I was *wondering* who pulled it out, making our bottle of wine go flat last night.

'You have to stop doing silly things like that when you're sleepwalking. You'll be the death of me one of these days, Dad.

'The black suit that was hanging in the wardrobe in the spare bedroom? What was wrong with your pyjamas? You know I bought that suit for... for future reference. I might not feel like going to Primark when your time finally comes.

'Now Dad, stop all that depressing talk. You know I don't like contemplating the inevitable before you – what's the term I'm looking for?

'No, I wasn't going to say before you kick the bucket. Have some decorum, Dad.

'Decorum? I don't know what it means either, but Mum always used to tell you to have some of it.

'Red satin? No, Dad, of course your bed doesn't have red satin sheets on it.

'No, it doesn't have four sides on it like a baby's cot. Have you taken your pills this morning?

'No, not *those* pills – I mean the turquoise one, and the hectagonal puce one.

'Puce? It's a colour, Dad. The colour your face turns when you forget to take your puce tablet.

'No, I didn't tell you to go and look at yourself in the mirror.

'Yes, I know all your best friends have popped their clogs, but that doesn't mean you'll be next. Why would that be guaranteed?

'Yes, Dad, your bowling-buddy's toes have turned up, blah-blah-blah. But you have *months* left in you, you daft old man.

'Why don't you go and watch *Countdown*, you like that?

'Dad, you can't stop watching TV in the afternoon just because they keep showing those funeral and cremation ads. That's a very defeatist attitude.

'Yes, I *know* it comes to us all in the end. Have you eaten your bran flakes?

'Yes, I *know* they make you poo. They do exactly what it says on the box.

'Somebody at the door? Why do you automatically assume that it must be the undertaker? It might just be the milkman, coming to complain about you leaving pee-stains in his empties.

'Sorry, Dad, that was inappropriate.

'Yes, I know Mum ran away with the milkman. But in her defence, you were in good health in those days. You only have yourself to blame.

'No, I'm not blaming you, Dad.

'No, don't worry, I won't stop. I'll try to score you some drugs outside the school gates. Mrs Shell usually lets us out of Home Economics a few minutes early on Fridays, in case there are cops around and *Mister* Shell has to do a runner.

'Yes, Dad, I'll do my best. Look, I have to go now, my lunch-hour is nearly over, FFS.

'What does that mean? Dad, I can't say that out loud in front of your impressionable ears – you're only thirty-three, FFS.

'Yes, that one means the same thing.

'No, I can't tell you that one, either. Look, I've got to go – I've just spotted that old bag Mrs Shell eavesdropping on me. She'll probably give me detention, unless I *accidentally-on-purpose* show her this big wad of your universal credit. She'll know where it's going to end up. Anyway, catch you later, Dad. I love you.

'Yes, I *know* you can't say it.

'Yes, I *know* you blame your parents.

'Yes, I *know* they didn't hug you, and I'm sorry. Now hang up.

'No, *you* hang up.

'No, *you* hang up.'

ONLY SIX MONTHS UNTIL CHRISTMAS

Tarquin and Nelly Kelly woke up with splitting headaches, and decided not to drink again until at least the festive season.
Tarquin put his glasses on and looked at the date on the *Clifftown Chronicle*, and he could hardly believe his eyes: there were only six months until Christmas. He found it hard to believe that twelve whole months had passed by since this time last year.
The shops in the centre of Clifftown didn't have any Christmas decorations, or even a single Christmas tree. Undeterred, Tarquin fetched the previous year's decorations down from the attic. Nelly put the Christmas tree up while Tarquin taped the bunting to the ceiling. They drowned their glee with a few Christmas drinks, and the following morning they put up the 'Merry Christmas' lights on the front of their house. Their neighbours would be dead jealous.
'All those copycats will have their lights up before the week's out,' Nelly predicted with a sigh.
'Today's the twenty-sixth of June,' Tarquin said. 'Six months from today it will all be over, and we'll be taking the decorations down again.'
'You always have to look on the gloomy side,' Nelly chastised Tarquin as the postman marched past their gate.
'No Christmas cards yet?' the failed 1970s pop star Mrs. Robinson shouted as she rode her pet emu around the next-door garden. She was grinning, so she had obviously received her first card already.
Thinking about the snowman he would soon be creating, Tarquin sharpened his spade in the crack of his neighbour's purple-feathered emu Guinevere's behind. Last year Tarquin had stood in the garden for three weeks waiting for the snow to fall, but by mid-July he had given it up as a bad bet. Come the winter, he had purchased a few extra freezers and filled them with snow. Now there were more snow-filled freezers in the Kellys' kitchen than there were spade scuff-marks in their next-door emu's underpants.
It's just as well that eating lots and lots of snow doesn't make one go a bit daft, or Tarquin and Nelly would have been up snow-creek without a shovel until long after Santa came to perform magic tricks

with the Christmas stockings hanging on their bedposts. Every year Tarquin and Nelly hung up their holy socks and stockings, and Santa climbed down their chimney with his magic needle and thread to generously stitch up all the holes in them. This year Tarquin had clean forgotten to cut his toenails, so he would be hanging out twice as many pairs of socks as usual. But then, that's what Christmas is all about. Maybe he could get Santa to sew his underpants as well.

It's great to sit down in front of a roasting hot fire with your winter woollies on, while outside the snow threatens to come and obliterate the blazing summer sunshine. Tarquin made sure that they would have a crackling fire that evening, by tearing up some spare planks of wood he had spotted in the attic. They were determined to have a lovely big turkey for Christmas dinner that year, even if it meant them having to kill it first.

'You can cook a turkey in ten minutes and it won't do you any harm,' Tarquin told Nelly.

Being vegetarians they would only eat the giblets – unless it was a female turkey and it didn't have any. Nelly would use the rest of the bird to make a nice big pot of vegetarian stew for their Christmas supper, and no doubt the two of them would fight over the eyes.

Nelly looked out the bedroom window and sighed. 'It hasn't started snowing yet.'

'Don't worry, dear, there's still six months to go.'

Tarquin wished he could make it snow for Nelly. If anybody deserved snow it was her. Sadly, it seemed as if the heatwave was never going to end.

Tarquin and Nelly were woken in the morning by a gigantic explosion. 'Stop making so much noise,' Nelly said, half asleep, 'my husband will hear you.'

'It snowed last night,' Tarquin screamed with delight. Nelly leapt out of bed and stared joyfully out the window. She kissed her husband like she had never kissed him before. Then she kissed him on the lips.

'Thank you, Tarquin.'

'Oh, it was nothing,' he said, feigning humility.

They put their wellies on and went out to make a snowman with the warm, foamy snow. Nelly gave him a pair of eyes. She couldn't believe her luck, finding those two coloured pickled-onions on the footpath. The ears were a sheer fluke. Pontius the Snowman was the best-looking snowman Clifftown had ever seen on a warm June morning.

Nelly heard on the news that two tankers full of compressed shaving-foam had crashed around the corner. Tarquin and Nelly had a snowball fight. Mrs. Robinson thought they were daft, they could tell by the look she gave them over the fence as she trotted up and down through the snow on Guinevere's back. She was keeping a tight grip on the emu's underpants because they kept falling down.

The postman had a whole sack full of mail for Tarquin and Nelly. Mrs. Robinson climbed morosely off Guinevere's back and trailed him into the house. One-nil to the Kellys. They had received seventy-one letters, and one of them even had a stamp on it. There were cards from both of Tarquin's parents, and all four of Nelly's (she was adopted by a barbershop-quartet when she was only nineteen), and from dozens of aunties and uncles who weren't related to either of them. Tarquin loved his aunties and uncles dearly, but not one of the stingy, impecunious old gits had sent him any money.

He and Nelly wouldn't need last year's snow, now that this year's snow was falling, so they removed it from the seventeen freezers in their kitchen and used it to build another snowman in their bedroom. Pontius II was the best snowman they had ever built in their bedroom.

Nelly was talking in her sleep that night. She raved about them having to get a bigger bird than Mrs. Robinson for their Christmas dinner. Tarquin didn't think that would be too hard, as Mrs. Robinson wasn't much more than four feet tall. Nelly wondered if an emu would fit in their oven.

The next morning, Mrs. Robinson's husband Sid was standing in his garden pretending to shave, with snow covering his lower face. Mrs. Robinson was shaving her legs. Tarquin fetched his razor and pretended to shave Pontius the Snowman. Nelly came out and shaved her legs, and then she shaved Tarquin's. After a while rain washed the snow away (snowman and all), and the drains were bunged up with chin and leg stubble.

Tarquin called his boss at the *Dehydrated Water Board*.

'I'm taking my Christmas holidays now,' he told him. 'I'll be back at work in the New Year.'

'Oh, that's OK,' his boss told him, 'just come back when you return to Planet Earth.'

When Tarquin told Nelly what his boss had said, she reckoned that his boss must have booked him a rocket-flight up to space as his Christmas present.

Mrs. Robinson phoned the police and complained about the snowman in the Kellys' bedroom spying on her as she sat naked in her garden trimming her emu's feathers. The police arrested Pontius II, carting him off to the Clifftown police station in a refrigerated black maria. Nelly sobbed that her only son had been taken before his time.

With all the kerfuffle about Christmas coming, Tarquin suddenly realised that he hadn't smoked for the last four days – it had totally slipped his mind that he was a hardened chain-smoker. When he mentioned this to Nelly she called him a 'silly', which he thought was below the belt. To teach her a lesson, Tarquin decided he would never smoke again. She would be stuck with an extra fifty pounds a week she wouldn't know what to do with – that would harden her.

Tuesday was cancelled when it was brought to the attention of the authorities that they had completely missed out last Wednesday, after Tarquin and Nelly got blitzed on Saudi Arabian lager and spent the whole day in bed. So the thirtieth of June this year fell on a Wednesday, although Tarquin couldn't see any point in the change, as it didn't bring them any nearer to Christmas.

A beautiful big turkey had escaped from a nearby farm. Like two modern-day Good Samaritans, Tarquin caught it and Nelly stuffed it. Where she found all that sawdust, Tarquin had no idea. 'Don't forget the giblets,' he said.

Not wanting to admit that she didn't know where one's giblets are, Nelly visited Doctor Curtains and told her that she had a terribly sore pair of giblets, to see which crevice the doctor would poke her stethoscope up. The doctor scoured her manuals before confessing that she was none the wiser. Nelly phoned her later that evening, only to be told that she had gone back to medical school for a seven-year refresher course.

Tarquin and Nelly were summonsed to appear in court on the first of July, as character witnesses for Pontius II the Snowman. They took the turkey to court for their snowman's breakfast, but Judge Curtains (no relation) said there was no eating in court and confiscated it, putting on his napkin and taking out his knife and fork.

Pontius II was visibly failing, Tarquin and Nelly noticed as the ushers pulled him up to the dock on the courthouse sledge. The cruel judge had removed his eyeballs (the snowman's, not his own), and had them sitting in a glass jar on his desk. Tarquin told Judge Curtains he was a sadist, but the judge told Tarquin to stop showing contempt for the court or he'd smash his face in.

Tarquin and Nelly bought a couple of choc-ices from the court usher, because he had no popcorn. Judge Curtains had prohibited eating, but he hadn't mentioned sucking – which showed that the law truly is an ass. The bald, fat, cock-eyed judge (who, incidentally, stank of pilchards and a small portion of mushy peas) complained that he had a dicky tum. 'How long did you cook that turkey for?' he asked.

'The snowman didn't cook it,' Nelly told him, 'it was me.'

'I was talking to you,' Judge Curtains said, with one eye still on the snowperson.

'I don't remember exactly how long it was in the pot,' Nelly replied. 'Nine, ten, maybe even eleven...'

'Oh, that's fine,' the judge responded, burping up a big mouthful of sawdust.

'It was nine minutes,' Tarquin whispered to Nelly.

'What the deuce are you writing?' the judge raged. The stenographer was writing away furiously although the case hadn't even started yet, bar the snacks. It turned out that he was writing his life story. Judge Curtains ordered him to write out five hundred times 'I must not write my autobiography in court.' When he had finished, the case commenced.

'All stand.'

The judge left the court, and then came back in buttoning up his flies. 'Ah, that's better!'

Nelly was depressed. She had just realised that six months from now it would be New Year's Day, and the Christmas festivities would be over for another six months. To drown her sorrows, she decided to change the snowman's name to Dishmop.

'That's a girl's name,' the judge grumbled when informed of Nelly's decision. 'All the court records say *The Crown versus Pontius II the Snowman*.' But Nelly was adamant, and so the dirty deed was done.

Judge Curtains traced a big puddle on the floor up to Dishmop the Snow-woman. 'Get to the toilet, you dirty barmpot,' he raged.
'Hold on just one minute,' he abruptly realised. 'Why would one member of the so-called *female* species peep at another sitting naked in her garden trimming her pet emu's feathers?'
– Judge Curtains dismissed the case, just as another court usher arrived from the optician's with his spectacles. He put them on and fell back in amazement when he spotted the lump of melting snow in the dock. 'I thought Snow-woman was only her surname?'
Judge Curtains held his stomach and demanded that the court usher bring him a bucket. It must have been something he had eaten. Tarquin and Nelly took Dishmop home in a different bucket, but she was beyond salvation.
Mrs. Robinson was lying naked in her garden, soaking up the rain. She kept staring up at the Kellys' bedroom window. God help any snowman who looked out at her, Tarquin thought. She had a huge Christmas tree in her front garden – the copycat.
'Eeh, Mrs. Robinson,' the postman shouted, 'Christmas is coming earlier every year. Are you not cold, love?'
'I'm just making sure nobody's watching me,' Mrs. Robinson explained. She was still staring up at the Kellys' window, as Tarquin noted with consternation when it showed her on the *Ten O'Clock News* that night. Nelly said she should be ashamed of herself, going on television with no clothes on like that and not letting the world see her big purple emu.
It was playing Bing Crosby's *White Christmas* on the radio. Everybody was getting into the swing of things at last.
Tarquin's boss had paid his Christmas pay into the *Trust Us!* Bank, but he had mistakenly written 'severance pay' on the paying-in slip. Tarquin decided he would sort that minor detail out in six short months. His new assistant, Sid Robinson, was almost as good a dehydrated water salesman as he was himself.
They took Mrs. Robinson away that morning. A crowd of her die-hard fans from the 1970s stood clapping three times between each word whilst singing 'Missus! Missus!' – She blew them kisses from the big yellow van filled with naked ex-pop stars. 'Good riddance to bad rubbish!' that's what her husband said as he clung to the back door and was dragged half way down Grim Street. Sid spent the remainder of the day playing *Mrs. Robinson's Greatest Hits* on

loudspeakers in his back garden (he was too shy to play it in the front garden, after his wife's antics). Tarquin was humming *Sid Left the Toilet-Seat Up Again* all evening.

There were no festive programmes on telly that night. Tarquin and Nelly listened to their *Greatest Christmas Songs* album for a while, but Nelly had to turn it off when it reached Mrs. Robinson's 1975 number ninety-three smash hit *Santa Claus Is Coming To Town, Sid.*

Tarquin and Nelly wrote and invited their parents to come and stay with them that Christmas. Hopefully the six of them would chicken out, otherwise Tarquin and Nelly would have to feign illness or death (again).

The postman delivered some more Christmas cards to the Kelly household, along with a leaflet pointing out that there were only another one hundred and seventy-four shopping days left until Christmas.

The Christmas spirit in the town centre was almost non-existent. There were no department store Santas and they were only just beginning to erect the fifty-foot Christmas tree outside the Town Hall. And yet meanwhile, across the Atlantic, Americans were celebrating the fourth of July as if it was the first day of Christmas.

Nelly tried to cash in her Christmas-club vouchers in the Clifftown shopping centre, but the old bat at the counter refused to believe that she was doing her Christmas shopping in July.

'Are you trying to tell us that we can't do our Christmas shopping until you say so?' Tarquin asked the old bag. 'Who do you think you are?'

She told Tarquin that she was his mother, and it was high time he stopped wishing his life away. 'Me and your *on-his-last-legs* dad won't be doing our Christmas shopping until the first week in August, like normal people.'

'It's my money,' Tarquin protested. 'You can't tell me what to do, Mummy.'

'Don't speak to your mother like that,' Nelly nagged him. 'Give us the money, you old trollop!'

'Don't let our Tarquin buy too many sweets,' his mother said while cashing in Nelly's Christmas-club chips, 'he's going to ruin his teeth.'

Tarquin bought Nelly a two-gallon home-made-custard starter-pack. It was hard to believe that a woman could reach the age of thirty-five without mastering the essential art of custard-making. Tarquin's mother had always warned him not to marry any woman who couldn't supply him with a big, steaming-hot plate of custard after a hard day's work. As he lay in bed that night he could still picture his grandad lying on his deathbed, tucking into the countless plates of custard his granny had lined up around the bed. Custard is an integral part of any marriage.

It was *Mrs. Robinson Day* on *Clifftown FM*. They played every one of her ninety-seven almost-hit singles, from *Sid's Eating His Breakfast* to *Come To Bed, Sid*. They even played *Voulez-Vous Coucher Avec Moi Ce Soir, Sid?* a record-breaking seven times in succession.

'This is the heaviest July snowfall since records began,' the newsreader said. Children were pulling their sledges up and down Grim Street, and Judge Curtains was rolling around in the snow with his pet dog Prancer, a king charles cavalier. Sid Robinson had built a huge snow-headstone in his front garden, with a carrot for a nose and *RIP Mrs.* and *Robinson* for its eyes. The gadabout was riding Guinevere in circles around the icy gravestone. He had dyed the emu's feathers red and white, and hung tinsel around its ears.

Judge Curtains was having a blazing argument with his dog. 'It's not Christmas for over five months yet,' he shouted. 'Eating turkey in July is unheard of in civilized society.'

Sid Robinson told the judge to stop shouting, or he wouldn't be able to hear his wife scratching her lovely pine box's lid through all the snow.

'I think Sid had done the dirty on Mrs. Robinson,' Nelly said. 'If I hear any scratching I'm going to call the police within seventy-two hours, and not a minute longer.'

Nelly was making jelly, little knowing that this Christmas she would be able to make custard to go with it. Tarquin could sit watching the telly non-stop while Nelly supplied him with a constant stream of jelly and custard. They listened to jazz on the radio for a while. Tarquin watched the telly while Nelly made the jelly. He scratched his belly, listening to George Melly. The kids on the street started yelling excitedly.

'Why is there such a brouhaha outside?' Nelly shouted in from the kitchen.

'I dunno,' Tarquin said, dashing across the room to look out the window. '*Holy underpants!*'
They rushed outside and stared up in astonishment at the reindeers pulling Santa's sleigh across the Clifftown skyline. It was as if all their Christmases had come at once...
'You were tossing and turning a lot last night,' Nelly told Tarquin, fluffing up her pillow. He checked his watch – it was still only the fifth of July. Sadly, they had to wait almost six months until Christmas.
Nelly wanted to go to Sunday Mass, but Tarquin said he hadn't been for so long that he couldn't remember all the right moves, all the subtle little ducks and dives in between prayers.
'They must have let Mrs. Robinson out of the funny farm,' Tarquin said sadly when he spotted the failed megastar next-door pruning her roses.
'All dressed up to the nines, I see,' said the 1970s icon.
'Yes indeed, Mrs. Robinson,' Nelly shouted back at her. 'And you're dressed yourself, I see.'
The summer sun was blazing out of the sky, and only a few houses had their Christmas trees up. Sid Robinson was prancing along Grim Street with a gigantic set of rosary-beads in his hands. He was jangling them around, trailing them along the footpath, and occasionally swinging them up in the air. 'Look at me,' he kept shouting, 'I'm dead holy.'
'Why can't you be as holy as him?' Nelly nagged Tarquin, as Sid thrashed his beads against the garden fences. They could almost smell the halo above his head.
Father Christmas said Mass. Sitting in the front row, Judge Curtains let out a huge rift and apologised to the priest, explaining that he had a dicky tummy. 'I'll dicky your tummy where you feel it,' Father Christmas ticked the judge off, showing him who was the boss in this jurisdiction.
'See me?' Sid Robinson shouted out, 'I'm dead holy, me.'
The choir sang hymn number 124, *Rudolf The Red-Nosed Reindeer*. Sid sang his wife's number ninety-seven hit-single version, ending every line with his own name.
After Sunday Mass, Tarquin and Nelly went to the Grinch's Left Eyeball for a few festive drinks. The barman thought Tarquin was slightly touched when he wished him a merry Christmas, adding, 'I

won't say Happy New Year, since there's nearly six months to go yet.'

Father Christmas popped into the pub for a celebratory half-pint of red wine, after what he bragged was 'Yet another result for God's boot-room boys.'

Sid Robinson commiserated with Tarquin on the untimely melting of Dishmop the Snow-woman. 'She was my best friend,' Tarquin sobbed into his beer. 'Why do only the good melt young?'

Sid started to cry. 'My bit on the side has moved out of town,' he blubbered. (Tarquin thought Nelly had thrown the first punch, although it may have been Mrs. Robinson.) 'Hermana, she's called. She has a bushy head of bright red hair, and she took it with her when she left.'

The police didn't pay any attention to Tarquin and Sid as they drowned their sorrows.

'Your snow-woman dies, and my extra-marital babe shoots the bolt,' Sid finally said at the forty-third attempt. 'Life is not worth living.'

'Bloody ambulance men,' Tarquin muttered. 'They can't even close the door on their way out.'

The TV newsreader was yapping about 'a madlady on the run from the Old Bill' after knocking another lady unconscious in a bar during an argument over who would have the biggest turkey that Christmas. Mrs. Robinson suddenly rushed back into the Grinch's Left Eyeball with a sledgehammer, which she used to impolitely thrash Tarquin about the head and ears, screaming, 'I'm going to have the biggest turkey! I'm going to have the biggest…'

Tarquin and Nelly were strolling hand-in-hand towards the Pearly Gates. They spotted a group of people in the distance, gesticulating towards them. Tarquin recognised the faces of the people he had always held dearest to his heart: Laurel and Hardy, the Marx Brothers, George Formby, Tony Hancock, Marilyn Monroe and Lynyrd Skynyrd. They were all there, furiously sticking two fingers up at Tarquin and Nelly and shouting, 'Get the Hell out of here! We don't want your sort around here, cluttering the place up!'

The light started to fade. Tarquin didn't even get a chance to ask Stan Laurel for his autograph, or to cop a feel of Monroe.

Tarquin woke up in a hospital bed, with Nelly in the bed next to his. 'Only three months until Christmas,' she groaned.

Tarquin shouted for the nurse. 'What date is it?' he asked her.

She said she would have preferred to have broken it to him gently, but he and Nelly had lost two months and twenty days of their lives.
'The twenty-fifth of September?' Tarquin worked it out. 'Brilliant!'
The more he shouted and clapped his hands, the worse the pain got. In the end they had to sedate him, and when he came to Christmas was another couple of days nearer. 'You couldn't knock me out again, could you?'
'Why, is the pain becoming unbearable?'
'No,' Tarquin said, 'I just want Christmas to come quicker.' – The doctor gave him another shot.
'That's not fair,' Nelly grumbled as she and her husband left the hospital on the twenty-eighth of September, 'you missed three days more than me in the build-up to the Yuletide celebrations. I've had to wait three days longer than you.'
No matter how they tried, they couldn't keep the nauseating well-wishers away from their door. The forty-third visitor, Sid Robinson, said he had prayed for the happy couple once every one-and-a-half-minutes. He said his wife had promised that she wouldn't do it again. By the time Father Christmas clumped his way up the Kellys' garden path, smoking so heavily that he was enshrouded in a thick cloud of smoke, they had had just about enough of it. Nelly threw a bucket of water over the priest, shouting 'Leave us alone, you vultures!'
After being let out of the quaintly-named 'Clifftown Funny Farm', Mrs. Robinson had resuscitated her pop career with the charity record *The Next-door Neighbours Have Been Duffed Up By A Madlady With A Sledgehammer, Sid*. All the proceeds would go to the song's unfortunate victims, Tarquin and Nelly. They were going to be rich... *rich*, I tell you!
Tarquin and Nelly traipsed around every record-shop in Clifftown, using their Christmas savings to snap up every last copy of the record. The more copies they bought, the more of their money they would get back. It was like backing the rank outsider in a one horse race.
The CD cover showed Mrs. Robinson standing between the unconscious Tarquin and Nelly, lovingly caressing the tubes poking out of every orifice in their bodies. Tarquin would have preferred them to be clothed, but Mrs. Robinson said their bare skin had been hidden by bubbles and smoke when she stood between them on last week's *Top of the Pops*.

In a rare lapse into silliness, it said on the local news, Mrs. Robinson had been given one hundred lines by the head psychiatrist for setting the parish priest's trousers on fire. The newsreader, Irma Goggins, added that only the actions of a quick-thinking neighbour had saved Father Christmas' goose. 'It was as if the woman had a bucket of water sitting on her doorstep, waiting for the priest to call.'

'I thought he didn't exist, Sid?' Nelly said in disbelief.

'I think you're still slightly concussed, dear,' Tarquin said.

They felt better after a crate of Irish stout left on their doorstep with a note from none other than – Father Christmas.

'He does exist!' Nelly yelled in jubilation. 'I knew it all along.'

It was the first of October, and they had contrived to miss yet another couple of days through sheer, bloody-minded drunkenness. It was almost as if some gigantic author in the scheme of things was attempting to rush the Kellys headlong towards Christmas. It wouldn't be long now.

The BBC had asked Tarquin and Nelly to appear live on *Top of the Pops* and dance to a redubbed disco-version of *The Next-door Neighbours Have Been Duffed-Up by a Madlady with a Sledgehammer, Sid*. Tarquin asked the BBC if he could sing Mrs. Robinson's old hit, *I Wish It Could Be Christmas Every Day, Sid*, but the show's producer told him not to be so silly, it was only October.

That Friday night they filmed Tarquin and Nelly lolloping around their garden. Mrs. Robinson was riding around her front garden on her emu's back, tugging suggestively at its underpants while miming to the chorus:

'*The loony grabbed that sledgehammer and bashed them on the noggins...*

I saw it on the news tonight, Sid, read by Irma Goggins.

Well bless my soul, I grabbed that thing and walloped the poor Kellys...

So shake that funky thang and dance, Sid, and we'll shake our bellies.'

The cameras kept well away from Mrs. Robinson's pug-ugly mush, although they did show her big purple emu to the viewing nation.

The lights on Tarquin and Nelly's Christmas tree were flashing on and off in time with the muzak. Next-door, Sid Robinson had a huge banner on the front of his house reading: '*STOP GOSSIPING*

ABOUT MY WIFE – SHE'S ONLY A TEENSY-WEENSY BIT LOOPY!'

When Tarquin and Nelly's song finished the cameras moved down the street to another garden, where U2 were performing their latest hit single.

Father Christmas was back at Tarquin and Nelly's door later that night. He told Nelly, 'I want to thank you for saving my life the other day, with that superbly-timed soaking you gave me.'

When he finished speaking Nelly threw another bucket of water over him, explaining to Tarquin that it wouldn't do him any harm.

There were dozens of teenagers standing around the front of Tarquin and Nelly's house on Saturday morning.

'Tarquin, we love you!'

'Tarquin, we want to have your babies!'

'Are they your *fancy-women*?' Nelly asked Tarquin. 'It looks like Christmas has come early for you this year.'

'Look at me,' the woman next-door shouted to the teenyboppers, riding her emu around her garden, 'I'm Mrs. Robinson!'

'No, look at me,' her husband Sid yelled, waving his rosary-beads around, 'I'm dead holy, me!'

Tarquin sat on his glasses, breaking the frame. He didn't fancy trudging through the lack of snow to the shopping centre for a replacement pair, so he made a cardboard frame from an old cornflakes box and stuck the lenses into it with sellotape. All the neighbours would be dead jealous when they saw him wearing them.

The local council wanted Tarquin and Nelly to switch on their Christmas tree lights that evening, and a telegram had arrived from the Queen inviting them to perform at the *Royal Variety Performance* on Sunday. Tarquin sent a telegram to Buckingham Palace saying 'I suppose so'.

He had just arrived home from the post office when a huge pair of soiled underpants dropped in through their letterbox. Emu dung dribbled all over the carpet Tarquin had bought for Nelly three Christmases ago last June. Who would be sadistic enough to drop a huge pair of y-fronts full of emu-faeces in through their letterbox? Nelly phoned the police.

As she rode proudly around the garden on her fine, upstanding pet's back, Mrs. Robinson directed the policeman to the Kellys' door.

'That's number two there,' she told him, 'the one with a big white number '2' on it.'

'Sorry,' the constable said, 'I can't see properly today because the wife sat on my spectacles, silly bag. I suppose I should have taken them off first.'

When Tarquin opened the door, the policeman said, 'Good morning, my name is Morecambe, Constable Morecambe. Where did you get those specs?' Tarquin said he had made them out of an old cornflakes box and sellotape.

'I think I'll try that,' said Constable Morecambe. 'Will rice crispies do?' After twenty-five minutes of niceties he finally got to the point. 'Yes, that's definitely emu dung,' he said after a right good old sniff. 'So you just cut out the holes and sellotape the lenses in?' – Tarquin made him a pair to shut him up.

'All the boys in the force will be wearing these before the week is out,' Constable Morecambe bragged, skipping down the path and leapfrogging over the gate.

It started snowing that afternoon – only this time the snow was cold, and Sid couldn't shave with it (not for want of trying). Mrs. Robinson's emu was in the garden, wearing new orange underpants. 'Is emu classed as meat?' Nelly asked Tarquin.

'I've never seen emu mince-pies or sausages,' he told her. 'Has the butcher ever asked you "Would you like to take a big slab of emu-rump home for hubby's tea, Missus?" – I think not.'

Clifftown's official Christmas tree outside the town hall was being guarded around the clock by none other than Constable Morecambe, wearing cardboard cutout glasses with the lenses sellotaped into the eyeholes. They made him look really authoritative – as did the council machine-gun he had perched under his arm, threatening to use it if anyone so much as looked sideways at the Christmas tree through funny eyes.

The mayor had received a phone call from a terrorist outfit calling itself the *Mrs. Robinson Guerrillas* (or maybe they spelt it *Gorillas*? It was hard to tell on the phone), threatening to blow up the Clifftown Christmas tree if 'those gits the Kellys' were permitted to perform the lighting-up ceremony instead of Mrs. Robinson. The mysterious caller had gone on to say, 'It's not easy, you know, re-writing other people's songs by adding my husband's name to the end of every line. Down, Guinevere!'

Tarquin cut the red ribbon and Nelly switched the lights on. Then she snatched the mayor's microphone out of his hand and started singing *Have Yourself A Merry Little Christmas, Sid*. Mrs. Robinson hadn't even covered that song, but by now it seemed only natural to add her husband's name to the end of every conceivable song line.

When Nelly treated herself to a joy-filled rendition of John Lennon's *Happy Christmas (War Is Over)*, the crowd continued to sing 'Sid' at the end of every line.

When Tarquin and Nelly arrived home that night they received a telegram through their living room window, wrapped around a brick. 'It's only from Mrs. Robinson,' Nelly said, 'threatening to sue me if I don't stop mentioning her husband in my songs.'

It was bitterly cold, so Tarquin lit the fire with some of the spare planks of wood he had found nailed up in the attic a few months earlier. Mrs. Robinson spent the night parading around her garden on her emu's back, miming to the songs from her 1970s album *Dark Side of the Moon, Sid*. Tarquin and Nelly didn't sleep a wink that night, and they had to go to Mass in the morning.

Father Christmas was halfway through his sermon when Guinevere the emu strode down the centre aisle with Mrs. Robinson lying fast asleep on its back. 'Stop in the name of the law!'

Constable Morecambe and a number of his colleagues, all wearing cardboard glasses with the lenses sellotaped in, ran after the emu. Mrs. Robinson woke up with a start. Holding on tight to her beloved sledgehammer, she leapt off the emu's back and took a shortcut out through the church's new stained-glass window, which depicted Father Christmas being met at the Pearly Gates by a yawning Saint Peter. Now there was a sledgehammer-wielding woman-shaped hole where the parish priest's whisky bottle used to be. The might of the local constabulary leapt truncheon-first out through the church window.

'Maybe you're only dreaming this?' Nelly said to Tarquin.

'Why me?' he asked her. 'This is more like one of your dreams.'

Tarquin curled up on the church pew and tried to get some much-needed shut-eye, hoping that it would wake him up. As he lay there he could hear Nelly blushing. 'People do occasionally fall asleep at Mass,' he heard Father Christmas groaning into his microphone, 'but this is ridiculous.'

In his semi-slumbers, Tarquin felt a crowd picking him up and carrying him out of the church. He imagined them laughing as they carried him home. He half-heard Nelly saying 'dump him on the bed,' and then he dreamt about her undressing him and putting him to bed. He turned over and went back to sleep.

Tarquin woke up at two o'clock on Sunday afternoon – he had only dreamt that he had been carried home from the church.

'I thought we were going to go to Mass this morning?' he said to Nelly, but for some reason she wasn't talking to him… and they had to appear on stage at the Royal Variety Performance that night!

Tarquin and Nelly were obviously the biggest stars on the Royal Variety Performance, because they were the first on the bill. They would be followed by the newsreader Irma Goggins, who was going to read out a selection of the year's most hilarious obituaries.

Tarquin and Nelly rolled around the stage like two time-weary pros, banging their hands up and down on their heads to give the impression that they were actually hurting themselves.

'The silly cow from number four, she thumped them on the bonces…
They thrashed around holding their heads, just like a pair of ponces.'

It suddenly struck Tarquin that the song's lyrics were none too complimentary about Nelly and himself. He had bought three thousand copies of the record but he had never really listened to it.

'Well Tarquin Kelly's always been more than a little rash…
So shake that funky sledgehammer, and give his skull a bash.'

They were up dancing in the aisles. All his life Tarquin had dreamt about being famous, and now here he was, thumping himself on the head while the Queen waved her tiara around and bopped.

Nelly grabbed hold of Irma Goggins' microphone and burst into song. Her Majesty instantly stopped jiving and held her head in her hands. 'Get off,' Tarquin thought he heard her scream.

Ten seconds later they were in a taxi, being rushed past the angry crowds thronging the streets.

Nelly had committed an unforgivable faux pas. It said on the taxi-driver's radio that, from the moment she started singing *O Little Town Of Bethlehem, Sid*, thousands of children across the country had leapt to their feet and asked their parents how long they had to wait until Santa came. The country as a whole seemed to despise the very mention of the word Christmas, as it meant them splashing out their hard-earned money on all sorts of useless gunk at highly inflated prices.

They paid Tarquin's parents a surprise visit on Monday morning.

Tarquin's mother opened the front door and shouted 'Merry Christmas!' She was wearing a purple party-hat and blowing a streamer. Tarquin's father was sitting in his armchair next to the Christmas tree. 'Hello, son,' he said. 'Are you not going to introduce us to your new girlfriend?'

'This is Nelly.'

'Merry Christmas, Nelly!' Tarquin's father shouted, taking a whistle out of his jacket pocket and blowing it. 'Why don't you stay for Christmas dinner? The turkey will be ready at three o'clock, as usual, isn't that right, Wilma?'

'As usual, Fred,' Tarquin's mother sighed, and Nelly followed her into the kitchen. There was an old *Morecambe and Wise Christmas Show* on the telly. On the mantelpiece there were seven Christmas cards that Tarquin and Nelly had sent over the past few years. Tarquin's mother kept them all, and his father was none the wiser.

'There are seven stuffed turkeys in the fridge,' Nelly came in and whispered to Tarquin. 'They'll probably be eating turkey from now until Christmas.'

Tarquin and Nelly had chips and beans for Christmas dinner number one. Tarquin's mother brought out ten cans of beer and a bottle of whisky, but she put them away again when her husband fell asleep in his armchair. She rewound the video, ready for when the old man awoke from his innocent slumbers. She told Nelly that she hated leaving Tarquin's father alone when she went to her Saturday job at the Clifftown Shopping Centre.

Tarquin and Nelly were about to go home, when Tarquin's father sat up and spotted them.

'Hello, son,' he said, with his usual warm smile. 'Are you not going to introduce us to your new girlfriend?'

Tarquin put his arm around Nelly's waist and did the honours.

'Merry Christmas, Nelly!' He gave them a quick blow on his beloved whistle, then said: 'Why don't you stay for your Christmas dinner? The turkey will be ready at three, as usual.'

As they were walking to the bus-stop, Tarquin slipped on an icy patch and banged his head on a rock.

He sat up in bed. Nelly and his parents were sitting by his side, wearing party-hats and blowing streamers. Father Christmas was standing holding a crucifix, and Sid Robinson was standing behind him waving his huge rosary-beads above his head. Mrs. Robinson and Constable Morecambe were taking turns at riding the purple emu up and down the hospital ward.

Judge Curtains was trying Constable Morecambe's cardboard glasses on. A couple of people were just leaving. Tarquin couldn't see their faces, but he thought they were newsreader Irma Goggins and Her Majesty the Queen.

Stan Laurel was sitting on the end of Tarquin's bed, eating eggs and nuts. He tipped his hat to Tarquin, but it flew through the air and landed on the emu's head. Nelly smiled at Tarquin's father when he invited her and Stan to join them for Christmas dinner at three o'clock.

Mrs. Robinson started singing her huge smash-hit number ninety-three hit single, *The Trail Of The Lonesome Pine, Sid*. Nelly, the constable and Tarquin's parents all joined in. Stan Laurel was doing his soft-shoe shuffle, like in *Bonnie Scotland* when Ollie sings *Shine On Harvest Moon*. It was only when Dishmop the Snow-woman burst in through the doors and started doing an Irish jig like Michael Flatley out of *Riverdance* that Tarquin suspected he was probably only imagining this whole peculiar scene.

Nelly was huffing when Tarquin came to for real, still wearing his paper party hat.

'You git,' she moaned churlishly. 'Your year between Christmases has just lost yet another thirty-seven days... now I'll never catch up with you.' She took Tarquin home.

It was the twelfth of November and the latest irritating fall of snow had melted at last. A white Christmas is a beautiful sight to behold, Tarquin thought, but one day a year is quite enough, thank you very much. While Nelly was out shopping, Tarquin took the Christmas decorations down. There would be plenty of time for all that sort of nonsense a month or so from now.

'Christmas is coming earlier every year,' Tarquin explained to Nelly when she came home. 'Talk about overkill.'

A lot of things had changed while Tarquin was otherwise disengaged. Mrs. Robinson had taken him and Nelly to court and sued them for miming her husband's name in vain in front of

Royalty. The court ushers had wheeled Tarquin up before Judge Curtains in his hospital bed, and he had been fined twenty-five pence for contempt when he refused to stand up as Judge Curtains entered the court, buttoning up his flies.

Tarquin removed the embarrassing *Merry Christmas* lights from the front of his house. Everybody was celebrating Christmas, this being mid-November, but he and Nelly didn't want to be seen as mere faces in the crowd.

On Friday the thirteenth of November, It suddenly crossed Tarquin's mind that maybe his boss hadn't been joking when he paid him his so-called 'severance pay' way back in the summertime? He paid his new doctor a visit to get a sick note, just in case.

The sign on the doctor's door said 'Doctor Herman Flying, 87', which Tarquin thought was ridiculous. Who cared what age the doctor was? He had a mop of bright red bushy hair, a matching beard and whiskers and a funny, deep booming voice that occasionally tailed off into a high-pitched squeal.

Doctor Flying asked Tarquin to take all his clothes off. Tarquin said he didn't like undressing in front of a man, so the doctor reassured him by revealing that he used to be a woman. To prove it, he showed Tarquin a snapshot of himself in bed with Sid Robinson.

'That's OK, then,' Tarquin said, whipping his kit off. But then he suddenly panicked. 'You weren't Mrs. Robinson, were you?'

'No, I was Sid's bit on the side,' Doctor Flying said. As he examined Tarquin's bits and bobs, he asked what was wrong with him.

'Nothing,' Tarquin said, 'I just want a sick-note, to tell my boss why I've been off work for the last five months.' – He would have recognised those ice-cold fingertips anywhere. 'Didn't you used to be Doctor Curtains?'

'Why *have* you been off work for the last five months?'

'Well obviously,' Tarquin explained, 'I realised there was only six months to go until Christmas.'

'You started getting ready for Christmas in June?'

'What's so strange about that?' Tarquin said, exasperated. 'I imagine the trees were up in every house on our street by the end of summer, although I can't be totally certain because I was unconscious for most of July, August and September – not to mention October to November.'

'The whole of Grim Street was festooned with Christmas decorations in the middle of summer?' said Doctor Flying. 'Grim Street is serviced by *which* reservoir?'

Tarquin answered, when further prompted, that he did indeed work for the *Dehydrated Water Board* and that Sid Robinson was indeed his assistant.

Doctor Flying made a quick phone call. 'Hi, Sid,' he said, 'guess who? Remember how your little bit of fluff said she was just popping out for a change, to see how the other half lived?' The doctor put the phone down. 'Sid hung up on me,' he sighed.

Just wait until Tarquin Kelly told everybody that the new doctor wasn't really eighty-seven years of age despite what it said on his front door, he cogitated to himself, walking past houses numbers eighty-five and eighty-three.

'Sid! Long time no see! I've just bumped into your old adversary, Doctor…'

'She's back in town?' Sid said excitedly. 'How does she look?'

'She's changed a little bit,' Tarquin said. 'Well, quite a few little bits.'

'Here, Prancer, here boy!' – A black-and-white king charles cavalier ran up Tarquin's garden path, followed by… 'Judge Curtains?'

'Silence in the garden!'

'Prancer doesn't really exist,' Tarquin told the judge. 'He only exists in my dreams.'

'Well, maybe you're dreaming now,' Judge Curtains suggested. 'Maybe that woman next-door, sitting on an emu's back and singing *The Doctor's Got A Big Surprise For Sid, Tarquin (Rap Remix)*, is just a figment of your imagination?'

Constable Morecambe strutted down the street. He was still wearing sellotape instead of glass in the lenses of his cardboard cutout spectacles. No, wait, Tarquin was convinced that he had only imagined the police constable using sellotape as lenses, during one of his comatose periods.

He recalled how Doctor Flying had intimated that everybody on Grim Street might be slightly touched because of the local water supply. If he wasn't mistaken, it was the only street in Clifftown where people insisted on having their water watered-down. Had they all been driven mad by the solid cubes of water they added to their tap water prior to imbibing it?

Mrs. Robinson was riding her emu up and down the middle of the road, singing a medley of her greatest hits with musical accompaniment by the sellotape-lensed-spectacles-wearing Clifftown and District Constabulary Orchestra sitting astraddle thirty-two emus borrowed from the local zoo.
'Look at poor Sid, decorating his house with his new electrified forty-foot Christmas rosary-beads,' Tarquin beamed excitedly. 'He's the only compos mentis man on the street.'
'Hey!' – It was Doctor Flying. 'I'm the only one around here who is qualified to speculate on the state of people's sanity around here!' Then he spotted Sid Robinson. 'Hi Sid,' he said. 'Sorry about the missing doo-dahs, and the new whatsit.'
'Her-mana?' Sid said, confused.
The doctor ripped off his red beard and moustache and scrubbed off his wrinkles – it was young Doctor Curtains again. 'That was my disguise for the Christmas party,' she yelled. 'What on earth were you thinking?'
'The Christmas party?' Sid asked. 'All right, so there are only six weeks left until Christmas… but, you left Clifftown four-and-a-half months ago!'
'Well,' Doctor Curtains sensibly explained, 'Christmas parties come but once a year. A little preparation doesn't go amiss, Sid. It took me quite a while to hand-paint all those wrinkles on my face, you know.'
'I thought you'd gone back to medical college,' Nelly shouted out through her front door, 'to revise on obscure body-parts and how to find them?'
When Doctor Curtains heard Nelly's voice her eyes suddenly bulged out of their sockets (if you'll pardon the medical terminology).
'I feel faint,' Doctor Curtains said in a daze. 'Or is it feint?'
'They're pronounced the same,' Tarquin said, as he kindly sat the good lady doctor down in the snow on Grim Street.
'It was June or July,' the doctor said, 'and this woman came into my surgery talking about Christmas. She said she had a terribly sore pair of giblets, and she wanted me to find out whereabouts in her body her giblets were situated.'
'That's ridiculous,' the boss-eyed Judge Curtains giggled as his dog licked his cauliflower ear. 'Everybody knows that one's giblets are situated between the left heart and the gizzard, slightly north-south

of the naughty thingumabob region, to use legal parlance. Stop it, Prancer!'

'Isn't this a great little street?' Tarquin thought out loud. 'If only Stan Laurel was here with us, this would be the most perfect little scene on Earth.'

'What?' Doctor Curtains asked him. 'The skinny one out of Laurel and Hardy? Isn't he dead?'

'Death is only relative on Grim Street,' Tarquin replied. 'Isn't that what Christmas is all about?'

'Christmas?' said Sid. 'But it's only the thirteenth of November.'

Doctor Curtains sighed and then popped home to change out of her green string-vest. Tarquin popped indoors to fetch cans of beer for everybody – even the thirty-two musicians.

They started to get slowly inebriated, and they were soon joined by Father Christmas. He explained that he had heard all the rifting from the church, so he ran out mid-confession to track the booze down. When Tarquin's thirteen fridges full of emergency supplies ran out, the whole damned caboodle of them staggered to the Grinch's Left Eyeball.

Father Christmas got very drunk and told Mrs. Robinson to stop messing around with her emu's head. 'Guinevere's a female,' he snarled. 'Female emus don't wear y-fronts, they wear pink silk panties.'

Judge Curtains revealed in a drunken slur that his full name was Prancer Curtains. 'But my friends just call me *Your Honour*.'

'That could confuse matters,' Constable Morecambe told the judge, while struggling to make a spare pair of spectacles out of beer-mats and broken pint-glasses. 'If I throw my big pointed hat behind the cigarette machine and shout "Fetch, Prancer," you and your dog might both scamper across the floor to search for it.'

Constable Morecambe ordered the barman – in the name of the law – to lock the doors and serve free-drinks-all-round for the rest of the night. Judge Curtains scribbled out a licence allowing the Grinch's Left Eyeball to remain open 'until the most senior legal representative present in the said bar begins to see pink elephants'.

Sid Robinson was throwing pint after pint down his throat as if tomorrow might never come, with a quick decade of the rosary between each sip.

Nelly woke Tarquin up early on Saturday... no, it was *Monday* afternoon. There wasn't an inch of sleeping space to be found on the pub floor.

Mrs. Robinson was sleeping on her emu's back. Guinevere obviously wasn't pub-trained, as she had soiled her baggy orange underpants. Doctor Curtains was wearing Sid's trousers. Sid was looking resplendent (although unconscious) in the doctor's mini-skirt and matching fishnet stockings, stilettos and pink g-string.

Tarquin and Nelly stepped carefully over the Clifftown and District Constabulary Orchestra's thirty-two prostrate bodies and left the pub, then fought their way past the thirty-two emus in the car park.

Tarquin popped into the corner shop to buy a dozen pairs of stockings for Nelly to hang on the end of their bed. They almost missed their house, not recognising the place without the woman riding a big bird around the garden of the house next-door. They finally tracked it down via the number on the front door.

Nelly was reading the *Clifftown Chronicle*.

'It says here,' she gasped, 'that scientists are now convinced that Jesus was born in March.'

'Eh?' said Tarquin.

'*Due to miscalculations with the calendar down through the centuries,*' Nelly read, '*the original Christmas Day was erroneously timed nine months (plus three or four years) too late.* That means we can't have our annual booze-up until just before Easter.'

Tarquin was in a state of shock. He had already waited the best part of five months for Christmas to arrive... did he now have to wait another four months?

'But Christmas in December is a national institution, like the FA Cup Final, Wimbledon and beans on toast!' Tarquin screamed, overcome with emotion. 'I need my beans on toast! People can't simply go changing time-honoured traditions willy-nilly like that. Nobody deserves to get plastered in December more than I do. It wouldn't have been so bad if they had told us after Christmas was over, so that we could at least have celebrated twice.'

'We could always pretend we don't know, and do just that?' Nelly suggested.

'It wouldn't feel right,' Tarquin told her, 'getting blitzed out of my head on the twenty-fifth of December, knowing that it wasn't the actual birth-date of Jesus Christ our Lord. I'm going to bed. Call me in four months.'

It was just before midnight on the twenty-fourth of December, and Tarquin and Nelly could hear their drunken neighbours out playing in the snow.

Gagging for a celebratory pint or ten, Tarquin said to Nelly, 'If Christmas falls in March, maybe the sixteenth of November was really the first of April, and scientists only said that as an April Fools' joke? Let's put our stockings up quick and get to bed, before Santa Claus comes. Tonight's the night that Santa comes and stitches up all the holes in the stockings and socks hanging on the end of our bedposts. I'm going to leave a couple of pairs of y-fronts out as well.'

'Santa won't be coming tonight, Tarquin,' Nelly said, as if she was breaking bad news to a child. 'There'll be no stitched-hole presents in this house tonight.'

'Why not?'

'Don't you think Santa reads the newspapers?' she explained. 'He won't be climbing down the chimney until March, on the Real Christmas Eve night.'

'Of course,' Tarquin realised. 'How silly of me.' He made a point of not hanging his socks and underpants on the end of the bed that night.

On the twenty-fifth of December, Sid Robinson threw an enormous snowball at the Kellys' living room window, shouting out 'Merry Christmas!' Tarquin didn't have the heart to tell Sid the truth. Instead he just told him that he wouldn't be back at work until April, in the light of recent events, and that he could continue covering as Chief Water Wetter until Tarquin returned.

As Nelly prepared their pretend-Christmas-dinner, Tarquin enquired: 'What about New Year? When do we celebrate that?'

'The first of April, I suppose,' Nelly said. 'Although the old first of April now falls in July.'

'And my birthday is at the start of September, instead of June.'

They were doing the washing-up when Nelly's parents turned up on their doorstep. They hadn't even replied to the invitation that had been sent to them in July (which now occurred in October), so that Tarquin and Nelly could hide or feign death, insanity or both – the bald pigs. The barbershop quartet made themselves at home, singing songs as Tarquin and Nelly decided to have an early night.

'There are crackers in one of the fridges,' Nelly told her four fathers. 'Let yourselves out when you've eaten us out of house and home, and we'll see you next Christmas. Good night, Dads.'

Through the bedroom window, Tarquin spotted Mrs. Robinson throwing the biggest turkey-bones he had ever seen into her dustbin. Her emu was nowhere to be seen.

Tarquin awoke on the twenty-sixth of December with a wonderful feeling.

'Boxing Day has always been the worst day of the year,' he told Nelly. 'But this year, for the first time ever, I feel great... because for once, the countdown is still on. You and I know that there's less than three months to go until Christmas, but everybody else has to wait a whole year.'

Father Christmas paid Tarquin and Nelly a visit, wearing a raincoat with the hood fastened up tightly to protect his head from the snow. When Nelly opened the door she instinctively looked around for her bucket.

'Sorry, Father,' she said, 'the bucket's in one of the fridges, filled with snow I collected in case of emergencies.'

'Why were you two not at Christmas Mass?' the priest asked.

'It wasn't Christmas Day,' Tarquin told him. 'It's not Christmas until March.'

Father Christmas argued that the actual birth-date of our Lord doesn't matter, it's the thought that counts.

Nelly went into the kitchen and filled her basin to scrub the potatoes. When he heard the water running, Father Christmas made a hasty retreat.

Nelly put the Christmas decorations up while Tarquin tended to the tree. 'Just think,' she said, 'three months from today it will all be over, and we'll have to wait another year (minus a day) until Christmas comes around again.'

Their neighbours were all taking their Christmas trees down.

'Shall we tell them the truth?'

'No, let's keep it our little secret.'

'Yes,' Tarquin agreed, 'why let anybody else join in the fun? We'll have our own private Christmas in March, and – to quote my good friend Mr. Laurel's good friend Mr. Hardy – nobody will be any the wiser.'

Some evil fiend had stolen the huge turkey-bones from Mrs. Robinson's dustbin in the middle of the night. 'Even the rubbish in your bin isn't safe any more,' Mrs. Robinson sighed.

On the bright side of things, however, Mrs. Robinson was at number one in the chart with *Bohemian Rhapsody, Sid*. Tarquin and Nelly invited the Robinsons down to the Grinch's Left Eyeball to celebrate. Sid Robinson had to take five trips to the bar to fetch each round, as he could only carry one drink at a time with the gigantic rosary beads in his hand.

After only one pint, Sid got down on his hands and knees in front of the beer-soaked bar. 'I've just missed Mass for the first time ever,' he sobbed, and suddenly Father Christmas marched into the bar with his fearsome 'You missed Mass' eyes. Mrs. Robinson stood on top of the pool table and sang, '*Sid's afraid of the big bad priest, the big bad priest, the big bad priest.*'

Tarquin and Nelly decided that they weren't going to let another drop of alcohol cross their lips as long as they lived. They sat and watched as everyone around them got sozzled and listened to Mrs. Robinson's raucous songs about her Sid, followed by dirges about how delicious her late, beloved emu Guinevere had been.

Tarquin was just reminding Father Christmas that it wasn't really Christmas until the twenty-fifth of March, when Mrs. Robinson – wearing a necklace made out of what appeared to be the bones of some unknown large bird-type creature – raged: 'March? Come on, Sid, we've got less than three months to find the world's biggest living turkey and wring its scrawny neck!'

Mrs. Robinson purchased the biggest turkey in the world towards the end of February. She christened it Dishmop II, in honour of the dearly beloved snow-woman that Tarquin and Nelly had lost in such unfortunate circumstances a few months earlier. By mid-March, Dishmop II was rarely seen in the garden without having Mrs. Robinson perched on its back, holding on tight to its green underpants as she rode it ragged around the lawn.

'Dishmop II is easily my favourite pet of all time,' Mrs. Robinson bragged, 'or at least since my pseudo-Christmas dinner. I'm still picking purple bits out from between my teeth.'

On the twenty-fourth of March, as the snow lay non-existent on the ground, Mrs. Robinson was pretending to cycle her gigantic turkey up and down the footpath of Grim Street.

All of a Sudden, Nelly caught Dishmop II in an enormous net – Mrs. Robinson and all. Spying through his super-strong cardboard and sellotape spectacles, Constable Morecambe leapt over the fence and caught Nelly in an even larger net – Mrs. Robinson and Dishmop II the turkey and all.

'Nelly Kelly,' Constable Morecambe said as he marched the whole gigantic net full of them towards the police station, 'I arrest you in the name of the law for attempting to kidnap your neighbour's pet turkey with a view to stuffing it and shoving it down your gullet, one horrendous forkful after another, probably smothered in tartar sauce, ketchup, mustard and dripping.'

As his voice faded slowly into the distance, the constable – his tunic festooned with buttons which lit up in multicoloured lights, with *Happy Real Christmas!* chalked brazenly across his back and a bell on the tip of his pointy blue hat – said, 'Mrs. Robinson, I arrest *you* in the name of the law as well, for cycling on a pedestrian pavement in the dark without a light on your turkey. The said turkey may, as a result, henceforth be taken away from you and duly stuffed by my good lady wife, and thereafter put into our oven for safe-keeping at a heat of 235 degrees centigrade.'

In lieu of a spell in jail, Nelly accepted the lenient Judge Curtains's alternative form of punishment and wrote out one hundred times, in her best handwriting, 'I must not try to kidnap my neighbour's pet turkey in a big net, with the intention of stuffing it and shoving it down my gullet.'

As Tarquin and Nelly filled their hot-water bottles that night, Tarquin's mother stuck a hand-written note through their letterbox sadly announcing that Tarquin's father had popped his clogs and advising Nelly not to overcook the twenty-three percent vegetarian turkey she had bought in the shopping centre the previous Saturday afternoon.

As they climbed into bed that night, Nelly burst into tears. Tarquin tried comforting her with a well-timed 'There, there,' But Nelly was inconsolable. 'I've got some jelly and ice-cream for tomorrow's dessert,' she sobbed. 'But yet again I'll have to let you down miserably on the custard front.'

Tarquin woke up in the middle of the night.

The socks and stockings and tights and suspenders and g-strings and jockstraps were securely fastened to the end of the bedpost. As Nelly had always said, you're never too old to dream. Life without dreams would be as pointless as non-stop dreams without a life to wake up into. If Santa Claus came every night, pretty soon Nelly would have been chasing him out of the house with her mop.

Tarquin heard an enormous crashing sound. It was as if somebody had just smashed all the tiles off their roof and leapt down through the rafters, taking half the house with him. If the hooligan was still in the house when Tarquin got up in the morning, he was going to throttle him to within 2.54 centimetres of his life.

Tarquin heard the attic door being blown open by the wind. Then he heard another big crash. A huge chunk of plaster fell from the ceiling, followed by a leg. Tarquin turned the bedside lamp on and Nelly sat up with a shocked look on her face.

'Red trousers?' she said, looking up at the stranger's leg. 'Real men don't wear red trousers...'

'Ho! Ho! Ho!' the man chortled as if he owned the place.

'Let's pretend we're asleep,' Tarquin suggested, closing his eyes and hugging his pillow.

'I beg your pardon?' Nelly asked him. 'Is that how you defend your wife from night-time invaders, by pretending to be asleep?'

'It's Santa,' Tarquin whispered, pulling the blankets up over his head. 'If he knows we're awake, he won't...'

Nelly faked snoring, and Tarquin copied her. There was a huge thump as Santa fell down through the ceiling directly onto their bed, with a loud groan. He clambered off the top of them, moaning 'My poor aching back.'

Ten minutes later Tarquin bravely poked his head out from under the blankets. Santa was sitting on the end of the bed, his red suit covered in dust from the ceiling plaster. Tarquin thought about all the wood he had found up in the attic – he hadn't noticed any floorboards missing while he was prying those planks up last June. Santa was humming quietly to himself as he sat stitching up the holes in Tarquin's socks and Nelly's tights. Then he moved on to the underwear.

Nelly peeped out from under the sheets. 'If only life could be like this all the time,' she whispered.

'It will be,' Tarquin promised, 'one day... just you wait and see.'
Santa put Tarquin's underpants down on the bed and turned around.
'Hey,' he said, 'you're awake! You're not allowed to be awake, that's cheating!'
'Tarquin and I were just sleep-talking to one another,' Nelly told him.
Santa opened his sack and pulled out an eight-millimetre cine-film projector. He plugged it in and took a reel of film out of his sack and played it, projected onto the bedroom door. The film of sheep leaping over a fence played on a continuous loop, until Tarquin and Nelly fell asleep.
'Did that really happen last night?' were the first six words that Nelly heard on the new Christmas morning.
'Well hardly,' she replied to Tarquin, staring disconsolately at the huge hole in the ceiling. 'We must have dreamt it, dear. Use your loaf.'
But hold on – all the holes in their socks and stockings and other smalls had been sewn up overnight as if by magic. Santa Claus *did* exist. Tarquin wanted to let the world know by wearing his underwear on the outside for the day, but Nelly wouldn't let him.
'Let's keep his existence our little secret.'
Tarquin realised that Nelly was right. They knew for certain that the great Santa existed, because they had caught him sewing up Tarquin's underpants and Nelly's knickers on a cold March Christmas night. But why let everybody else learn their secret, thus spoiling their fun?
Nelly was overjoyed when she opened the wonderful Christmas present Tarquin had bought her less than nine months earlier. With her custard-maker's starter-pack she would be able to make custard as if it was going out of fashion.
They spent Real Christmas Day throwing custard-pies at their neighbours, who ran indoors and came back out two hours later with their own home-made custard-pies to throw back at the Kellys.
Tarquin and Nelly had custard on toast for supper that night, and they had custard instead of milk on their cornflakes on the Real Boxing Day morning. By the time they reached Real New Year's Day on the first of April, Tarquin's tongue was becoming sick of the sight of custard.

Father Christmas turned up on Tarquin and Nelly's doorstep on a sunny April morning.

'You wanted to see me?'

'Come in, come in!' Nelly replied, guiding Father Christmas past a bucketful of custard.

'Well?' he said. 'What do you want with me this time?'

'We'd like you to perform a blessing, Father,' Tarquin said. 'We've been in this house for over four years, and in all that time you've hardly blessed as much as a crate of beer in our freezers.'

'I don't bless beer, I drink it,' Father Christmas snapped. 'You haven't invited me here to bless your beer, I hope?'

'Don't be silly, Father,' Nelly said. 'We'd hardly invite you into our home to bless a crate of beer. Would you like a drink?'

'I wouldn't mind a glass of whisky.'

'No whisky, Father.'

'Vodka?'

'No vodka.'

It took about an hour for Father Christmas to hit the jackpot.

'Okay, okay,' he begrudgingly said, 'I'll settle for a nice cool pint of custard.'

Tarquin and Nelly and Father Christmas lolled around the house drinking custard to their hearts' delight, and the wise old parish priest blessed The Kellys' vat full of custard for them. Now they would be able to die happy, even if goblins invented the ultimate fighting-weapon and blew every last lump of custard into kingdom come and it never crossed Tarquin and Nelly's lips ever again.

Tarquin and Nelly woke up with splitting headaches, and decided not to drink again until at least the festive season.

Tarquin put his glasses on and looked at the date on the *Clifftown Chronicle*, and he could hardly believe his eyes: it was the twenty-fifth of September. There were only six months until Christmas. Tarquin and Nelly found it hard to believe that twelve whole months had passed by since this time last year....

NICE WEATHER FOR HAMSTERS

The TV weathergirl said there was going to be freak weather that weekend. Sean Byrne looked at his wife Ciara and laughed. Then he thought of something funny.
'That brunette bimbo I fancy was in the pub again last night,' he said.
'Did you tell her you love her?' she asked.
'Of course I did,' Sean snapped. 'What sort of *animal* do you take me for?'
He tried to remember his exact words to the angelic tart. *You silly git, I love you.* That was it, right on the button. 'I think the cat must have her brain,' Sean said.
'Don't worry,' Ciara comforted him, 'there are plenty of fish in the sea.'
'Yes, I suppose so, love.'
The local news was on TV. The main story was about fish dropping out of the sky in Ballinamallard.
'Plenty of fish in the sea,' Sean repeated Ciara's words, before having a quiet chuckle to himself.
Ten minutes later he looked at her and laughed again. 'What's for dinner this evening?'
'Fish fingers.' – She didn't see the irony of it all.
'Maybe if you stopped calling her a silly git she might show a little interest in you.'
'Has the cat got your brain?' Sean asked. 'I know you're none too clever, dearest, but I'm sick of old refrains.'
She didn't know what he meant by that, and that made two of them. *Think before you speak*, Sean thought to himself, shutting his mouth. It was raining. It was coming down in bucket-loads. A bucket smashed against their front window and shattered the glass. Sean leapt to his feet and ran to the window, just in time to see the window-cleaner landing flat on his back in the front garden.
'You'll pay for that broken window, you gormless cretin,' Sean shouted at the window-cleaner as the paramedics put him on a stretcher. The middle-aged man threw his squeegee at Sean and told

him to go and boil his head.

'I suppose if he told you to go and jump in the River Lagan you'd do that too?' Ciara said cuttingly, as Sean boiled a big pan of water on the stove. He thought about the whole scenario for a minute.

'I wasn't going to boil my head, honestly.' He thought she believed him. He took his red Manchester United socks off and boiled the stench out of them. 'Only three hours until ten o'clock.'

'Why,' Ciara asked, knitting a new pullover for their beloved hamster, 'what's happening at ten o'clock?'

Her stupid words didn't even warrant a reply. Did she think he could predict the future or something?

'Silly git.'

Sean suddenly noticed that it was snowing, and it was coming down in shovel-loads. But they were only plastic – more like the spades you use to bury your wife in the sand at the seaside. 'How the hell did you get out, that last time?' he asked Ciara. She didn't know what he was talking about, so he had to go through the whole monotonous chore of telling her what he had been thinking about before speaking out of the blue.

'I bet you'd know what I was thinking about if it was wearing skimpy lingerie,' Sean complained, not unnaturally. 'You only read my mind when it suits you.' In fact, he thought to himself, she couldn't even read her *own* mind, never mind his.

Ciara cut him dead. She was on to the hamster's pockets. Soon they would have the best-dressed hamster in Belfast, bar none. 'It'll keep Ming warm in this winter weather,' Ciara remarked, glancing out the window at the thunder and lightning. The freak-weathergirl was on the box again.

'The weather has gone to pot since that ugly lass started doing the forecasts,' Ciara groused.

'Don't be such a bigot,' Sean nagged, 'you'll be like that yourself one day.'

He looked out at the plastic spades sticking out of the melting snow.

'You'd pray for that at the seaside,' he said caustically. 'But does it ever happen? Does it *****!'

'Mind your tongue,' Ciara whined, as Sean shaved his upper-lip. He couldn't even go to the bathroom in peace, without her following him in and plopping herself down on the loo to keep an eye on him. He looked at her sitting there, pulling the paper off the holder on the door.

'This is very degrading for me,' he told her straight, blushing.

'I've seen men shaving before, you know,' Ciara carelessly replied. 'And all razors look the same, you know.'

Sean looked out the bathroom window and saw lightning striking the church spire. It had stopped snowing, but now it was raining cats and dogs. The cats were peeing on the snow, and it was turning into slush. Sean hated slush, especially of the soggy variety. Nice dry slush was all right... something he could get his teeth into. Lightning struck the wet slush, electrocuting half a dozen people running down the street.

'The next time you buy me shoes I want rubber soles, darling.' – That told her. That certainly put her in her place all right.

Ten o'clock came and went without anything strangely peculiar occurring. The shocking normality of the situation amazed Sean, although he wasn't at all surprised. He had sneakily listened to the weather forecast at the end of the news that afternoon, while out painting his side of their neighbours' back-garden shed bright red to teach them a lesson in property law, and the weathergirl said things would 'improve for the worse' at twenty-two hundred hours. Sean ought to have known better than to take a silly weather forecaster's word as read.

At a minute past ten, the weather went downhill rapidly. Then the wind blew it back up the hill again, straight into Sean and Ciara's front garden.

There were all sorts of things falling out of the sky: haystacks, cows, barnyard doors, farmers, you name it. There must have been a tornado nearby. A pig landed on their roof and commenced eating out of the guttering. Sean telephoned the USPCA to get it down safely, but the line was engaged so he shot it down with his father's hunting rifle. Bullseye. No sooner had Sean put his winter woollies on than the clouds blew away and the sun blazed down from the sky.

'Where are my flip-flops?' he asked.

'You probably left them in your fancy woman's bedroom,' Ciara said.

Sean rubbed his chin in contemplation. He hadn't left them there, had he?

'I don't think so, love... I'm pretty sure I've worn them here since.'

'Oh, so you admit it!'

'Of course I do,' Sean said forcefully. 'I wore my flip-flops last night. Why deny it?'

There was an urgent weather-flash on the TV. The police had requested that all farmers – and other assorted people with ordure between their toes and aromas that brought tears to normal people's eyes – should return to their farmyards to check for missing livestock. The weathergirl Orlaith Paisley was pointing her big stick at a picture of two sheep and a duck on the screen behind her. The sheep seemed to be sniggering, but the duck had a nonchalant look in its eyes. It knew when it was on to a good thing.

'That duck knows where its bread is buttered,' Sean said.

'Well, maybe you can learn from your betters,' Ciara replied, cutting Sean to the quick.

It was raining straight pink bananas, unusual for that time of the year.

'The brunette bimbo in the pub will be out reaping in that fine harvest,' Ciara said. 'Oops, I've dropped a stitch.'

'Must you keep talking about my bit on the side like that?' – She was beginning to irritate him. 'Can you not forget about the *present* for one solitary second?'

The slush had melted in the heat, turning into a river of pink bananas and plastic spades, and all she could think about was how her husband got his kicks when her all-encompassing back was turned. God, she made him so angry at times. The eyes in the back of her head were really beginning to wear him down. Why couldn't she just live and let live, like his extracurricular woman did?

'You don't want me to have any fun,' Sean sulked manfully.

'Must I tell you my feelings?' – The weathergirl was back again. She was staring straight out of the screen into Sean's eyes. 'Must I put into words the way I feel about you?'

'Is she talking to *you*?' Ciara was becoming suspicious.

'I suppose you'll be blaming me for the *weather* next.'

'Well,' Ciara said, 'we didn't have weather like this back in the old days, before you started boiling your smalls three times a day.'

There was no arguing with her. Sean could see the tornado coming down the road, and it was all *his* fault. There was a sudden total eclipse of the sun – Sean Byrne's fault, needless to say. He couldn't win.

Ciara put the hamster's pullover on. God, Sean wished that he were a hamster. The wife never knitted pullovers for him. All he ever got were woollen underpants, as itchy as hell. Ciara obviously hated him.

'I bet you wouldn't hate me if I was a hamster, a gerbil, or even a rat. I bet you'd knit me pullovers then,' Sean sighed, fetching his leather jacket from the back hall. 'But what am I thinking about – there's a tornado coming! I'm off to the Vodka-Swiller's Handbag for a pint of Guinness.'

'Like hell you are, you clampet!' Ciara said softly, tucking the spoiled hamster's pullover into its trousers. She was making Ming look effeminate. 'If this house is going to be sucked up into the air, I want you to be in it at the time.'

'I'd rather be sucked up in the pub...'

'You'll be sucked up where I tell you,' Ciara informed Sean pertinaciously. 'You're not leaving me here with only that hamster to defend me.'

The tornado was hidden behind a black-and-red chequered rainbow, the likes of which Ciara hadn't seen since Ming was in nappies.

'What about my brunette bimbo?' Sean sobbed. 'You don't care a toss about her.'

Ciara looked thoroughly ashamed of herself as she told Sean to go and boil his head, quickly adding that she was speaking rhetorically. 'If that thing is as big as it looks, your bint will be up there with us.'

Urgent weather-flash: Lock up your daughters! Orlaith Paisley had a crazed look in her eyes. Ciara noticed that she was both a brunette and a bimbo. *And* she was doing the forecast from their local pub. The game was up.

'The two of yous have rigged this whole thing,' Ciara caught on. 'The pair of yous are trying to get rid of me, by fixing the weather. I know how those TV companies work.'

It was raining lemon meringue and semolina. Ciara knew that Sean knew she had a morbid fear of lemon meringue and semolina. Somebody up there had timed the script badly. An amateur television button-pusher was going to destroy his romance with his angelic slut weathergirl, before he even got to show her his seven home-made DVDs filled with great weather forecasts of the twenty-first century.

'Your dinner's ready,' Ciara shouted in from the kitchen, five or six hours after she had told Sean that he would be having fish fingers. Her and her bloody knitting had thrown his whole body-clock out of kilter.

'I'd swear that you don't love that hamster,' Ciara sighed in self-sympathy.

'Of course I love it,' Sean protested vehemently. 'I just love my brunette bimbo in a... *different* way.'

'Weathergirls come and go.' Ciara had a point. 'But me and my... *our* hamster will always be here for you to fall back on in times of crisis. Just remember that, the next time you're feeding your bit on the side slivers of cheese.'

Sean knew when he was beaten. He phoned the local pub's weather-centre and asked to speak to the woman who pulled all the strings.

'Cancel the freak weather,' he told the silly git he loved with all his loins, 'the wife has pulled the old *lonely hamster* ploy on me.'

Orlaith Paisley told Sean that total eclipses of the sun don't grow on trees, and that he would pay for that evening's entertainment with his hide.

'It's six of the best for you, my boy.'

'Fair enough,' Sean begrudgingly accepted. He hung up and gleefully rubbed his hands together. 'I suppose I can't win them all.'

The weather was turned off at the mains and Sean, Ciara and the hamster went to bed.

'It's not fair,' Sean sulked heroically as they hit the sheets, 'how come the hamster gets a new pair of silk pyjamas, and I have to wear my baggy underpants to bed every night?'

'He's only trying to make you jealous,' Ciara explained. 'Just ignore him.'

Easier said than done, Sean meditated, tossing and turning all night. It was a safe bet that his brunette bimbo wouldn't have let the hamster sleep in the middle. And she wouldn't have spent the night rubbing the hamster's cheek pouches in such a suggestive manner.

'I'm going to have that new newsreader in the pub tonight,' Sean informed Ciara as the three of them sat watching her reading the morning news.

'Don't forget to tell her that you love her,' Ciara said.

'I won't,' Sean replied with a smile. 'Thanks for the tip, sweetheart.'

THE SILLY GHOSTS

My grandma was convinced that, in the dead of night, the ghost of my deceased grandad paid a visit to the sleeping-quarters of the local nurses' home. She was an extremely jealous woman, was my grandma. She just couldn't wait to die, so she could keep a beady eye on her late husband's shenanigans.
Even in death she wondered what the old codger was getting up to, and with whom. She despised the idea of him hovering unseen above the frisky young nurses' showers, having the time of his life. What did he think death was, for God's sake, a non-stop party? She would soon put a stop to that!
I never saw anybody looking as contented in a coffin as my grandma did. 'I can't wait to get one of my own!' she shouted excitedly as the mourners dragged her out and put the genuine corpse back into his or her casket, every time my befuddled grandmother gatecrashed a wake.
She was so intent on dying, that in no time at all she became an absolute expert at feigning her own death. She would lie on the floor of our old house for days on end, with her arms folded across her chest, never seeming to breathe. My mum and dad confidently predicted that Grandma would die before the winter was out, as she was a sure-fire expert at playing dead. She looked for all the world just like a real-life corpse, especially when we had visitors.
One night in particular, a couple of our neighbours didn't know which way to look when Dad invited them in for a few drinks, and Grandma went to sleep in the middle of the living-room carpet, just like a genuine dead body.
As the height of winter approached Grandma started to smell our house out, so Mum and Dad dumped her body out in the back garden.
Funnily enough, it was at around that time that Grandma finally went to join Grandad in the land of eternal rest, as the vicar called it. I was sure I could hear Grandad moaning as his widow was buried in the ground beside him. And that got me wondering: was she still his widow, now that she was dead as well?

Not long after Grandma went to rest in peace, Grandad became a restless spirit. He obviously longed to get as far away from Grandma as possible, but she was having none of it. She chased him through our old house with her ghostly frying-pan at least once a fortnight.

Occasionally she caught him and knocked him out cold (as she had done many times in life, Dad said), leaving his ghostly spirit lying unconscious until he faded away into the ether at sunrise. And to make matters worse, Grandad's ghost was always stark naked. We didn't know where to look. After a few weeks of this malarkey, Mum and Dad were too embarrassed to let anybody enter our house at night.

If I live to be forty, I'll never forget the night my late grandma walloped her deceased husband on the head with a heavy shovel. At the time it seemed really funny. But the following night, Grandad's unmoving body was still lying on my bedroom floor. The next night his dead widow, using the self-same spectral shovel, buried Grandad's ghostly corpse beneath my bedroom floorboards. Grandad's interred corpse hovered spookily in the air of the kitchen below.

After that it reappeared there every night, seemingly rotting away as time drifted slowly by. We had to keep the kitchen curtains tightly shut at night, so that nobody would see Grandad's ghostly remains hovering there. On more than one occasion it nearly put me off my supper.

Six months passed before the body gradually faded away to nothing, leaving Mum and Dad free to open the curtains once again. But throughout all that time, Grandma had been prowling around our house every night, bawling out, 'What have I done? Oh, woe is me!'

Eventually Dad decided to borrow the vicar's Ouija-board, to try and exorcise his mother's tormented spirit. I know old people can be silly at times, but Grandma's behaviour was getting beyond a joke.

Me and Mum and Dad joined hands with the vicar around the Ouija-board. It was second-hand and it had no X, but it would be alright, as long as Grandma didn't try to spell out her erstwhile favourite word, xylophone.

On the first night nothing unusual occurred. But on the second night Grandma's ghost strolled casually in through the wall, sat down beside us at the table and asked, 'What are we playing?'

At that precise moment, her late, late husband's head bounced up through the middle of the Ouija-board. He yelled, in an earth-shattering voice fit to rouse the dead: 'BOO!' It was a really frightening sound, mind you, not your everyday, common-or-garden 'Boo'.

Grandma fell straight through her chair, as if she had never seen a ghost before. Obviously she couldn't quite believe the astonishing sight confronting her – but my grandad was fully dressed!

It was a really long time since anyone there present – or past – had seen the old man respectably attired. His widow's ghost instantly became suspicious, and asked him who the hell he was dressing to impress.

'You've got yourself a fancy woman, haven't you!' Grandma snarled, leaping angrily to her feet. It was like a madhouse. The big nightly chase began once again, every bit as crazy as before – except that now Grandma seemed to be a little less unhappy, and her predeceased was definitely a little less unsightly. Grandma had already killed Grandad once after he died, I don't think she wanted to kill him again just yet.

From that day on, Grandma and Grandad were often heard to laugh and joke with one another as they ran around our house… and sometimes he was chasing her! Mum thought they were trying to rekindle their love for one another. 'Although,' she added, 'perhaps it's a little late in the day for all that stuff and nonsense.'

After a while their ardour cooled down, and they started strolling arm in arm around our old family home, exchanging the occasional gentle peck on the cheek.

Ultimately we could see them sitting comfortably in a couple of ghostly armchairs in front of our living-room fire, watching the flickering flames, at long last truly happy in their ways. At which major turning point in their long relationship they faded away into the eternal ether, never to be seen again.

Well, here's hoping!

LINE OF SIGHT

You won't have any trouble believing the story I'm about to tell you, although with the benefit of hindsight, you may wonder how the hell I ever managed to tell it to you. I'm wondering about that myself as I speak… but hey, mine is not to reason why.
I was sitting watching a blockbuster movie in the cinema when, out of the corner of my eye, I spotted the silhouette of somebody arriving at the end of the aisle.
He turned his head this way and that, looking all around him, before shuffling all the way up the empty row of seats in front of me.
I was the only person in the whole tier, and yet he seemed to zone in on me, planting himself and his big head directly in front of me. The absolute tyrant!
He was a good six inches taller than me (at the time), so I could no longer see the screen. All I could see was his massive big noggin. The cheek of him!
I could feel the blood pumping into my head, throbbing through the veins in my neck. It sounded like a really good scene, but I couldn't see the screen.
Champing at the bit, I opened my rolled-up leather jacket and took out my trusty companion. Luckily for me I had, only that evening, put four new batteries into it.
I really enjoyed the rest of the film, even though, admittedly, I had seen it before.
I left just before the end credits started rolling, not wanting to be there when the lights came on – although, truth be told, I couldn't for the life of me think of one good reason for my innate fear, as I had nothing to hide.
Hiding my beloved implement in my rolled-up brown leather jacket, I stepped out into the cold, cold night air.
As I stood at the bus stop, as luck would have it, a carrier bag came blowing along the street. God is obviously on the side of the just, I thought to myself with a smug chuckle as I picked it up and put my faithful friend into it. I wrapped myself up snug and warm in my jacket, thanking the good Lord for small mercies.

Five minutes later I boarded a double-decker bus.

I went up to the top deck, which was quite deserted. People weren't going out as much as usual these balmy nights, for some obscure reason. Some men and women have no balls.

A couple of young thugs came upstairs at the next stop and – of all things! – sat down on the pair of plastic seats immediately in front of me.

Of the two sides of the otherwise empty deck, they chose to block my line of sight. How ignorant can you get?

They were laughing and joking, and stuffing their faces with chips smothered with what seemed like gallons of tomato ketchup. I couldn't see a thing but their heads and the ketchup. I was blinded by redness, and I felt like a raging bull.

As I got off the bus, ketchup was trickling down the stairs. Some people have no decorum, I thought to myself, looking at the equally abhorred driver and tut-tutting.

It was on the news again. There was a madman running loose around town, doing inexplicable things to 'poor innocent' people (to quote the newsreader).

I couldn't understand it, it sounded perfectly reasonable to me. What the hell did they expect? Surely the 'evil' ones were those who were ignorant enough to block the poor man's line of sight with their big clumsy careless heads? Some people have no respect for the innermost needs of their fellow men.

I opened my carrier bag and looked at my pride and joy. Was that blood etched deep between the grooves? Suddenly it all made perfect sense.

I had always had a deep fear of being deprived of my inalienable rights as a human being, a profound loathing of people who selfishly shunned my desire to see whatever my God-given eyes wanted to see. It was as if they were trying to blind me, trying to take my most vital, my most beloved sense away from me, as if they were lord and master over it. But I was too strong for them. Oh yes. My mind had never felt more powerful than it did at that moment in time.

I was walking past the huge mirror on my living-room wall, lovingly caressing my beautiful plaything. Suspicious, I stopped in my tracks and stared into the mirror. I had a gut feeling that somebody was looking at the back of my head. I struggled to see behind myself, but my big head was in the way. I tried moving it to one side, but I couldn't. I was desperate to see past the head that was barbarously blocking my line of sight.

I pushed the switch down, seething with indignation, and the chainsaw whirred into motion. I should simply have turned around, I thought to myself as my head rolled along the floor. I was right, there was somebody standing behind me, and he was covered from head to toe in a long black cloak... or gown... or whatever the correct word is. I can't think straight, because all the blood has just rushed out of my head....

BILLY THE ELEPHANT

Billy the elephant climbed out of his girlfriend's bed and blushed – he couldn't find his pants.
Sharon had already left for Belfast City Zoo. In a panic, Billy ran out onto the Ormeau Road and asked Sammy the monkey if he had seen his pants. Sammy put his hand in his pocket, pulled out his handkerchief and blew his nose. He rolled his wee eyes and walked away, scratching himself as he walked.
Billy approached Paddy the giraffe.
'Have ye seen my pants?'
Paddy pulled up the neck of his polo-neck jumper and stared at the elephant.
'Your pants?' Paddy said. 'I've never been so insulted!'
The giraffe strutted away with its big lolloping legs and an insulted look on its face.
Billy went up to Ciara Clackett, the proud lioness.
'Bout ye, Ciara,' he said. 'I don't suppose you've seen my pants on your travels?'
Ciara reached down and rubbed a piece of fluff off the hem of her miniskirt. 'Here's me wha?' she snarled. She buckled her shoes, put on her flowery hat and marched away, looking scundered.
'Aw!' Billy the elephant shouted into the wilderness. 'Has nobody seen my pants?'
Just then, Jimmy the hippopotamus came clumping his way out of the River Lagan, covered from head to toe in mud. He was boggin'. He rolled on the grass in Botanic Gardens to wash it off, and Billy noticed he was wearing a turquoise bathing costume.
'Have ye seen my pants, Jimmy?' Billy asked.
Jimmy guffawed. 'Pants, Big Lad?' he said, quickly taking off his bathing costume and putting on his blue shorts, white T-shirt and red fedora. 'I've told ye before, Billy – you're an elephant. Elephants don't wear pants, so they don't.'
'Oops,' Billy said, feeling like a buck eejit. 'Dead on. I must have been blootered last night. At's us nai.'

Billy dandered up the Malone Road and went to the Botanic Inn for a hair of the dog. Sadly, the hallion bouncers wouldn't let him in because he was wearing trainers.

SAY CHEESE AND DIE

So anyway, that's enough gossip for now. I'm sure you're tired hearing about how my best friend's party narrowly lost the general election last month, as you've probably read all about it in the papers. I promise I won't mention him again.
Now let me describe this picture to you, as promised. I'll send you a copy as soon as my scanner is fixed – it wore out and died a death while I was busy printing all those election leaflets for my friend. Oops sorry, ha-ha.
Sitting on the ground at the front of the school photograph are six girls and two boys. Incidentally, one of the boys was killed in a hit-and-run incident six or seven years after the picture was taken, and – now that I come to think of it – the other died from a brain tumour a year later, when he was only eighteen.
Of the six girls, one died of the dreaded cancer when she was in her early twenties, and another somehow managed to fall off a ship into the Irish Sea when she was only a teenager; the girl on the far left came to an unfortunate end when she crashed her car into a double-decker bus on the streets of London on the eve of her twenty-fourth birthday, and the girl on the extreme right died of a heart-attack at the age of thirty-two; the other two girls passed away together on a plane that flew all the way across the ocean only to crash in Canada ten years ago this week, as it happens.
The boy sitting on the first chair on the left died less than a year after the photograph of his year-seven class was taken, and nobody but his family ever really knew the true cause of his demise. I remember it was a cause of much intellectual debate on street-corners at the time. The boy sitting next to him, the class Fat Boy, became a soldier when he grew upwards and inwards; it won't surprise you to learn that he was killed in an explosion in some foreign land about a decade later. The girl sitting beside him lived to the grand old age of thirty-four before being struck by lightning.
The next girl along – the third child from the right – inexplicably drowned in her own bathtub at the age of nineteen, although at the time she was stone cold sober with her eyes wide open (so they tell

me – I wasn't there at the time, ha-ha). The two boys on her opposite side died in motorcycle accidents four years apart, the first of them some ten years after the picture was taken.

There are eight children standing behind the six seated ones, with the ill-fated teacher Mrs Daly in the middle. On her right (to the left of the picture, lest there be any confusion) are two sets of twins, one of them identical girls and the other a sister and brother. The latter passed away when he fell into his sister's grave and broke his poor neck while helping to lower her coffin into the ground after she died in child-birth at the age of twenty-nine. The identical twins, Sally and Jane, on the other hand, died fifteen years apart; Sally fell off a swing in the park just behind the school at the age of twelve, and Jane struggled on all the way to twenty-seven before she was blown off the side of a cliff while enjoying the holiday of a lifetime in Switzerland.

On the other side of Mrs Daly stood her four favourite pupils. To her immediate left was her devoted redheaded son who, sad to relate, committed suicide the day after his mother was gored to death by a bull while participating in the Pamplona Bull Run in Spain eleven or twelve years ago. The little blond boy standing next to him is still alive. And on the very right at the rear are a couple of girls who died in extremely tragic circumstances while still only in their early twenties. One of them, the girl in the corner, was infamously kidnapped and subsequently murdered by a jealous ex-lover when she moved to one of London's suburbs to try and get away from him. The other girl, Pamela Somebody-or-other, grew up and became a drug dealer on the capital's streets for a number of years before being shot in the back of the head by a member of a rival gang. Such a tragic, senseless waste of a young life, as I'm sure you'll agree.

The boy who survived it all? Well now, that was me. I guess I was just lucky. As a matter of fact, I was always the lucky one in my family. I'm now looking up on the wall at a picture of me and my family, taken twenty-odd years ago. My father left this mortal coil when he nearly crashed his car into a white van, and at the next set of lights the white van man's crazy-eyed passenger jumped out onto the road, smashed the windscreen and stabbed him repeatedly. My father had just bought a brand new car, and was taking it out on its maiden drive.

It turned out, ironically, that the enraged white van passenger who stabbed him was my uncle Brian. He said he would never have carried out the atrocious act of barbarity had he known that his own brother-in-law was behind the wheel of the car. When his only sister discovered that he had killed her husband, she was naturally distraught beyond words. So distraught, in fact, that she... well, I'm sure I don't need to tell you what she attempted to do to her brother in the court, what he did to her in self-defence, and how two of my brothers tried to defend her and lost their lives in doing so. My other brother became convinced that our family was cursed, and in order to escape the curse, he took a lethal overdose a couple of weeks after the funerals.

My sisters and I felt almost embarrassed as the national media focused on us, as if we were some kind of freaks just because all around us had died so horrifically. It was almost as if they thought we should have been dead too, Barbara and Helen moaned repeatedly, like a couple of doom, gloom and despondency merchants.

I won't bore the pants off you with the manner of my sisters' deaths. I can't even remember how Barbara died, now that I come to think of it. Suffice to say, I stand alone as the last surviving member of my family, with the picture on my living-room wall being the only remaining testament to the fact that the other members ever set foot on this planet or any other.

It's funny, but not a single fellow pupil from any of my dearly departed brothers' and sisters' classes have passed away, by either natural or unnatural causes, in the twenty-odd years since the last of our schooldays came to an abrupt conclusion. In fact as far as I'm aware, all of their teachers throughout the years are still alive and kicking to boot. And yet when I look in my collection of family photo albums I'm hard pressed to find a picture of myself standing alongside anybody who is still breathing as I write.

There is one picture in particular of which I have always been very fond. It shows me and my Uncle Terence standing in a field filled with cows, just before the terrible outbreak of Foot and Mouth Disease during which all his cattle had to be destroyed. Seeing his life's work go up in smoke in an instant utterly destroyed my uncle, and he shot himself in the head three or four weeks after that picture was taken.

As my late wife said to me while lying on her deathbed eleven short weeks after the wedding photograph that still takes pride of place on top of my television was taken, perhaps I'm jinxed. The priest posing between me and Sheila on another photo in the album said something along those lines as he was being rushed to hospital after celebrating my wife's funeral mass, or so I've been led to believe.

Anyway, I can't sit here scribbling away until the cows come home (especially not my Uncle Terence's, ha-ha). Today is my big day, at long last. I am being honoured for my services to charity (that's another story, and I don't have time to go into it right now).

At the request of my good friend P----- F-------, an esteemed member of His Majesty's opposition, I am now going to the Houses of Parliament to have my picture taken with the entire government, before meeting the Prime Minister and all his Cabinet for yet another photo-shoot. I sincerely hope that everything turns out fine this time.

By the way, dear friend, as you can see I have enclosed, in the envelope with this letter, the photo of me standing beside you at the party in the gentlemen's club in Chelsea last month. I hope it finds you fit and well, and that it isn't marked 'return to sender' yet again.

EARLY MORNING CALL

Ciara Byrne tapped her husband Sean on the shoulder. 'The phone's ringing, honey.'
Sean switched on the bedside lamp and looked at the alarm clock. 'It's... *ten past four*,' he exclaimed, exasperated. 'Who would ring us at such an unearthly hour?'
'You'll have to go downstairs to find out,' Ciara replied curtly, rolling onto her side. 'You can tell me who it was when I wake up in the morning.'
It was probably one of Ciara's Belfast knitting-club buddies, ringing for a laugh after a night on the razzle. Sean pulled the pillow up over his head to stifle the noise, and went back to sleep.
'Get up and answer that phone, you clampet,' Ciara sat up and said. 'It's been ringing non-stop for twenty minutes.'
'It's not for me,' Sean said. 'None of my mates ring at half past four in the morning. It must be for you, sweetheart.'
Ciara had that look in her eyes again. Sean would probably have to cook his own dinner on Saturday, if he didn't perform his manly duty of attending to anything that made a sound after the lights went off. But he wasn't going to be intimidated.
'I'll tell you now, I'm not answering that phone.'
'Well it can bloody well ring all night, then,' Ciara snarled, sticking resolutely to her guns.
It was 5AM. Sean was having trouble getting back to sleep. If he went downstairs and took the phone off the hook, he would be able to return to his contented slumbers. But could he resist the urge to stick the phone against his ear to discover the identity of the strange caller? He thought not. The phone could ring until hell froze over as far as he was concerned.
He spent the next hour tossing and turning. Thank God it was the weekend – he could have a long lie-in in the morning.
'Are you not getting up to watch *Football Focus* on the telly?' Ciara asked after poking Sean in the spine with her sadistic elbow. It was just after twelve o'clock in the afternoon.
'Why are you still in bed?' Sean puzzled. In their nine long years of

marriage he had never once seen Ciara in bed after ten o'clock.
'I'm not getting up first,' she said. 'I let the dog out the back a couple of hours ago. I'm not going to walk past that phone again until you've answered it. It could be anybody ringing.'
'Whoever it is,' Sean said, 'they're very keen for *one* of us to answer it.'
'Yes, probably you.'
'Not on this occasion,' Sean replied stubbornly. 'Most of my workmates hang up after the phone rings eight or nine times... not for eight or nine hours, non-stop.'
'It's probably a wrong number,' Ciara suggested. 'Give me a shout from the bottom of the stairs if it's for me.'
'I can stay in bed all day, if need be,' Sean said. But he had to get up a couple of hours later, when the noise of his stomach's incessant rumbling began to drown out the sound of the telephone. He walked down the stairs and marched straight into the living room. He was frying a couple of eggs and a potato-waffle when Ciara walked into the kitchen, her arms tensely folded.
'Well,' Sean said inquisitively, 'Who was it?'
'Who was what?'
The phone was still ringing away in the background!
'You lazy...' Sean took his frustration out on his eggs.
'Don't go and answer it just yet,' Ciara pleaded caustically. 'Leave it for another...' she looked at her watch, 'fifty minutes. Then it'll have been ringing for twelve solid hours, a new world record.'
'It can ring for the next week for all I care,' Sean said. 'It's not my turn to answer the phone. I answered it yesterday, when your friend Mrs Kenny rang, whingeing about her missing husband.'
'I'm just going out into the hall, to fetch my slippers from beneath the phone table.'
'See who that is while you're out there,' Sean said, trying to trick Ciara. And when she walked back into the living room: 'Could you not have answered the bloody phone while you were crouched down next to it?'
'You passed it yourself and didn't answer it.'
'A mere technicality,' Sean explained. After eating his waffle and eggs he passed the phone another couple of times, going up and down the stairs to and from the bathroom.
'That thing is still ringing,' he announced as he passed Ciara in the

hall.

'I wonder who it could be?'

'Whoever it is, I hope they hang up soon,' Sean said. 'I want to make a phone-call at some stage this afternoon.'

'Well, then, you'll have to answer the phone and tell the mysterious caller to try again later,' Ciara chanced her arm.

'No can do,' Sean said. 'If I answer the phone now, the person on the other end of the line will know I'm in the house. They'll think I was extremely ignorant, letting the phone ring for such a long time before answering it.'

'Pretend you've just walked in through the door.'

'Are there any cotton-wool buds in the first-aid kit?' Sean asked, rooting around. 'Ah, here they are.' He shoved a bud in each ear to drown out the racket. 'That's better,' he shouted. 'That ringing was beginning to drive me up the wall.'

Ciara stuck up two hands followed by two fingers, to let Sean know that twelve hours had elapsed. 'It's not for me,' she mumbled to herself.

'I could lip-read that,' Sean grumbled.

He turned the TV on, with the volume up at full blast so that he could just about hear it. Ciara sneaked up behind him and pulled the cotton-wool buds out of his ears, and the ensuing blast of noise almost deafened him.

'Jesus,' he screamed, 'you sadistic git!'

Ciara couldn't help laughing. 'Sorry, dear, I forgot the phone was ringing so loud.'

'The phone?' Sean snapped trenchantly, grabbing the remote-control and turning the TV down, 'Are you crazy, woman?' – He could hear the phone ringing. 'That's probably your psychiatrist, calling to ask why you skipped your last appointment.'

'Very funny,' Ciara said in a deadpan tone of voice. 'Ha-ha indeed.'

'No, but seriously, can you imagine if it really was a psychiatrist calling?' Sean said. 'Would he come to the conclusion that we were both of sound mind, at this moment in time?'

'What,' Ciara protested, 'just because our phone has been ringing non-stop for the past twelve hours and we haven't answered it? You wouldn't classify that as insane behaviour, would you?'

'Not on my part, no,' Sean said, as Ciara made herself some tea and toast. 'It's not as if we're afraid it might be bad news.'

'Maybe it *is*,' Ciara speculated, nibbling her toast and marmalade. 'Otherwise why would they hang on so long?'

'I don't care,' Sean said. 'Whatever the person on the other end of the line has to say is totally irrelevant. The only matter of any importance is: who is going to answer the phone, me or you?'

'So,' Ciara said, 'if I answer the phone and it's the last woman on earth, calling to tell us there's been a nuclear war while we've been sitting here phone-watching, all that will matter is... *you win*?'

'It's not a case of winners and losers,' Sean argued, 'it's the principle of the thing.'

Ciara let the dog in for his dinner, but he scratched on the door a few minutes later as the ringing sound was driving him up the wall. Sean let him out the back, and a knock sounded on the front door.

'I suppose you're not going to answer that either?' Ciara asked, going to the door in a huff. It was only their neighbour Mrs Kenny. She said she had tried ringing to say she was calling round but their phone was constantly engaged.

'Do you want me to get that?'

'No, it's for Sean.'

Mrs Kenny looked at Sean, sitting with his fingers stuck in his ears.

'Why don't they just hang up?' she asked after another ten minutes had elapsed. 'They must realise you're not going to pick the phone up. Would you like me to unplug it for you?'

'Don't you dare!' Ciara said. 'It might be an important call.'

'When did it start ringing, if you don't mind me asking?'

'Ten past four,' Ciara said.

'Oh, that was only about fifteen minutes ago,' Mrs Kenny replied in all innocence. 'So when did you come up with the brainwave not to answer it?'

'If it's bothering you that much,' Sean snarled, 'you know where the door is.'

'No, I'm just wondering what's so important about not answering the phone,' Mrs Kenny said. 'Why is that one call in particular playing such a big part in your lives, leading the two of yous to refuse to even acknowledge that the phone is ringing?'

'You're dying to know who it is, aren't you?' Sean said.

'Of course not,' Mrs Kenny replied. 'The longer the phone keeps on ringing, the less I care about who is on the other end of the line. I'm just curious about which of the pair of yous is eventually going to answer it.'

'Our thoughts exactly,' Ciara said.

'Do you know what I wish?' Mrs Kenny said a few minutes later. 'I wish I had your permission to answer the phone, so that I could refuse to do so... so that I could feel like I was doing something constructive, by not doing anything.'

'OK,' Sean decided. 'We'll give you permission to answer the phone, as long as you promise not to take us up on it.'

'I won't take you up on it,' Mrs Kenny agreed, 'but please don't make me promise.'

'Deal.'

Despite his extreme kindness in allowing her to answer the telephone in theory, Mrs Kenny could tell by the look in Sean's eyes that he would break both her arms, if need be, to prevent her from answering the phone in real life. Still, it was the thought that counted. Mrs Kenny's visit certainly hadn't been in vain, because now she had permission to answer her friend's phone, as long as she didn't rip the arse out of it by actually doing it.

'I suppose you've been through all the permutations in your head,' Mrs Kenny said, 'working out all the people who could possibly be ringing, minus the ones who, for one reason or another, it couldn't be?'

'Of course I have,' Ciara sighed. 'What do you take me for?'

'The Widow Erinsborough would love this whole scenario,' Mrs Kenny over-dramatized. 'Can I invite her round?'

'Don't touch that dial!' Sean shouted, as Mrs Kenny moved towards the front hall. 'Go anywhere near that phone, and I'll –'

'Sean!' Ciara screamed, 'don't threaten to kill my friend!'

'But if she picks that phone up...' Sean yelled, in an absolute furore.

'She wouldn't dare,' Ciara snarled. 'If she so much as breathes on our phone, she won't know what has hit her.'

Ciara thought she detected a glimmer of fear in her friend's eyes.

'I'm sorry, Mrs Kenny, did big bad Sean frighten you?'

'I wasn't going to answer the...'

'There, there,' Ciara said, 'he's harmless. Oh, by the way, have you heard from your Mike lately?'

'No,' Mrs Kenny said with a sigh. 'He's still gallivanting around the universe in that feckin' flying-saucer, like a child in a sweet-shop. At least ET called home, but my husband never phones me.'

'Could you ladies please keep your voices down? I can't hear the phone ringing.' In so saying, Sean curled up in his armchair. 'I'm just going to have a short nap. Feel free to answer the phone, Ciara... but don't, under any circumstances, let your friend get it.'

'I wasn't going to touch it,' Mrs Kenny pleaded. 'I wouldn't answer your phone now if my life depended on it.'

'It would if you did,' Sean muttered beneath his breath with a blatantly-false smile on his face, which made Ciara chuckle.

Mrs Kenny desperately wanted to find out who the mysterious caller was, before it was too late and they hung up. Her best friend's husband had virtually threatened to have her bumped off if she answered the phone, but if she were to strike first, she could claim self-defence. The ring, ring, ringing sound was beginning to drive her insane... why couldn't somebody *please* put a stop to it?

Sean and Ciara appeared to be asleep. Mrs Kenny stood up, trying not to make any noise. Some of life's questions simply have to be answered, and 'Who is on the other end of the phone?' is the most searching question of them all. Mrs Kenny didn't want to spend the rest of her life wondering who it might have been. Maybe it was her husband ringing from Ursa Major or Ursa Minor or Timbuk-Bloody-Tu.

Sean woke up in a panic. He had dreamt that Mrs Kenny answered the phone while he was asleep. The irritating woman was nowhere to be seen.

Perspiring greatly, Sean tapped on Ciara's head. She sat bolt upright on the sofa.

'Where's Mrs Kenny?' she said, panicking.

'I think she has escaped!' Sean said, spotting their dog fast asleep in the corner. 'Mrs Kenny must have let the pooch in.'

'Did she answer the phone?'

They pricked up their ears and crossed their fingers. The phone was still ringing, thanks be to God.

'For a minute there,' Sean gasped, 'I thought the ringing had stopped while I was asleep. I had a horrible nightmare in which...' he choked, 'in which your *friend* answered our phone.'

'Where is she?'

'Who cares, as long as she's gone,' Sean said, unable to contain his

relief. 'I don't think we'll be seeing her again.'
'I should think not,' Ciara said, looking at her watch. 'The phone has been ringing for eighteen hours now. I wonder who it is?'
'Don't start that again,' Sean said as he fed the hamster. 'What business is it of ours, the identity of the caller? Just because our phone is ringing, that doesn't give us the right to confiscate the soul of the person on the other end of the line.'
Ciara reflected for a moment. 'What did I say?'
'Well I'm definitely not answering it,' Sean finally declared, breaking Ciara's line of thought. 'Not after all this time.'
The happy couple spent a typical evening watching TV until bedtime. Only the phone's interminable ringing made it seem different than any other day in their contentedly conjoined lives. But Sean wasn't going to answer it, and Ciara certainly wasn't.
'You were the first to hear it ringing,' Sean bandied words, 'you should have got out of bed and answered it last night.'
'You were nearer the door,' Ciara wisely argued. 'And besides, it's your turn.'
'No it's not,' Sean remonstrated, with a passion belying his usual impassive disposition. 'I answered it when your friend Mrs Kenny phoned to ask what our hamster wanted for his birthday.'
A crazy thought fleeted across Sean's mind as he and Ciara cuddled up beneath the sheets. 'What if Mrs Kenny answered the phone while we were asleep, and then rang us up so we wouldn't know that the call had been intercepted?'
Ciara's face turned white. 'Surely nobody could be that cruel?'
'You can never be too sure – there are some pretty sadistic people out there.'
'Maybe that's her on the phone now? Go and answer it, to see if it's Mrs Kenny or not.'
'No. She's your friend, you talk to her.'

Sean was woken at 4AM by a sharp elbow to his ribs.
'The twenty-four hour mark is fast approaching,' Ciara explained. 'I thought I'd better wake you up, so you can hear the phone ringing in a brand new day.'
'Phone?' Sean said, 'What phone?' – It had been ringing so long that it was beginning to blend into the background.
Throughout the whole of his life to date, Sean had never before

achieved such an outstanding goal with such ease. He closed his eyes and tried to picture his name in the book of *Guinness World Records*. What a man, people would remark down the ensuing generations, what a cool customer. Sean Byrne had blatantly ignored a ringing telephone for one, two, or maybe even *three* whole days. People for decades to come would idolize him as they pictured him lying in bed listening to the phone ringing while, maybe ten thousand miles away, the unknown caller stood shaking, sweating, begging God to make the great Sean Byrne please pick up the phone.

He woke up in a cold sweat. What if the caller suddenly hung up? What if he didn't get to become the cool customer who eventually picked the phone up – after it had been ringing non-stop for twenty-five hours – and said, 'Hello, the Byrne residence?'

For every hour the phone rang Sean would look an even bigger hero – but every hour the threat of it suddenly stopping ringing would grow larger and larger. He had to pick the receiver up a mere matter of seconds before the caller was about to hang up. But for how many more hours would the mysterious caller be willing to hang on? It was the ultimately delicate balancing act for the master tactician.

Never before in the history of mankind had a simple human being reached so great a height, with such an imminent threat of falling flat on his face. If Sean came up trumps on this occasion, he reckoned, his very name would be lauded around the world until the end of time.

His heart skipped a beat – had the *phone* just missed a beat? He leapt out of bed and scrambled down the stairs, reaching out to pick up the phone before it was too late.

'Who's there? Why are you calling me? Why have you stayed on the line for over twenty-five hours?'

Keep your voice down, Sean told himself, *Ciara will be listening!*

'Hello, Sean Byrne... Hello, Sean Byrne superstar...'

– IT'S THE DEVIL TRYING TO TEMPT YOU!

Sean moved his hand away from the phone. It would seem such a shame to answer it now, after waiting such a long time. Hearing the caller's voice would probably be a huge anticlimax after all the excitement.

He heard clumping footsteps – Ciara was coming down the stairs.

'I'm going to answer that phone,' she said decisively. 'I can't take it any longer, the tension is killing me. What sort of person sits by the phone for a whole day and night, listening to it ringing on and on, without bothering to answer it? I have to find out who it is.'

Ciara reached out to pick up the phone, as if Sean's thoughts and feelings counted for nothing. Just as her fingers touched the receiver, he pulled her hand away.

'It's too late,' he yelled. 'We've let it ring for too long, we can't possibly answer it now. Think of the consequences.'

'What?' Ciara implored. 'What could possibly be worse than this?'

'What if it's a wrong number?' Sean said. 'What if somebody rang us up in a drunken stupor last night, and forgot to put their phone back on the hook?'

'At least then we'd know the truth of the matter.'

'That telephone,' Sean said, 'has given me the best twenty-five hours of my life. Every minute it keeps on ringing is yet another minute I've spent in ecstasy, wondering who is calling. Life is boring when you know all the answers. Do you really want it all to end with you picking the phone up and saying *Sorry, wrong number*? Can't you see how sadistic that would be?'

'This whole situation has blown up out of all proportion,' Ciara said. 'Come to think of it, I might have arranged for an early morning call yesterday. Maybe I ordered it for four hours too early? Let's take it off the hook and go back to sleep.'

Sean knew when Ciara was trying to humour him.

'I don't *care* who is calling,' he said. 'The identity of the person – or *thing* – on the other end of the line is not important any more. All that matters is that we are here, our phone is ringing, and it's up to you and I whether or not we see fit to answer it. The decision is ours, and ours alone. Nobody can ever take that choice away from us. We can decide not to pick the phone up, if we prefer. The choice belongs to *us,* and nobody else.'

'*We*… as a partnership!' Ciara could see everything clearly now. As long as their telephone kept ringing, they would remain bonded together in both body and mind, as an inseparable entity. The stranger on the other end of the line was (perhaps subconsciously) trying to split them up. But they weren't about to let it happen.

'If we *ever* answer that phone,' Sean elaborated, 'we will deprive ourselves of our whole future freedom of choice. We are only truly free until once that choice has ultimately been made.'

Sean's words sounded hauntingly ominous to Ciara's ears. They would probably have to spend the rest of their fatefully-interconnected lives sitting by the phone, making sure nobody answered it, making sure it never stopped ringing… otherwise their lives together would cease to have any meaning.

WRITE TO THE DEATH

Jimmy Komorowski's heart missed a beat as he reread the bulletin posted on deadgoodwriters.com by an eagle-eyed site member. It was hard to believe that this could be true, it seemed too far-fetched. But the three deaths had been verified by reputable Internet news sites – their veracity was beyond doubt.

One New York inhabitant, an accountant in his late twenties by the name of Martin Hardiman, had been found drowned to death in his own bathtub. Not so peculiar, you might think – but he was tethered to a wooden chair, fully clothed, lying on his back with his nostrils and mouth just below the water-line.

In the bulletin posted by an anonymous member, Hardiman's demise was compared with that of a second writer from another continent.

Manchester, England. Ruth Morrison – a lady in her early forties, although she looked about twenty in her on-screen picture – was found dead in a public swimming pool when the local baths opened their doors that morning, UK-time. As he read, Komorowski thought this was getting weirder by the minute.

Ruth Morrison's arms and legs were bound to a wooden chair with thick hemp. But – and here's the rub – these two homicides were, it seemed, only the tip of the iceberg.

Henry Bolsover could quite easily have been mistaken for a flood victim, were it not for the fact that it hadn't rained in Chicago last night. His elderly wife went to the bathroom and returned to find water halfway up the stairs, way past head height on the ground floor. She yelled for assistance from the bedroom window. When a passer-by helpfully threw a brick through the downstairs window water flooded out of the house. Mr Bolsover was found dead in his armchair, with his eyes still glued to the TV, although it had switched off when the plug blew a fuse. Nobody could figure out how the water had got into the house or where it had come from – all the faucets in the kitchen and bathroom were turned off. It was as if the water had appeared by magic, Komorowski thought, reading between the lines.

The names Hardiman, Morrison and Bolsover had set alarm bells ringing right across the fast-moving American website. Mainly because – coincidence? – they were the names of three of deadgoodwriters.com's most regular contributors. Jimmy Komorowski himself had had many online conversations with them over the six months since he first registered with the site, and as a result he considered them good (albeit virtual) friends.

A quite sizeable percentage of the many writers from around the world who logged on to the site on a daily basis and now instantly recognized the names checked out the home pages of the writers in question – as did Komorowski – to see if they could find any clues as to the triple tragedy.

The three writers had made their final entries on the site only yesterday evening, each of them posting an entry to the latest short story competition. The rules were simple: 'Write a short story about a fictional character, in any genre. The character is to be called – to pluck a name out of thin air – Helen Singleton. No collaboration is permitted.'

Reading the three stories served only to intensify the already intriguing mystery. Hardiman's Helen Singleton was a witch; Morrison's Helen Singleton was a witch; and Bolsover's Helen Singleton was a witch. Coincidence? It could be explained quite easily, of course – this being the Hallowe'en season, it was natural that witchcraft was a subject on every writer's mind. However, there were other similarities in the three stories that weren't so easy to explain, unless the writers had – which they surely had – put their heads together and plotted their characters out beforehand.

In all three stories, Helen Singleton was born in the small town of Billhook, Massachusetts in 1749, and died in the same town in 1786. She was accused of witchcraft by thirteen people, who then strapped her into a ducking-chair to see whether or not she floated. She didn't sink to the bottom of the river in the wooden chair, which proved, in her accusers' eyes, that she was indeed a witch. The unfortunate character was subsequently burned at the stake on the night of 31 October 1786. The same night in all three stories.

Jimmy Komorowski's computer made an unearthly whirring sound, but he ignored it. He didn't find these facts too astonishing on reflection. It was common knowledge that people suspected of being witches were put into dunking-chairs, and burned if they floated. The only real oddity was the fact that they had all given the same years of birth and death, and based their stories in the same small Massachusetts town – especially since the writers themselves lived in New York, Chicago and Manchester, England. Still, Komorowski was sure there must be more to this than met the eye.

What was it, he wondered, some peculiar sort of suicide pact? Had the three authors created their own personal witch-torturing dunking-chair-type deaths simply to get their kicks? This seemed highly implausible, unless all three of them were mentally unstable.

Komorowski spent the remainder of the afternoon and early evening checking out the other competition entries. The case for the prosecution became indelibly stranger and even more incomprehensible with every story he read. He stared at his computer screen as the rain beat down, almost unnoticed, on the window of his suburban apartment.

Susan Kennedy from Portland, Oregon, had written a story about a witch (1749-86) who was dunked and then burned at the stake in Billhook, Massachusetts. Apparently her local police force were thinking along the same lines as Jimmy Komorowski, for they had attempted to contact Miss Kennedy, only to discover that she had died in a car crash shortly after posting her story on deadgoodwriters.com late last night. She had crashed into a willow tree, a protruding branch of which had smashed through the windshield and cut straight through her heart. The car had then burst into flames, and Miss Kennedy's body was burned practically beyond recognition.

Another eight people had participated in the competition – each of them writing virtually the same plot, in the same setting, on the same date, with only the exact words each individual used to tell his or her own particular version of the story changing from screen to screen. The fact that the paragraphs and sentences weren't alike made the story they told seem all the more plausible, as they obviously hadn't been copied from a central source.

The amateur authors had all written about the fictional Helen Singleton's death, and they had all died since posting their stories on-screen last night. Each of them had died either by fire or by water, the same choice they had given the character they had – so they believed – created.

Komorowski's computer sounded really peculiar. It was making crazy banging sounds, as if there was a rat bursting to get out from behind the screen. But he had much more important things to think about.

He had another reason for taking interest in this fascinating sequence of events. He had lived all his life in the small town of Billhook, Massachusetts. He had the feeling that the twelve deceased writers had made the name up, not knowing that it really existed; just as the website moderator had created Helen Singleton's name at random.

Komorowski had heard about the sad plight of the Billhook Witch many times throughout his life, of course, as nothing much ever happened in the nondescript middle-of-noplace town. All the children at school recited the roll-call of names as if it was a proud part of the area's history.

The people who tried, convicted and ultimately slayed the alleged witch had the same surnames as the wannabe authors who had subconsciously written her life-story for posterity. Out of a baker's dozen tormentors, only one of the writers knew the names of his brethren. Only one knew his hometown existed, and that Helen Singleton was a genuine historical figure. Only one had named the guilty parties.

While being tethered to the fire just before the flame was put to it, Helen Singleton had – according to his forefathers – vowed, in all earnest, to come back one day in the distant future – 'in ways not yet dreamt of' – to kill the relatives of her slayers at a time when it would terminate each of their family lines once and for all. Just as they had ended hers for ever and ever.

Jimmy Komorowski couldn't vouch for the other twelve, but he *was* well aware that he was the last of his direct family line… although, thanks to God's mercy, the Billhook Witch had obviously decided to let him go.

But why? Why had she spared him? Was it because he was the only one who actually lived in the town, or because he was a much better writer than the other twelve? They were rank amateurs compared to Jimmy Komorowski. He, after all, was the only one to end his story with an actual threat made by Helen Singleton to the writers who told her story.

He looked at his story on the computer screen again. As the tapping on the screen intensified to an almost unbearable level, he scrolled down to the last paragraph and read the words:

'My death shall be avenged, ye vile wretch. By my own hand I shall make amends for the vast wrong done to me by your forefather. I shall, in a matter of moments, leap forth from this lighted-up glass and burn thee to death the very moment you finish reading these words.'

TWO WRONG NUMBERS

'And besides,' Louise said, pausing to wipe her lips on a napkin, 'I don't see any difference between chance and fate.'
The waitress smiled with everything but her eyes as Louise and Harry ordered the exact same meals they had eaten the last time they came to the best restaurant in Belfast.
'Chance is when something peculiar happens. Fate is when it happens twice.' In so saying, Harry leaned back in his seat and reflected on the events of that stifling July evening one year earlier.
He had been watching TV in his Lisburn Road apartment when the telephone rang. 'I'm sorry,' he tried telling the woman on the other end of the line, 'I think you have a wrong number.' However, she kept on talking as if she couldn't hear him. Without pausing for breath, the stranger told him all about the terrible day she had had at work, and no sooner had her rant ended than she hung up the phone. What a peculiar woman, Harry thought. And then the phone rang again.
He had no idea why, but he was delighted when he picked up the phone and heard the same voice again. He was sitting waiting for the lady to apologize for dialling the wrong number the last time, but instead she said 'and another thing,' and then she recommenced telling him about all her problems. She informed him that her TV had a terrible reception, her sausage-dog was badly in need of a bath, and her mother hadn't phoned her all week although it was her turn to ring.
'And why did you not call me, when you knew I was in a foul mood?' she demanded to know. 'Sorry, I must sound like a terrible bore, do I?'
Harry opened his mouth to speak.
'Anyway,' the stranger said after taking a swift, deep breath, 'I suppose I'd better stop taking up all your time with my problems. I'm sure you have better things to do than sit listening to me chatting away all evening.'
'Not at all,' Harry said, 'I'm quite enjoying it.'

All of a sudden he could almost hear her thinking. Upon listening, for a change, she obviously hadn't recognized his voice.

'I take it that's not you?' she said.

'It *is* me,' Harry argued.

'Oh my goodness,' she said.

'It wasn't me the last time you rang, either,' he told the mysterious lady.

'Whoever you are, you must consider me a real grumpy cow,' she said with a guilty chuckle. 'You must be the most polite man in Northern Ireland – anybody else would surely have hung up on me, not once but *twice*. I hope I didn't say anything I shouldn't have done, naming names?'

'No,' Harry said glumly, 'you didn't even tell me your own.'

'Louise McKeever,' she now revealed, and Harry told her his name. Before either of them knew what was happening they were swapping addresses and email addresses and revealing their respective marital statuses. Harry was delighted to hear that Louise was single too, although he wasn't quite sure why he was so delighted to hear it. She told him her approximate age, adding, 'Tomorrow is my birthday. I don't suppose you'd like to…?'

'I'd love to,' Harry said. They arranged to meet in a restaurant in Belfast city centre the following evening, and Harry told Louise his mobile phone number. While taking out her pen, Louise said that she intended to buy a mobile the following week, but in the meantime he could make do with her office number.

She rang him twice on Friday morning – the first time to check that she had written down the correct mobile phone number and that they were still on for that evening, and the second to tell him about 'something and nothing' that had happened to her in the office that morning. He phoned her back that afternoon, to chat about something so insignificant that he hadn't bothered mentioning it to his work colleagues.

He put on his Sunday best and waited in the restaurant at the prearranged time. He was standing alone at the bar, taking a sip from a cool glass of beer, when a woman behind him said 'Hello.' He turned around and beheld a vision of beauty.

'Louise?' he said.

She smiled and said, 'We meet at last.'

They felt utterly at ease in one another's company from the very first moment they met, like two people who had shared a lifelong friendship. Their tastes were very alike – they both had the same steak dinner, and the only difference in their desserts was that Louise preferred lemon ice-cream to Harry's vanilla.

'What if you had accidentally rung some other man yesterday?' Harry said while driving Louise to her home two miles from the city centre later that night. He answered the puzzled look in her eyes by elaborating, 'You could easily have misdialled the last digit instead of the second-last.'

'Isn't life strange,' she replied.

'It certainly is,' Harry said, and the two of them laughed heartily.

They vowed to meet up again the following Friday. Indeed they would probably have left it at that, had not fate intervened again on Tuesday evening.

Half an hour after arriving home from his accounts office, Harry decided to phone one of his colleagues to see if she wanted to go to the local bar for a quiet drink or five. He looked up his friend's mobile phone number and dialled it, but he was surprised when a woman's voice answered. 'Hello?'

'I'm sorry,' Harry fumbled, 'I must have rung the wrong number.'

The woman in question reflected for a few seconds, before saying, 'Is that who I think it is?'

As Harry scrambled his brain into action, trying to make some sense out of bizarre reality, the gentle-voiced lady said, 'How did you get my number? I have just this minute walked out of the O2 shop with my new phone in my hand. I don't even know my *own* number yet.'

'Louise?' Harry gasped.

Twelve months later, Harry still couldn't fully comprehend the strange events that had occurred that mystifying week. Upon checking the number he dialled, he had discovered that he somehow managed to key in each of the last three digits wrong. And yet it had turned out so right.

'Fate is when it happens twice,' Louise repeated Harry's words to him, swallowing her last mouthful of steak and wiping her lips on her napkin. 'Now I see what you mean. Sometimes two wrongs do make a right.'

The two of them laughed as one.

'Would you like a dessert?'

'Not this time,' Louise said, tugging Harry's arm towards her and glancing at his watch to check the time, before feeling around in her handbag for her purse in order to pay the bill. 'I don't want to get too big for that lovely white dress I'm wearing next week. Oh Harry, only seven days to go until the best day of our lives! Isn't it exciting!'

THE MERCEDES

And that, as they say, was the end of that. His lifelong dream had died unfulfilled along with him.
'I'm sorry for your troubles,' said the perspiring butcher (who, incidentally, wouldn't appear again in this story), reaching out to shake the hands of the widow and her two bottle-blonde daughters, who he reckoned must have been in their early forties. He was standing outside his shop, which he had closed as a mark of respect when he saw the funeral car approaching, followed by a respectfully silent line of good friends, neighbours and relations of the deceased.
Pauline Doherty looked at the butcher and nodded, and her eldest daughter Geraldine tightened her arm's grip around her waist. Virtually the whole town appeared to have turned out to mark the sombre occasion, reminding the grieving widow of just how popular a couple she and her husband had always been.
It was in the playground of St. Christopher's Junior School that Pauline had first encountered Johnny Doherty, or at least that was the scene of her earliest surviving memory of the skinny blond kid.
After all these years she could still remember what a show-off he was as a child, and how he always had to go one better than the other boys in his class at school. That particular afternoon they were taking it in turns to boast about what make of car they were going to drive when they grew up, and they were all being relatively realistic – but not Johnny. He bragged that he was definitely going to end up in a Mercedes. Even at seven years of age Pauline knew that if his dream came true it would be the first time such a grand car had ever set its wheels on Ballybothar tarmac.
'A Mercedes indeed, Johnny Doherty!'
'I will!' the blushing boy turned on his heels and yelled at his eavesdropping neighbour. 'Just you wait and see!'
Pauline couldn't remember precisely what she had said in reply to Johnny's boast, but she reckoned it was probably something along the lines of 'In your dreams'.
'He was never done talking about that car,' Pauline reminisced with her daughters in a private moment among the hubbub at the wake in

their house the night before the funeral. 'Nearly every day, practically until the day he died, he told everybody within listening distance that he just *knew* he was going to end up in a Mercedes. He swore blind that he could feel it in his bones.'

Pauline did her best to smile and look happy to see all the mourners – most of whom she recognised – traipsing through her house as if they owned the place. To avoid causing a commotion, she decided not to mention the fact that some of the people attending the wake had never once set foot through the door of the house while Johnny was alive. Neither did she mention the fact that three or four of the people gleefully prancing around her home on the saddest night of her life appeared to be three sheets to the wind and enjoying themselves far too much, considering the gravity of the situation. They had clearly misunderstood when friendly neighbours informed them that they were going to 'celebrate' the deceased's life.

As more people arrived and the noise of shouting, singing and clinking glasses in the living-room became more deafening with every passing minute, Geraldine and Michelle slinked into the kitchen for a little peace and quiet – better late than never, as their dad used to say all the time.

They closed the door and sat facing one another at the table and thought back to old times. They quickly found themselves reflecting upon the many cars their father had owned – one at a time – over the last four decades or more. There was the green Cortina, Michelle said, and Geraldine recalled the white Escort; then there was the sky-blue motor and the fancy red one, an off-grey hatchback and a silver four-by-four, and another two or three cars that had no standout distinguishable features.

'Your dad only ever wanted for one thing in life,' Pauline said in a reflective mood, with the look of happy memories in her eyes, when she joined her daughters a few minutes later. Thankfully, unlike the adjoining living-room, the kitchen hadn't yet been invaded by an army of mourners with smiling faces.

'Is that why you married him?' Michelle asked. In reply to the glazed look in her mother's eyes, she elaborated, 'To ride in the Mercedes he said he was destined to end up in?'

'I wouldn't say he believed it was his *destiny*, as such,' Pauline said as she chipped in and did her bit, helping the girls to make another batch of egg-and-onion sandwiches to satiate the appetites of the

long line of people coming to pay their respects. 'It was more the case that he had high hopes of one day escaping from his factory job and becoming a wealthy man. Some people thought he was a snob for wanting to drive a better car than theirs. I ask you, is it wrong to want to better yourself?'
Geraldine and Michelle shook their heads in unison.

Pauline focused her eyes on the coffin in the back of the funeral car. She was trying her best to keep in step with the daughters holding her hands, and the eighty or so people walking immediately behind them – a number of whom were undoubtedly nursing bad hangovers after sitting around the open-top coffin all night, telling rude jokes that would have made Johnny blush, had he been alive to hear them.
'The funny thing is,' she said quietly, 'I could never tell two cars apart. I remember your dad telling me, in the early 1970s, that there were two different makes of Mini, but they both looked exactly the same to me. I couldn't see any difference between the Cortina and the Escort we bought to replace it – or was it the other way around? To be honest,' she smiled, realising that she was the only person in the funeral procession talking, 'I couldn't even tell the difference between the cars in your dad's two favourite films, *Herbie* and *Genevieve*. Truth be told, I wouldn't recognise a Mercedes if one were to drive over my foot as I speak.'
'Look, Mum,' Geraldine said, 'there's one now.'
Pauline glanced around to see which direction Geraldine was looking in, but she was looking straight ahead. She could see in through the bars on the fence of St. Christopher's Church and there were no vehicles at all in there, nor were there any parked outside the graveyard wall on the opposite side of the road.
'I didn't realise that either,' Michelle said, looking bamboozled. 'But then again, like Mum I've never driven a car, so they all look the same to me.'
Pauline suddenly caught on what they were talking about.
'Do you mean to say that *this*…'
Geraldine looked at her mother and nodded her head as they turned into the churchyard, and Pauline gave a gentle smile of recognition.
'Fate has a peculiar way of coming back and slapping people in the face to show them who's boss,' Pauline said, as her husband's final

journey ended. 'It looks as if your dad's life-long dream has finally come true.'

Geraldine and Michelle didn't know what to say. In a most peculiar way, their father's dream *had* come true – although it was a little too late in the day for him to be able to enjoy it.

'I suppose it's true what your dad used to say.'

'What was that, Mum?'

'Better late than never,' Pauline said, as Johnny's brother and a couple of neighbours removed the coffin from the car. A few friendly faces looked on as Pauline wiped a solitary tear from her eye, but ne'er a soul suspected that she was struggling not to laugh out loud at the ironic turn of events. She was certain that, had he been able to, Johnny would have been laughing louder than anybody else attending his funeral that cold November morning.

EPILOGUE

Mary Cunningham was the luckiest woman in the world. She lived in the house nearest the graveyard, so she got to see every funeral in town, free of charge. Nothing cheered her up like a good death.

It was a bad week. She had gone to ten o'clock mass every morning, but not a single person had died. 'Some people have nothing better to do with their time than stay alive,' she muttered to herself as she grumped and groused her way around the house. She looked out the back bedroom window at the rain pouring down on the sadly deserted graveyard. There wasn't a single mourner to be seen, more's the pity. It wasn't fair, why had people stopped dying all of a sudden? What the hell was keeping them?

To this day, she still couldn't believe it. One and a half years he had kept her waiting. She had been in love with him for all of the eighteen long months since they first met, and yet he had spent all that time playing silly mind games – for over five hundred days. He must have thought Mary was going to live forever, if he could afford to waste a huge percentage of her golden years like that.

What a pity he wasn't buried in the graveyard yet, she thought. She would have loved to kneel down beside his grave and tell him: 'I haven't decided yet, dearest, but I'll make my mind up pretty soon. And I promise, just as soon as I do, you'll be the first to know.'

Mary drifted happily off to sleep every night with the mental images of the dead faces of all the people she had known when they were alive. It always cheered her up to think of the ones who had scorned her, at one time or another, lying just below her back garden, being eaten by worms.

He had been widowed at the same time as her. Precisely the same time, as a matter of fact, as his wife and her husband had been involved in a head-on crash. Which was quite lucky, in hindsight – had their spouses not killed one another on the road, Mary and Jimmy would probably never have met.

She wanted his body, even before they had nailed the lids on the coffins. He was in his early seventies too, but she wasn't worried about that; he was far better looking than the man his late wife had erased from existence. But why had he spurned all her advances? Even when she pinched his bottom while giving him a consolation kiss at his wife's funeral (the grave closest to her house, spookily), Jimmy hadn't taken the hint. She had slept alone that night, as she had every night since. It was as if the man was brain-dead. Or maybe he was dead in the trouser department? That didn't bear thinking about.

She felt guilty for cursing him. It was wrong of her to wish Jimmy dead and buried, just so she could kneel down by the side of his grave and say: 'Are you sure you wouldn't rather still be in the land of the living, sharing my bed, instead of being down there in the cold, cold ground?' It would have come to nothing and she knew it.

She was just passing by her front bedroom window a few minutes later, not staring out of it, when she happened to see a woman in one of the houses across the road standing glaring out her living room window. Dying room, more like. You'd have thought, what with her remaining years being so limited and all that, she would have found something better to do with her time. She was probably jealous, because Mary could see the graveyard from her back bedroom window and she couldn't. She had to walk to the end of the street, cross the road and go down the next street whenever she wanted to visit all her old friends, whereas Mary could just stand at the window and wave to them, singing la-la-la and laughing. Some people won't take death for an answer.

She told herself to stop it. What would the neighbours say? They could have been forgiven for thinking her obsession with death was taking over her life. But then, they merely existed, whereas she had a hobby. Death kept her young, fit and agile, it kept her brain active far better than their crosswords and jigsaws.

There was a woman in the graveyard. Mary saw her when she went upstairs to use the bathroom. I wonder who she is? She thought, intrigued.

Apart from death, Mary's only other vice was sweets. She loved mint imperials. And chocolate éclairs. And sherbet strawberries. Brandy balls usually made her feel slightly dizzy – tipsy, ha ha! – so she tried to avoid them except at Christmas. And that was only a couple of months away again. My, how time flies, she thought to herself, moving to the back bedroom window as it made a far better vantage point.

It was still raining – perfect. She loved looking at the graveyard when mourners were getting drenched through to their skin – the worst of both worlds.

The woman was pacing up and down the footpath between the graves, as if she couldn't decide which one to visit. She was spoilt for choice – Mary knew the feeling, she had often found herself torn between one old acquaintance and another when it came to kneeling down and thanking God for taking them. It was just as well she never told people exactly what she was praying for, ha ha.

Memo to self: must stop talking to myself. At times she thought she was losing it, always sending private messages to herself.

The woman was kneeling down in front of a grave, having at last made up her mind whose passing to grieve. Now she was lying prostrate on the grave bed. Either she dearly loved whoever was buried there, or she was one hell of a poseur. There was nobody else in the graveyard to see her posing, and there was no point in posing without an audience, so maybe she suspected that Mary would be watching her every move? If so, she must have been paranoid.

Look at her, lying there in the rain, showing off. She ought to have been... no, wait a minute, she wasn't moving. That was odd, Mary thought. She went down to the back hall and felt in the pocket of her green coat. She took out her little black book and found her favourite phone number on the first page.

'I'd like to report a death,' she proudly told the local undertaker. 'No, I don't know who she is. She's at plot – let me just refer to my map – plot 14A in the graveyard. And please hurry, I think rigor mortis might be about to set in.'

He didn't even need to ask who was calling, he said before he hung up. She wondered what he meant by that.

Ten full minutes elapsed before Mr. McKee arrived on the scene with the local police sergeant. They looked up at Mary's back bedroom window, as if they expected her to be standing there. Did they think she had nothing better to do with her time? She opened the window to try and hear what they were saying, but all she could catch was the odd word being blown away by the wind. It had stopped raining, so she went and stood outside in the back garden. This was going to be fun.

'She was always staring out that window, the silly old bat.'

'Yes, so I've heard.'

'Every time I buried somebody there she was, staring down with a huge smile on her face.'
'Who alerted you?'
'I beg your pardon, Sergeant?'
'Who phoned you, to tell you about the body by the graveside?'
'You know, I have absolutely no idea. At first I thought I knew, but on reflection I was obviously wrong. She would have been standing up there now, watching our every move.'
'Or she would have had her ear pressed against her back garden wall, trying to hear what we were saying.'
'She didn't do that as well, did she?'
'Yes, according to her neighbours. Some of them saw her doing it from *their* bedroom windows.'
'You'd better alert Jimmy, he'll be heartbroken.'
'Jimmy?'
'My brother. He told me last night that he was going to propose to her this evening, now that a suitable period of mourning has elapsed for both of them. Mind you, thank God she went first.'
'Why do you say that, Mr. McKee?'
'She loved Jimmy dearly,' the undertaker said. 'She would have killed herself if anything bad had ever happened to him.'

Printed in Dunstable, United Kingdom